DR. BETHUNE'S CHILDREN

DR. BETHUNE'S CHILDREN

A novel

XUE YIWEI

TRANSLATED FROM THE CHINESE
BY DARRYL STERK

This is a work of fiction. Any resemblance to actual persons, living or dead,
events, or locales is entirely coincidental.

Prepared for the press by Timothy Niedermann
Cover design: Debbie Geltner
Cover illustrations: Cai Gao
Layout: WildElement.ca

Printed and bound in Canada.

Library and Archives Canada Cataloguing in Publication

Xue, Yiwei, 1964- [Bai qiu en de hai zi men. English]
        Dr. Bethune's children / Xue Yiwei ; Darryl Sterk, translator.

Issued in print and electronic formats.
ISBN 978-1-988130-51-4 (softcover).--ISBN 978-1-988130-52-1 (EPUB).--
ISBN 978-1-988130-53-8 (Kindle).--ISBN 978-1-988130-54-5 (PDF)
        I. Sterk, Darryl, translator II. Title. III. Title: Doctor Bethune's
children. IV. Title: Bai qiu en de hai zi men. English

PS8646.U4.B3513 2017   C895.13›6   C2017-902038-2
                                                 C2017-902039-0

The publisher is grateful for the support of the Canada Council for the
Arts, of the Canada Book Fund and of the Société de développement des
entreprises culturelles (SODEC) for its publishing program.

We acknowledge the financial support of the Government of Canada
through the National Translation Program for Book Publishing, an initiative
of the *Roadmap for Canada's Official Languages 2013-2018: Education, Im-
migration, Communitie*s, for our translation activities.

Linda Leith Publishing
Montreal
www.lindaleith.com

Dedicated to
Yinyin and Yangyang,
whose deaths unveiled the mystery of *must*.

"You see, Pony, why I *must* go to China."

Norman Bethune, farewell letter to his last lover,
January 8, 1938

"Comrade Bethune's spirit, his utter devotion to others,
without any thought of self, was shown in his great sense
of responsibility in his work and his great warm-
heartedness towards all comrades and the people …
…A man's ability may be great or small, but if he has
this spirit, he is already noble-minded and pure, a man of
moral integrity and above vulgar interests, a man who is
of value to the people."

Mao Zedong, "In Memory of Dr. Bethune,"
December 21, 1939

"You are all Dr. Bethune's children."

Yangyang's mother, in conversation with the narrator,
November 18, 1974

AUTHOR'S NOTE
TO A CANADIAN COLLEAGUE

You may be aware that Norman Bethune was married and divorced twice in his life, both times to the same woman. Before their first marriage, Dr. Bethune promised his future wife that, though their union might make her life "a misery," it would "never bore" her. Both marriages were childless.

Almost five years after his second divorce, he said farewell to all his lovers and joined the communist cause in China, "making light of travelling thousands of miles" as his great friend, Mao Zedong, put it. Dr. Bethune never anticipated that this would be a road from which he would never return. Nor did he ever imagine that his relationship with China would turn him into an icon.

Dr. Bethune became one of the most idolized foreigners in China, ranked closely behind the four great revolutionary mentors—Marx, Engels, Lenin, and Stalin. And, unlike his previous marriages, his marriage to China blossomed and bore fruit. As a "noble-minded" man, a "pure" man, a man who displayed "an utter devotion to others"—as his great friend famously described him—

this Canadian doctor posthumously begot tens of millions of children with his spirit, rather than his semen, at the other end of the earth from the nation of his birth.

We are all Dr. Bethune's children, the madwoman once said to me. Thirty years have passed since that day, and I still tremble at the memory, for she had identified what all members of my generation have in common.

I've long wanted to write the story of Dr. Bethune's children, but I have always hesitated. I knew the facts but felt unable to explain them. I feared that the cruel limits of reality would confine my imagination and restrict my freedom of expression, so I waited, deferring the re-emergence of the past and postponing the realization of what it had meant.

Then I heard that the madwoman had died. This saddened me—I felt sorrow for her son, Yangyang, and her adopted daughter Yinyin, especially—but it also inspired me. In that moment, reality and imagination became one, and I now knew how to tell the story of Dr. Bethune's children.

Most of us are still alive and living in China, some in positions of great influence. But the three of his children who appear in my novel are exceptions. Two are no longer living, each having died an unnatural death for reasons related to their spiritual father. Yangyang committed suicide just before the end of the dark period in China's past known as the Cultural Revolution, while Yinyin died as one of the "accidental casualties"—this was the government's term—on another grim day, June 4, 1989.

I am the only survivor of the three, and I fled China in the early 1990s, taking these memories of pain and loss with me. My journey took me in the opposite direction from that of the legendary doctor. I reached Vancouver via Hong Kong and eventually settled in Montreal, a city Dr. Bethune lived in for eight years. I've been here ever since, inhabiting the past and the present, both of which are haunted by the spectre of Dr. Bethune.

I came across a farewell note in Dr. Bethune's papers addressed to his last lover, the artist Marian Scott. "You see, Pony, why I *must* go to China," his note begins. And this, to me, is the great mystery in his life—and in the lives of all his children. Why *must* Dr. Bethune go to China? Why *must*? Through my writing I was starting to understand this mystery, which could not be approached in any other way.

My dear colleague, we write in different languages, but this *must* is our shared inspiration. It is sure to stimulate the same surprise in both of us, allowing our imaginations to transcend the boundaries of language and discover a wider and stranger space for literature.

China and Canada have Norman Bethune in common, and *Dr. Bethune's Children* can become part of both our collective memories. This is the reason I am writing this book, a book for China and Canada to read—and read together.

CONTENTS

A scholar of Chinese history, I am now living in Montreal. My research on education in the Japanese-occupied territories in China prior to World War II has been well received, and some of my newspaper columns have attracted some attention. My Montreal Gazette *article on Dr. Bethune, in particular, prompted people to rethink this extraordinary figure, who is fading from popular memory both in Canada and in China.*

A few months ago, a publisher in Beijing invited me to write Dr. Bethune's biography, saying he wanted an "authentic" biography based on papers I had read in the Norman Bethune archive. This biography was planned for release on November 12, 2009, the seventieth anniversary of Dr. Bethune's death.

I accepted the publisher's proposal to work on the biography, but I took exception to his insistence on authenticity. I think there must be bias in every biography. To a great extent, a bias, or even a lie, is a form of authenticity in a work of literature. I pointed out in my Gazette *article that the Norman Bethune "archive" can be divided into two parts, one of which is preserved in China and the other here in Canada. The Chinese part is derived from the famous memorial by Mao Zedong, which all the "children of Dr. Bethune" had to memorize. It finds a source in the power of*

1

the imagination. Dr. Bethune's Chinese archive is more authentic to Chinese readers than the archive preserved here at McGill University in Canada—and it's more meaningful, as well. Dr. Bethune's Chinese papers are part of Chinese history, part of Chinese culture, part of the modern Chinese mindset. Instead of exaggerating the superficial contradictions between the two archives, I believed that, in the biography I was about to write, I should seek to discover the inner links between them, in which a kind of historical authenticity is concealed.

Even though my philosophy of history was unfathomable to my publisher, he respected my creative freedom. He anticipated that my bias and the Dr. Bethune archives on which I was about to draw would bring the biography great success.

The first two months of preparatory work led to some good results, and I had soon completed a third of the research. I was so satisfied, so gratified, that I was not aware of the coming of winter. But winter did come, as I discovered when I heard my neighbour's moans in the wee hours one night. My neighbour is a gorgeous Lebanese woman. Her boyfriend was transferred to Hong Kong three years before. She visited him in Hong Kong in the summer, and he came to Montreal on vacation in the early winter. They enjoyed making love in the middle of the night, a sensitive time for me, when I was almost ready to fall from fragile slumber into deep sleep. Her moans of pleasure lasted a long time, exciting me physically but depressing me mentally. They evoked in me a dejected nostalgia. I bemoaned the absurdity of my existence.

I knew that this would continue, night after night, and that the result would always be the same. The next day, all day long, I would be in a daze, incapable of focusing on my research and

2

writing. I tried to reset my circadian clock so that I could get a sound sleep, inured to my neighbours' behaviour, but it didn't work. What I thought of as my neighbours' remarkably robust "combat capability" eventually defeated me. Classic symptoms of depression soon appeared. I began to lose my passion for the biography. I lost my appetite. What's more, I started to suffer auditory and visual hallucinations. One night, not long after I went to bed, a sharp pain shot through the back of my head, towards the right side, followed by another stabbing pain, and then another, even more intense. It was a migraine. Soon my neck got so stiff I couldn't turn my head. I struggled to get up and put on my clothes, and then dragged myself toward the Jewish General Hospital, about two kilometres away.

Sitting in the Emergency waiting room, I could still hear my neighbours' wild moans, which gave me sadness of a very particular kind in the intervals between the stabs of pain from my migraine. Beset by hot and cold flashes, I felt I was drifting away from the present, away from life, away from myself.

I was distracted me from my neighbours' moans when a shabby old woman in ragged clothes walked into the waiting room, dragging a little cart filled with empty bottles and old newspapers behind her. I thought she looked familiar, but I couldn't place her. She walked toward the reception window, as if in her own world, speaking neither English nor French, muttering a slew of what seemed to be profanities at the hospital employee behind the window. The employee didn't even lift her head. And that didn't bother the old woman at all. She turned back and went on cursing to the air for a while before dragging her little cart away.

"She loiters here every day, that mad old woman," I heard

the employee explain in a loud voice through the window to an approaching patient. Another throbbing pain assaulted the back of my head, again on the right-hand side. I strained to turn my neck to look towards the entrance of the waiting room, where I'd last seen the old woman as she walked out.

It couldn't be. Was I imagining it? I closed my eyes in shock. I realized I wasn't asking myself this question. I was asking Dr. Bethune, who had just appeared before my eyes. His spectre had started visiting me two months earlier and would look at me with a lost expression, making me hesitate between belief and doubt. I always closed my eyes.

Now an intense impulse squeezed the pain of out my head. I wanted to talk to him, to tell him everything that we, his children, had experienced, everything to do with the impact he had had on our lives. It had been nearly forty years since I first heard his name, and this was an impulse I had never felt before. Yes, there he was in front of me. I could see his expression clearly, even with my eyes closed. He looked so much like the portrait stuck on the wall of my elementary school classroom. "Can you tell me where I've seen that woman before?" I asked softly.

This was the first time I'd addressed him directly, in the second person. I had known about him for forty years, and I had always felt a connection with him, but I had never felt as close to him as I did at that moment. Using the second person gave me a deep-ened sense of intimacy. I was excited, thrilled. A miracle followed: the pain in my head stopped, just like that. Memories of the past flooded in. I had so many things I wanted to say, to tell him, but I wanted to address him directly. Biography or some other form of writing about him suddenly seemed so distanced, so inauthentic.

I had to speak to Dr. Bethune face to face, to write to him as you. *Only in this direct, personal manner could I present our mysterious yet magnificent relationship.*

I walked out of the waiting room, full of gratitude. My steps were light. I felt a sense of clarity. I had changed completely from the man who came into the waiting room. I wanted to get home as quickly as possible.

I just wanted to get back to my apartment, turn on the computer, open up a new file, and save my memories on the hard drive. I wanted to start talking to you.

It is November 18, 2007. So many years have passed. "Dear Dr. Bethune. . . ."

A FOREIGN COUNTRY

Dear Dr. Bethune, I have just returned from the hospital. On my way home, I swung into the supermarket at the corner of Côte-des-Neiges and Queen Mary.

You're probably wondering what a supermarket is. There will be many more unfamiliar words that may be obstacles in the way of your understanding my story. I will do my best to avoid such obstacles, but there's no way I can avoid all of them. I've been wondering if I should stop and provide a simple definition every time such a word appears, but I think this would be impractical, disrupting my train of thought and our conversation. In fact, most of these unfamiliar words will not stand in the way of your understanding. And etymology will guide you. A supermarket, for example, is obviously a kind of market. Context should help, too. To make it easier for you, I will make a list of all the new words, a custom dictionary you can consult if you get stuck.

It has been nearly seventy years since your departure, which is long enough for a language to change dramatically, not to mention a city. Yes, I live in Montreal now, but it is certainly not the same Montreal as the city you lived in. The buildings, the streets, the residents' complexions and languages, people's memories and desires—all are very different from the ones you once knew.

The differences between the two cities with the same name have also been accentuated by your departure and my arrival. Nearly seventy years ago, when you left Montreal, you had become a well-known figure here, but you had not gained national recognition, let alone international fame. You became a legend in your home country because you left and never came back again. And my arrival in Montreal bore witness to the legend you had created. Montreal is a city of migrants, and I am one of the myriad foreigners who live an expatriate life here. Though one of many, I am still special, because of you. I came here because of you, because of your presence in China, because of your experience in China as a foreigner. Sometimes I feel I am just your reflection, wavering on the river of time. Were this city not your city, I would not be here now—no way. I remember the farewell note you sent to your "Pony," the note you wrote after boarding the passenger steamer bound for China. I can highlight our connection by imitating your sentence structure. "You see, Dr. Bethune, why I *must* live in your city?" I am one of the countless children you begot in China. You are the father we all keep searching for.

I sometimes wonder if I am the only one who came to this city because of you. The special connection between us often makes me imagine your life in this city—operating on a patient, delivering a political speech, painting a self-portrait, even making love to your anxious wife or one of your various lovers. And I imagine you reclining on a comfortable sofa reading *Red Star Over China* by Edgar Snow. (Who now remembers Edgar Snow?) I know it is this book that stimulated your interest in my country and inspired you to join the revolutionaries trapped in the barren northwest after the Long March. I imagine how you pictured your life as foreigner in my country. Did the China you had imagined conflict with the China you found in reality? You were reborn in my imagination. This is very significant to me, since it was you that made me come to this city. One day, when I was sitting in a bookstore, the expression on your face as you were packing up to leave Montreal appeared to me. You certainly did not know that you would never come back to Montreal. No worry or anxiety showed on your face. I imagined you putting the famous typewriter into a shabby crate.

Dear Dr. Bethune, let me tell you why I went to that supermarket. It wasn't just to make a purchase. I rushed to the dairy shelf and reached down for a two-litre bottle of whole milk. I checked the expiration date on the seal and then walked toward a cashier. I will tell you why this purchase mattered a lot to me. Before writing to you, I have to admit, I was not in a good frame of mind. In fact, I was feeling disappointed. My disappointment had nothing to do with the purchase itself. I felt disappointed because . . . I will tell you the reason in good time. I believe that you will understand why, which will again demonstrate the special connection I have with you and your city.

8

I am writing to you, finally, like a volcano about to erupt. I have so many things to tell you. I need to transfer them from my brain to my computer. There's another term that you have never heard before. I am not sure whether you can guess from the Chinese translation what this is. The literal translation of computer into Chinese is "electrical brain." You're probably still confused. OK, you can think of it as a typewriter. Of all the possessions you left to posterity, your typewriter is the one I find most touching. As a foreigner in China, you could not live without your typewriter. Through it you could communicate with the world far away from you and overcome your loneliness. The typewriter understood your language and thoughts. In fact, only your typewriter could understand. You can think of this "electrical brain," this new machine I am using to talk to you as a kind of typewriter. (By the way, the phrase "new machine" reminds me of the substitute teacher of the Physiological Hygiene class I took in high school, which is one of the stories I want to tell you.)

About an hour and a half ago, I sat down at my desk and switched on my "typewriter" to write to you. Why is it necessary to switch it on? This phrasal verb hints at the difference between my "typewriter" and the one you used when you were in China on the front line of the war against Japan. You lived in China for about twenty months, the loneliest time in your life, as I now know. You wrote many letters to your comrades and friends in Canada on your typewriter, but you only received a few replies. You also used the typewriter many times, to write to your great friend, our Chairman Mao, as I learned from his well-known memorial to you. The memorial also mentions that he replied to you just once. Just once! And he never knew whether you received his reply or not. Did you get it?

Yes, my "typewriter" needs to be switched on to function. Now that I'm writing to you, I realize I will be more disappointed even than you were, because it is impossible for me ever to get your reply. I want to write down all of the things that we children of Dr. Bethune experienced. I know, had it not been you—had you not gotten on the passenger steamer in Vancouver on January 5, 1938, had you not walked into that historically significant cave dwelling at the end of March, had you not been sent to the front line in May, had you not cut your finger in November of the following year, had you not departed from the world due to infection, had your death not startled your great friend, and had he not published an eight-hundred-word memorial a month after your death—then we, your offspring, would not have experienced all the things we have experienced. My life would not have been like this. Our lives would not have been like this.

You may still be wondering about my "typewriter," which can only be operated after it is powered up, switched on. At the loneliest time in your life, electricity was hundreds of miles away. This was your own choice. You chose privation over civilization, believing that your choice would prove to be the road to progress. I know that when you were in China, you performed surgery under kerosene lighting. Your eyes started aging, and despite the light of your lamp, more and more of the world fell into shadow.

You may also be surprised to learn that my "typewriter" has a certain degree of intelligence, which is why it is called an electrical *brain*. With its intelligence, my "typewriter" knows that I am writing a letter now. A considerate query just popped up on its screen. (Yes, this "typewriter" has a screen, like a television, another device you may not have heard of before). The question on the screen is: "Are you writing a letter?"

"Yes, I'm writing a letter," I tell my "typewriter," "but it's to Dr. Bethune, an outstanding surgeon, a staunch revolutionary, an unsuccessful artist who kept on pursuing women without ever finding love, a fighter who couldn't communicate with his comrades, a loner who kept on writing letters but seldom got a reply, a foreigner who wanted to go home but had to die before his dream could come true." A sudden wave of emotion makes me pause. "He passed away almost seventy years ago. For me, he's a spectre that appears every now and then. How can you help me write my letter?"

Dear Dr. Bethune, I can't follow chronological order in my narrative of the past. I can't complete a true biography of your life just by using the papers in your archive. All the things I want to tell you are fragments of memory, some of them vague, like tombstones on which the epitaphs have mostly been effaced. All I can do is present my memories in fragmentary form, hoping that, as a great surgeon, you will know how to suture the pieces together into a life, my life, which represents the lives of all your children.

Dear Dr. Bethune, we both settled in a foreign country. I know I will die in your country as a foreigner, just as you died in mine. Your death was a big deal, "more weighty," as your great friend emphasized, than Mount Tai, while mine will be as light as a feather. But, no matter how weighty our deaths were or will be, death is our common homeland, the place we will ultimately meet.

A DOG

Dear Dr. Bethune, yesterday I ran into Bob at the entrance to my apartment tower. He's the neighbour I'm most familiar with, and the most talkative. He's a man in his late seventies now, and every time I see him, he wants to have a long conversation. We hadn't seen each other in a long time. If I hadn't been in a hurry to write to you, I would have asked him how he'd been. But last night I didn't want to get tied up. I just wanted to politely shake his hand, exchange a few pleasantries, extricate myself, and return to my room and my "typewriter."

Bob did not relax his hand. He mentioned the massacre he had just seen on television and complained that "the world has gone mad." I didn't say a thing. He's got a talent for turning small talk into desultory conversation. I didn't want to talk to him. I just wanted to make up an excuse so he would release my hand. To my surprise, he did something even more dramatic. He suddenly embraced me and started crying, broken-heartedly. Taken aback, I reminded myself not to ask him what had happened.

"My little girl is dead!" he sobbed.

I was shocked, because I knew how important Bob's

"little girl" was to him. She was his only companion since his wife's suicide. He had told me many times that without her he never would have survived and wouldn't be able to keep on living. He said she was his only spiritual support.

"What happened?" I asked, a bit reluctantly.

Bob cried even harder at my expression of concern.

I tried to move Bob's head off my shoulder, but he just wouldn't let go of my right hand. He told me she had refused food for four days. In the end, he took her to the vet, and she was diagnosed with cancer of the kidneys, late stage. And then she died, not even a week after the diagnosis.

Bob described this as the biggest tragedy of his life. Which was to say that it was worse than his wife's suicide. After burying his little girl, Bob had gone on a trip around the world. First he went to South America, then to Oceania, Africa, and Europe. Finally he returned to North America. He'd only been back in Montreal for three days. In Asia, he'd mainly gone to countries he'd not visited before like Vietnam, Cambodia, and Japan. But he had made a two-day stopover in Shanghai, his third trip to China. He found the prosperity he witnessed there disgraceful.

"Will you consider getting another one?" I asked without thinking, immediately regretting it because I didn't want to prolong our conversation.

My question made Bob all the more upset. "I've never considered it. I'll never consider it! It's impossible!"

14

he said, wiping the tears from his cheeks with the back of his hand. "I loved her too much," he said, pausing. "That kind of love is irreplaceable."

Dear Dr. Bethune, I could feel your gaze, pressing me not to keep talking to Bob. I twisted out of his embrace, patted his shoulder, and offered a few words of consolation, and then headed for the elevator. Before he saw me, Bob was obviously on the way out, but now he changed direction and followed me to stand in front of the elevator. Then he walked into the elevator with me.

"Will you go to the Olympics in Beijing?" he asked me, repeating the question he had first asked me four years previously, the question he asks me every time we see each other, a rhetorical question that needs no reply. Whether I said yes or no, Bob would always follow with the same remark. "The Olympics are going to cause a lot of trouble for China," he said in seeming earnest.

Bob fixed his eyes on me, not even glancing at the buttons. I pressed the button for his floor for him. He smiled and said that he wanted to accompany me to my floor and then go down and continue his walk. It wasn't the first time. I often wonder whether this company is for me or for himself. Dear Dr. Bethune, I was reminded of your "utter devotion to others without any thought of self."

By the time the elevator door opened on my floor, I was sick and tired of Bob's attention. "What trouble will the Beijing Olympics cause?" I said, angry. This was the first time I had ever responded to Bob's Beijing Olympics obsession. My response was also a rhetorical question.

I didn't wait for him to reply.

But my response provoked Bob even more. The pain of losing his "little girl" left his eyes for an instant. "I don't know what trouble they'll cause," he said, looking at me proudly and holding the door of the elevator for me. "But I know there'll be trouble." Then, even more earnestly, he added, "A lot of trouble."

My first long conversation with Bob had taken place in strange circumstances. That evening, I'd called my mother to wish her Happy Mother's Day and heard the news of Yangyang's father's disappearance. The news was unbearable and had left me feeling anxious. To calm myself down, I'd walked loops around our building, trying to breathe deeply. On the ninth loop, a stately Belgian shepherd blocked my path. I stopped and knelt down to pet it. Then I heard a forthright voice from somewhere nearby. "Her name is Sheila. She's my little girl."

I stood up and walked over to an older man sitting on a bench beside the lawn. Out of politeness, I praised his daughter's noble appearance and elegant manner.

The old man motioned for me to sit down on the bench. He told me his name and the floor he lived on. He said he knew I was Chinese. His friend Simon had told him. Simon is another neighbour. I often see him in the sauna by the swimming pool. Like Simon, the old man said he liked China and the Chinese people.

I was a bit hesitant, because I wasn't interested in talking to anyone at that moment. Especially not about

China. The news of Yangyang's father's disappearance had left me disturbed by my memories of China. "I'm waiting to see how that madwoman will carry on!" my mother had said at the end of the call, her voice animated. Not even at such a disastrous moment was she willing to utter Yangyang's mother's name. Instead, as obstinate as ever, she kept calling her "that madwoman." I found it almost unbearable. I knew that any disaster that befell Yangyang's family was good news to my mother, news she thought deserved to be broadcast far and wide.

My hesitation had no impact on Bob's mood. He started telling me all about his happiest trip to China. "It's hard to believe it's been eight years," he said, about to launch into a brisk reminiscence, motioning again for me to sit down by his side. "I've always liked Chinese people," he said, a sincere smile flashing across his face. "Even though they eat dog meat."

I sat down on the bench, feeling overwhelmed by memories of Yangyang's father. I was not the least bit interested in probing Bob's rather unsavoury topic of conversation. But then his expression turned serious. He looked me over and asked me solemnly, "Have you ever eaten dog meat?"

I civilly told him I hadn't. It wasn't actually the complete truth. The complete truth would have been, "Sort of." About forty years ago we visited the home of a friend of my father's, where we were served "stewed dog meat." At the time, I was feverish. And dog meat, normally a tonic according to traditional Chinese medicine, is considered poisonous to a feverish body. Though my father and his friend said this wasn't to be taken seriously, my mother insisted. She wouldn't allow me to eat at the beginning. But a compromise was successfully reached at the end. My mother agreed to let me taste the broth with a chopstick. Thus, strictly speaking, I have "sort of" eaten dog meat.

Bob's face relaxed at my reply. Then I told him that even though Chinese people do not consider eating dog meat barbaric, not many have actually had the opportunity to try it. "Because there are a lot of Chinese people, and very few dogs," I said, trying to be witty.

"Why so very few dogs?" Bob laughed and answered his own question. "Because your ancestors ate too many."

I didn't find it this amusing.

Then Bob shared that well-known claim about Cantonese-speaking people—that they'll eat anything with four legs except the table. He told me about how he'd seen endangered animals in cages in the entrance to a restaurant in Guangzhou City for the patrons to choose. Bob found this completely unacceptable. Other than that, Bob felt a deep respect for Chinese culture. He said he liked everything that was "Made in China."

"Is it because you've been to China that you like things Chinese?" I asked.

Bob waved his hand and said, "Quite the opposite. I went to China because I liked all things Chinese."

"Then how did you come by your fondness for Chinese things?" I asked.

Bob didn't reply directly, but asked another question instead. "Have you heard of Dr. Bethune?"

This was a question I'd often been asked in Montreal. In the past I never considered it a serious issue. But now, feeling unsettled by the news of Yangyang's father, it seemed a weighty matter indeed. It made me feel like the world was shaking. One scream after another burst through the partitions of time, exploding out of the depths of my memory. I could even see the frightened expression on Yangyang's mother's face. "I'm waiting to see how that madwoman will carry on!"—my own mother's voice over the telephone echoed in my ear. I was ashamed of her stubborn indifference towards the mother of my childhood friend.

Bob stared at me, waiting for my reply.

"Of course," I said. "Mao described him as a 'pure human being.'"

It was impossible for Bob to know about the pain I endured between his question and my reply. But he clearly knew the source of the words I quoted in my reply. His eyes lit up. "He was my idol when I was a boy. My very first idol."

Bob's declaration surprised me, because it could almost have been a part of my own reply. How could a political hero in China play any part in the childhood of an elderly Canadian? Dear Dr. Bethune, you were my childhood idol. Your portrait was stuck to the walls of my classroom in elementary school, while photographs of likenesses of Marx, Engels, Lenin, Stalin, and Mao hung over the blackboard. Your Canadian compatriots could not possibly have had the same experience as we had. In fact, you were our ideal not just in our childhood. You were also in the words we memorized, in our daily lives, and in our far-reaching imaginations. You were part of us.

I had no intention of opening the gates of memory to my childhood and letting Bob in. But Bob immediately dragged me into his own childhood. He said he clearly remembered one cloudy afternoon when his father took him to St. Catherine Street to take part in a gathering to celebrate your return from Spain. Bob's father was a member of the Communist Party. That day, he made a point of wearing a red scarf, "and he gave me a red scarf to wear, too," Bob said proudly. Riding on his father's shoulders, he saw you from a distance. Of course, he did not understand your speech, dear Dr. Bethune. But your gestures and the applause that you got were etched in his childhood memory. You became the first idol in his life. And his second idol, his father, was also born of that gathering. A week later, abandoning his wife and four kids, the second idol threw himself into the Spanish Civil War, too. Three months later, he lost his life in battle near Catalonia. Bob was proud that he had such a heroic father. He said that in his heart his father had never died. He still remembered how it felt to ride on his father's shoulders the afternoon of your return.

Bob admitted that he only understood your true greatness after he grew up. He was a clerk at Revenue Canada at the time. One day, after noticing a supervisor reading your biography, Bob went out to buy a copy for himself. That biography, which was basically a work of propaganda, intensified Bob's esteem for you. It drew him closer to communism. He said he'd never joined the Communist Party, because he thought being a communist would be the hardest thing in the world, given the way the world has gone. But he was firmly convinced that a socialist system, far superior to capitalism, was the most humane social system possible.

We talked until deep in the night. Or rather, Bob talked deep into the night. I was surprised that I would, so many years later and on the other side of the earth, hear someone say that "socialism is superior to capitalism," the "truth" our politics teacher in high school proved with "facts" in every class. "The acorn doesn't fall far from the tree," I said, trying to sum up Bob's relationship to his father.

Who knew my commonplace would induce such an emotional change? "Not necessarily!" He sounded sad. "The world's not the same anymore." I could see his cheek twitching. "Young people today are more and more selfish. They don't have a sense of responsibility, or morality. Nobody would take Dr. Bethune as a role model anymore."

"If you had a son, he might be different," I said, trying to reassure him.

"I have a son." His voice sounded cold. "He's not even average. He's not the least bit like me." He stood up, called his little girl, and left without saying goodbye.

21

I didn't understand why my pleasantry would cause Bob to lose all interest in our conversation. Still sitting on the bench, I watched Bob walk away, looking every inch a broken-hearted father from behind. Then I thought of Yangyang's father. Why had he disappeared? Where had he gone?

The day after that first conversation with Bob, I ran into Simon in the sauna. He'd already heard about my encounter with Bob. I was going to ask about Bob's son when Simon brought up Bob's wife. Two other old Jewish men in the sauna joined in. The three old men praised Bob's wife as the most beautiful woman they'd ever seen. But that was the only thing they agreed upon. When it came to when she had committed suicide and why, they all remembered differently. One remembered that it happened less than ten years ago, and he was sure that she had killed herself because Bob was involved with a middle-aged woman living on the same floor. Simon and another old man recalled that it was more than a decade ago, but they didn't agree on the reason. Simon thought it was because their son hadn't lived up to expectations, while the other old man was sure there was some kind of inherited tendency. As far as he knew, Bob's father-in-law had committed suicide in a German POW camp on the eve of VE Day.

The three old men remembered that, after his wife's funeral, Bob had joined a package tour to China. That was the second time he had gone to China. The first time had been the year before he retired, when he went with his wife. Simon remembered very clearly that Bob went to see the Three Gorges, which he would mention to anyone he met that year, urging his friends to go and see it soon, before the mythic landscape was flooded for the massive hydroelectric engineering project.

After he came back from that second trip to China, Bob's life returned to normal. He didn't move to a smaller apartment on a different floor as he had planned to do before going on his trip. This might have been because the middle-aged lady he was supposedly having a relationship with moved away before he came back. Every morning, like clockwork, he would go down and walk his little girl. He was just as talkative as before, but he never mentioned his late wife to anyone.

Certainly not with me. I only knew about her tragic end from Simon, and I never mentioned her to Bob himself. But I did happen to see his son one time.

I was returning from the central library not long ago when I saw Bob standing in the doorway to our apartment tower with a middle-aged man who was tall and thin and tired-looking. Bob called hello, but did not introduce me to the man. I waited to one side for him to say goodbye.

After the man left, Bob did not immediately turn his head. He watched him walk away, and, as if talking to himself, said, "There he goes."

I knew who he was referring to. I recalled our first conversation and did not inquire further.

"He's nothing like me. He doesn't believe in himself.

Or should I say all he believes in is drugs." He was still staring at the retreating man and seemed to be talking to himself. "The only reason he came to see me is because he needs money. That's our father-son relationship. We no longer have anything to talk about except my pension."

He kept staring into the distance, as if into the obscurity of the past. I did not know how to call him back from the sense of despair he must be feeling.

"A dog," Bob said. "A dog that has lost its way."

I patted Bob on the shoulder. Only then did he remember I was standing there. He looked round with tears in his eyes and sadly shook his head.

At that moment, I almost mentioned Yangyang's father to him. Compared with a father who had lost his son forever, Bob should feel lucky, because his "dog" wasn't really lost. It knew where its home was when it got hungry. Yangyang's father's pain might prove some small consolation to Bob. But I did not say anything. I did not want to gaze into the dark obscurity of the past, something I had refused to do for many years. I walked with Bob in silence into the building.

In the elevator, Bob's mood took another sharp turn. He smiled slyly and repeated his rhetorical question, "Are you going to the Beijing Olympics?"

A SPECTRE

Dear Dr. Bethune, today Bob mentioned an article in *The Globe and Mail* about Chinese coal miners. He's very angry about the bad working environment and living conditions the miners have to endure, so dreadful in comparison with the prosperity he witnessed in Shanghai. He thinks the gap between rich and poor in China is dangerously wide. "China is the biggest capitalist country in the world today," he said, in all seriousness.

I don't know if that's his own opinion or if he was quoting from the newspaper. "Don't forget that China is a People's Republic under the control of the Communist Party," I reminded him, partly as a provocation.

"So it's the biggest capitalist country under the control of the Communist Party." Bob said, incensed.

I didn't know how to react.

"I don't care what the country is called. I care about the economic reality!" Bob continued. "I love China, but I hate capitalism."

Recalling that he once said that he was happy that the world had entered the "Made-in-China" era, I asked, "Do you also hate capitalism when it's made in China?"

He didn't answer.

Dear Dr. Bethune, can you, as a member of the Communist Party, imagine and tolerate the fact that the country you devoted yourself to can now be called "the biggest capitalist country in the world"? Having left China almost two decades ago, I don't feel personally connected to the huge changes taking place there, but there's one thing I'm sure about. When I left China, it was a socialist country both in name and in practice. Of course, at the time, the debate between socialism and capitalism had died down, as per the famous "cat theory": no matter whether it is a white cat or a black cat, if it can catch mice, it is a good cat. It doesn't matter whether the country adopts socialism or capitalism, in other words, it's fine so long as it works for China.

The year before I left China, 1989, was the fiftieth anniversary of your death. That year, so much happened both in China and around the world. Socialist regimes in Europe fell one after another, like dominoes. (You might not find this news too shocking, considering that most of those regimes hadn't even come into existence in your lifetime.) The Soviet Union, which you were obsessed with, was on the verge of collapse, as well. I know you once visited the first socialist country in human history, and I know how important that visit was to you, how it inspired your conversion from individualist to communist, how it heralded the final and fatal move of your life when you travelled those thousands of miles to join the communist cause in China.

I have many things to tell you about what happened that year. But let me return to Bob, whose view of China is not completely unreasonable. You would find the way China has evolved unimaginable. In today's China, money, which you despised, has become the symbol of ability and happiness. Doing things "without any thought of self," as your great friend described your own spirit, is now seen as either idiocy or hypocrisy.

Maybe a linguistic detail can help you better understand China's change. You were used to people calling each other "comrades" in China. But today, the most popular way of addressing someone is as "boss." Maybe this is a sign of capitalism. My mother is very unhappy about it. She says being called "boss" gives her the creeps. When I was a child, "boss" only referred to someone who exploited others. If your parents or any of your relatives was a boss, you would feel ashamed of them; if you were a boss yourself, people would think that you deserved to die ten thousand deaths or at least make a confession in the hope of clemency. But today, every Chinese person wants to be a boss. And anyone in a position of power is called "boss." A government officer is "boss," a school headmaster is "boss," a magazine editor is "boss," a doctor, a concierge, a bus driver. Even those who don't have any power at all call one another "boss." If you ask a stranger for directions, you had better call him "boss." Businessmen (real bosses) are the most respectable group of people in China. They command children's respect and stimulate their imaginations, just as you aroused ours in the past. You are our father not because of your means, but because of your spirit.

In a society like that of China today, how many people would pay attention to coal miners working and living under wretched conditions? They don't represent China, and China doesn't represent them, either. Bob cannot understand this. He believes that the spectre he met at the beginning of *The Communist Manifesto* is still haunting the good earth in China.

That spectre did haunt the good earth in China when I was a kid. We were born into a new society and grew up under the red banner, as adults never failed to remind us. We were the inheritors of the great communist cause. The symbolism of communism was all around, encouraging us and inspiring us. But in the 1980s, those symbols disappeared from view, and today, they have even disappeared from China's collective memory.

In Montreal, however, the city you used to call home, one does come across the relics of communism. This is a side of this city I find confusing but exciting. Pictures of the hammer and sickle and workers with huge fists and muscled arms, portraits of the revolutionary mentors, the cover of *The Little Red Book* of Mao's pithy sayings, the opening and closing lines of *The Communist Manifesto*. These words and images often appear in announcements pasted on telephone poles or in the brochures people hand out at the entrance of the metro station or the supermarket. These are signs that connect this city with the city where I lived as a child, as one of Dr. Bethune's children.

In my distant hometown, *The Communist Manifesto* opened the door to Western civilization for me with its famous first line, "A spectre is haunting Europe, the spectre of communism." *The Communist Manifesto* was the *Harry Potter* of its time. From the very first sentence, I learned of the existence of the spectre and even of the continent of Europe, and about the impending globalization of communism. I imagined that when the workers of the world united, only one language would be needed, and only one chairman would be necessary. I imagined that the language would be our mother tongue, the chairman our Chairman Mao.

I remember one evening on my way home from school when I recited that first sentence to myself, it suddenly occurred to me that the beauty of a language was in its metaphor. "Ah, a spectre!" I felt a strange shudder from the bottom of my heart. In our value system, a spectre was an evil presence, like a demon, while communism was the noblest ideology and could only be compared to an angel. How could our great revolutionary mentors juxtapose an angel with a demon, proclaiming opposites in the same breath? "The word *spectre* is a metaphor," our principal explained one day across the public-address system. "Comrade Marx and Comrade Engels, our revolutionary mentors, sagaciously wield rhetoric as a weapon in the revolutionary cause."

That was the first time I heard the word *metaphor*. And the "spectre of communism" was the first metaphor I had ever known. Every time I come across some relic of communism on the streets of Montreal, I always think of that afternoon thirty-some years ago and that strange shudder from the bottom of my heart. I am proud of my "red" childhood. It was an extraordinary experience to be "born into a new society" and to "grow up under the red banner." It taught us the power of metaphor much earlier than children who grow up under the Star-Spangled Banner or the Maple Leaf.

I relive my red old days in Montreal from time to time. There are big parades and rallies every year on May Day. Last year, coming out of a bookstore on University Street, I came across a parade of protestors, whose anti-capitalist slogans disoriented me, as did the solemn notes of "The Internationale." All of a sudden different space-times seemed to overlap with one another. I felt as if I had entered a fairyland. In my childhood, "The Internationale" was the only Western song we were allowed to sing. We even knew the names and nationalities of the lyricist and the composer. We knew, and were able to recite, their tough lives and harsh struggles. The music of "The Internationale" shocked us and encouraged us to be ready to give our lives, just like the revolutionary martyrs. The lyrics also strengthened our awareness of globalization. We looked forward to the day when the ideal of internationalism would be realized.

I kept following the parade. Dear Dr. Bethune, I know you marched in the parade several times on May Day here in Montreal. I imagined your every step and facial expression. I imagined that all strangers all over the world would become close comrades long before their deaths, just because of this somber anthem.

As Dr. Bethune's children, we had similar parades and rallies. We sang "The Internationale," shouted anti-American slogans such as "Stand with Panama! Down with America!"—a slogan first shouted in 1964 to protest American suppression of student protests over the Panama Canal. In the eighties, however, formal commemorative activities gradually disappeared, and now the May Day holiday, the third biggest holiday after the Spring Festival (Chinese New Year) and the National Day holiday, has become a time for nouveau riche Chinese to travel and shop. Their travelling and shopping destinations have extended from Beijing, Shanghai, and Hong Kong to Paris, London, and New York.

The spectre of communism no longer haunts China. China today is no longer the country to which you once devoted yourself. China today is no longer the country that buried you with honour and turned you into an icon, either. If your spectre is still hanging around, it is haunting your homeland, not China. Yes, it has followed me to Montreal. It often appears before me. It is listening to my description of the dusty past, a past in which it figured but of which it has no knowledge. Dear Dr. Bethune, I am going to tell you stories of the other China, which is a red China, a poor China, a China thousands of miles and decades away, a China that was full of sound and fury (though I hope it signifies something)—the China that Bob idealizes.

That other China had started fading away the year before I left China. One night after the Spring Festival that year, my wife told me, her lips close to my ear, that she wanted to write about her own life. I turned to her to kiss her fearful eyes. "Let me be your only reader," I said softly.

She knew I was using a figure of speech, as our great mentors did. She knew what I really needed and what I really meant.

A PIECE OF WORK

Dear Dr. Bethune, if you had lived to a hundred, you would have experienced the tumultuous year, 1989. I do not know whether the communist dominoes falling in an instant would have prompted you to re-evaluate your attitude toward life. Perhaps they would. But life is but a dream, and your dream had come to an end half a century before. You were lucky not to be tortured by the shattering of your illusions.

Nineteen eighty-nine was the most sorrowful year I can remember, the year of my own disillusionment. In the early summer of that year I read the strangest work in my life and then confronted the most intimate death. That death had an inevitable relation with my first bereavement, which is to say, an inevitable relation with you.

That stifling evening, when martial law was declared, my wife turned off the television before I had finished watching the headlines. She leaned her cheek on my shoulder. "What kind of world will our child grow up to know?" she asked.

The result of a test in early April had confirmed her

pregnancy. I made no reply. "Let's go to bed and have a nightmare," I said.

We lay on the bed, staring at the ceiling. For a long time, neither of us spoke. When I turned around to turn off the light, my wife stopped me. "I have important news to announce," she said.

"Who are you for, the people or the government?" I asked in jest, mimicking the stiff voice of a television news announcer.

"I am for the people's government," my wife said, always able to appreciate my humour. But then she turned serious. "I do have important news to announce," she said.

"What news can be more important than this?" I said despondently, pointing at the silent TV set.

"My first story will be published in July," she said excitedly.

One night after the spring festival, my wife had told me that she wanted to write about her life. I had not expected news of a publication so soon. "Where did this urge to write about your life come from?" I asked. This was a question I had been wanting to ask her ever since that night.

My wife touched my lips with her fingertips. "You have beautiful lips, you know," she said. She seemed reluctant to answer.

"Tell me," I insisted. "Why do you suddenly want to write about your life?"

My wife looked at me seriously. "I've always wanted to write my life. There's nothing sudden about it. The only thing that's changed is that I want to write it right now."

Then she confided that she had gone to a famous fortune teller with her best friend when we were visiting her in Hankou during the Spring Festival. Her friend, who was a successful career woman, had felt that her boyfriend was acting indifferently towards her, and she was desperate to know the future of their relationship. At her insistence, my wife asked her fortune, too. The fortune teller frowned at her lot. He listed several of my wife's life experiences, to her great surprise. He even foresaw that she would soon become pregnant. And that she would have a boy. But the biggest disaster in her life was right in front of him. "Do you want to know the truth?" he asked. My wife said, "Of course." The fortune teller said that although she was tough enough to survive the worst natural disaster, she wouldn't make it through a "man-made disaster."

"What man-made disaster?" my wife asked.

The fortune teller, shaking his head, said all he saw was darkness, that he could not see what was happening in the darkness.

"What about my child?" my wife asked. "What will happen to the child if I don't survive?"

"He's your child," he answered, obscurely. "He will stay with you."

What my wife told me was disturbing, making that horrible night even more horrible. "Nothing's going to happen to us," I said, trying to comfort her. I emphasized "us" intentionally, instead of saying "you." "Don't mind what the fortune teller said," I added.

At a loss, she nodded. She told me that her friend regretted having brought her to that fortune teller. My wife comforted her friend by saying that she never believed anything a fortune teller had ever said. But this time she truly believed the fortune teller's words. On her way back to her friends' house that day, she had decided to write a novel based on her life.

"Why a novel and not a memoir?" I asked.

"Because my life in itself would seem fake. I want to package it in fiction to make it more believable," she said.

I liked this odd explanation. "Nothing's going to happen to us," I said. I rubbed her shoulders, comforting her.

My wife cared even more about what the fortune teller had said after her pregnancy was confirmed. She quickened the pace of her writing, eventually producing thirty-two interrelated stories. In the meantime, she sent a revised version of her first story to a well-regarded avant-garde literary magazine, that had just told her that it would be printed in the July issue.

"Can I take a look at your manuscript?" I said. "I can't wait any longer."

My wife held me tight. "You can't?" she said, mischievously.

I asked her to be serious. "I really want to read it right here, right now," I said.

"On a night like this," my wife said. "We all need some entertainment to lighten up."

Of course, I fully understood the importance of the kind of entertainment she was alluding to. Since the last time, the day before my wife's pregnancy was confirmed, I had not had any desire for sex. It had been two months. My life had been taken over by news reports, insecurity, fear. I felt depressed, and I was exhausted, physically and mentally. I can't go on like this, I thought.

I gazed at my wife desperately. "I have imposed a curfew on my groin," I said, not knowing if I was making a sarcastic comment about the current political situation, or just mocking myself.

My wife laughed. "Come on," she whispered tenderly in my ear. "Let's break the curfew, just this once." Her fingertips were gliding over my chest, recalling my memories of sexual desire.

But my body was not aroused at all. My fear made me nervous. I could not feel any instinctive passion. All I could feel was shame. "Aren't you afraid that the child might know?" I asked, embarrassed, trying to use this excuse to relieve the pressure of my shame.

"I want him to know," my wife said, stubbornly. "He should know how he came into the world."

I needed another excuse, not the one I had used in April, when I quoted the first line of "The Waste Land" to brush her off. I thought of the topic she had just avoided. I asked her to give me time. I asked her to let me read her work first. "Then we can celebrate its publication," I said.

My wife saw through this. "If you read the whole story, we will not have time to celebrate," she said. She got a manuscript from the drawer of her desk. It was the prologue to her novel. She said the prologue could stand on its own and would be published along with the first story. She said I could read the prologue, which was entitled "The Past at Present."

When I left China, I took this amazing manuscript along in my backpack. My wife's words have evoked my deepest respect for her life and my guilty conscience over her death. From that historic afternoon when I first saw her to that historic night when I unknowingly bid her farewell, my understanding of her inner trauma was so superficial. That is my lifelong regret.

Dear Dr. Bethune, you do not yet know what role you played in our relationship, do you? You were our matchmaker. Forty years after you left the world, it was you who brought her into my world. "She can also recite 'In Memory of Dr. Bethune.'" Yangyang's mad mother's quavering voice on that historic afternoon still echoes in my ears.

To show my deep gratitude for you, dear Dr. Bethune, please let me, on behalf of all your children, transcribe this incredible story for you.

> Her life changed completely overnight. It was
> 1976. She had no idea what was going on. A group
> of soldiers from the People's Liberation Army had
> taken her to a noisy tent. She was surrounded by
> some doctors and nurses who were treating her. It
> was the first time she had had medical treatment
> without her parents present. "Where are they, my

father, my mother, and my brother?" she asked in a weak voice.

"Stop asking such silly questions," one doctor said, weeping. "You should know better."

A few days later, she was placed in a group of children who had all been told not to ask silly questions.

"We are going to take an airplane," the middle-aged woman who took care of them said in a lively tone.

Few of the children reacted to the woman's words. But the girl asked, in a trembling voice, "Why are we going to take an airplane?"

The woman, facing her, shouted, "You are going to have a new home soon. Each of you. You are flying to your new home." She emphasized the word flying.

None of the children seemed excited.

She stared out of the window all the way to the airport, at the ruins of the city. She still had no idea what had happened. She still wanted to know where her parents and brother were.

The middle-aged woman turned up the transistor radio in her hand, trying to distract the children from the ruins. Suddenly, she cried, "Nadia Comăneci! What a beautiful name!" She walked up and down the aisle, telling us excitedly, "She is from our sister state of Romania. Her achievement is our achievement," her voice drowning out the sound of the radio. "Let's give this pretty big sister a big hand! Let's give our socialist sibling a big hand!"

Not even one child applauded.

Only several months later would she realize what had happened that night. She would realize that she had been through one of the most severe natural disasters in the history of her socialist fatherland, one of the most severe earthquakes in world history. She would realize that, not as fortunate as she was, her family members had perished with about two hundred-and-forty-thousand others. She would also realize what people were talking about on the radio. The very first perfect score in the history of gymnastics. She not only came to realize the existence of the Olympics, but also heard the name of the host city for the first time. The name would become an integral part of her life, part of her. Every time she entered her hometown in a nightmare, she would always hear voices from the ruins talking about that North American city. She would be awakened in shock by that pleasant-sounding name: Montreal! Montreal! Montreal! That pleasant-sounding name would become a mark of her identity as an orphan.

Dear Dr. Bethune, I wonder how you feel after reading this. Its bold, direct style is completely different from that of your own writings. You were not a revolutionary in terms of literary style, but the style of this piece is quite revolutionary. Do you like it? Even if you like this kind of writing, I am sure it is difficult for you to enter this little girl's world. She escaped by accident from the most dreadful disaster. She heard by accident about the city where you lived and I was going to live.

When I entered my wife's maze-like world, her head was leaning against my chest. I could not see her face and had no way of knowing whether she was looking at her right hand, which was caressing my abdomen. From her breathing, I could hear her desire for me. I was deeply moved by her writing style. I could not help reading it again. Not surprisingly, the second, closer reading inspired an impulsive desire in me, a desire for intimacy. I did not want to leave that world. I wanted to hide in the deepest and warmest corner. Finally, I felt it. I felt my body awakening. Putting the sheets of paper down, I held my wife's face in my hands. I had a lot of questions in mind, but did not ask even one. I gazed at her curiously, as if she had become another woman. She seduced me with a charm that I had never experienced. "Do you like it?" she asked in a whisper. I seemed not to have heard her anxious voice. Burying my head in her breasts, I sucked hard on her nipples.

Her body had also been suppressed for two months, and now her nipples could finally stand erect with dignity. It was a moment she had been waiting for. She closed her eyes in satisfaction. My tongue was like a sail, tacking sensitively around her desire, and her body was like a tenacious tide that appealed to me with a rare amplitude. I knew gigantic tidal waves would soon overwhelm us. It suddenly occurred to me that my wife's quivering body was a literary work in a new genre, with countless details awaiting my exploration. I did not want to miss out on a single one. "I want to read every sentence, every word, every punctuation mark, every space." I said, making forceful entry into the labyrinth of her body. I had a liberated craving for knowledge. "I want to read you," I said. "Every part of you."

As tears trickled down from the corner of my wife's closed eyes, she asked, anxiously, "Do you like it? Do you like it?"

My wife would never know that her story was not published. One day before I left Beijing, I received a letter from the editor of the magazine, saying that times had changed and it would be "inopportune" to publish anything so forthright. *Inopportune* was the word that same editor had chosen to refer to the massacre that occurred in the centre of Beijing in 1989 at Tiananmen, beside the mausoleum of your great friend. However, the editor complimented my wife on her talent, calling her "promising." He encouraged her to persevere in writing, saying that good works would stand a chance of being published "in the future." He could not have known that the future had flatly rejected his promising author.

Dear Dr. Bethune, I can't keep on writing, for I can no longer see the words on the screen. Those words are now swimming around like a school of hungry goldfish. I remember the night when we got married, and my wife woke up terrified from a nightmare about her father's goldfish bowl. She told me that her father was famous for rearing goldfish in her hometown of Tangshan. However, two days before the earthquake, all his fish suddenly died. He called this unfathomable occurrence a "fiasco." "He never knew the actual cause of the fiasco," my wife said sadly, pressing her naked body against mine.

A MAN WHO IS OF
VALUE TO THE PEOPLE

Dear Dr. Bethune, I just came back from the lookout by rue Camillien Houde on Mount Royal. From there you have a bird's eye view of the eastern half of Montreal. The most conspicuous landmark is of course the Olympic Stadium. Like my wife, I heard about the Olympics and about this bilingual city in North America as the host of the games in 1976. The Mandarin pronunciation of the city's name, *méng tè lì ĕr*, was very pleasing to the ear. To me it sounded like the name of a woman who could be trusted. And the Chinese translation of the name carries the meaning of "utter devotion to others," which seems to hint at its essential connection to you.

But it was not until 1989 that I happened to learn of your connection to the city. In that year, my wife's best friend invited us to go to Hankou to spend Spring Festival with her family. That was the first Spring Festival we spent as a married couple. You also spent one Spring Festival in China, so you should know of the importance of the festival in Chinese people's lives. It is a festival for family reunions. But because of our marriage, we were

44

cut off from both our families. We became "homeless." So we gladly accepted the invitation. We had no idea that it was the only Spring Festival we would spend together. I had no idea that during that Spring Festival, my wife would hear from the fortune teller that a great disaster was looming over her.

On the train back to Beijing, we started talking to a Canadian sitting across from us. He taught in the Department of Political Science at McGill University, so of course we talked about you, dear Dr. Bethune, and I learned for the first time of your connection to Montreal. In the past, we had always just connected you with Canada. The mention of Canada would make us think reflexively of you, and vice versa. In the Chinese people's lexicon, your name is a synonym for Canada. That conversation linked you for the first time to a *city*. At the time, I did not know that city had already been linked to my wife through the disaster that would orphan her. Neither did I know that that city would be the next stop in my life's journey. It might even be the last stop. Your past, my future, and her imagination. This is the way the city took us in and gave us refuge in the maze of time.

I had noticed my wife's interest in Montreal, which I thought a bit strange. But I would never have connected her interest in Montreal with her childhood trauma. I remember at the time, on the train, she asked what the Olympic Stadium looked like, and that the Canadian took from his bag a postcard with that very building on it. He gave it to us. I remember my wife looked it over,

45

then looked at me, charmed. "It is totally different from what I had imagined," she murmured.

I wanted to know what she had imagined of that building and of the entire city of Montreal. Later on, looking down from the lookout on Mount Royal, I felt an even more intense desire to see that. I felt lonely. I have lived in this city for so many years without knowing whether my life was anything like what she had imagined.

Dear Dr. Bethune, did you, too, feel a deep sense of loneliness in this city? Now I know you not only divorced the same woman for the second time in Montreal, but also met the love of your life there. Did the consolations and tortures of love have any impact on your politics? This is a question that has always troubled me. You became a Communist Party member in Montreal, left the city to participate in the Spanish Civil War, and came back to hatch the idea of a Chinese adventure. Was there any necessary relationship between all this and the women in your life? How could your "Pony" see that you *must* go to China?

I think I've gotten off topic. The reason I mentioned the rue Camillien Houde was that I wanted to discuss the person it is named for.

Camillien Houde, the most controversial mayor in Montreal's history. He won his third election the year before you went to China. But I've never seen any mention of him in the Norman Bethune archives. I know you were willing to throw yourself into revolution, but in spite of this, did you ever vote in a democratic election?

That was the year when you were at your political nadir. You were despondent. You were called back from Spain. Crowds welcomed you on the streets of Montreal as a hero, but you knew that you had already lost the trust of the Communist Party, the "organization." How or why did you lose the trust of the organization? Was it something you did in Spain? And was losing the trust of the organization similar to losing a women's trust? Now I think these are meaningless questions. The important thing was that you were called back from the front line of the Spanish Civil War in 1937. This is what might be called a historical necessity. Had you not been called back, you would not have walked in to your great friend's cave the following year, and you would not have died in the Wutai Mountains the year after that. And had you not died in China, you would have left hundreds of millions of children spiritual orphans.

I understand your sadness and disillusionment. The crowds that gathered to welcome you home seem not to have brought you consolation or comfort. But you should know that your appearance changed so many people's fates. Bob's father went to Spain and died on the battlefield because of you. Bob may have been the youngest person in the crowd that welcomed you that day. At the time he was only six. Now, over seventy years later, he preserves the memory, perhaps the only one who does. And maybe one of the reasons he's lived so long is to pass this memory on to me, one of Dr. Bethune's children. That evening, when he talked to me about you, about

47

your place in his memory, I felt once again the mystery of life and understood even more clearly why I *must* come to this mysterious city.

The welcome the crowds gave you must have reminded you of a similar welcome two years previously, when you returned from a visit to the Soviet Union. Historians think that it was that visit that confirmed your faith in communism once and for all. You became a communist, someone who, in your great friend's words, "is of value to the people."

Dear Dr. Bethune, I have many questions about your visit to the first socialist country. What did you see in a country in which Stalin would soon carry out the Great Purge? Your political transformation reminds me of the author of *Animal Farm*. Like you, the English liberal Eric Blair went to Spain to fight against capitalism and for the socialist cause. He left because he was wounded in action. He never went to the country Stalin ruled, but he relied on his imagination to get to the truth (that it was metaphorically an animal farm) and critique it from a liberal perspective as the author George Orwell. But how is it possible that one person's imagination could get closer to the truth than another person's observation?

In fact, quite a number of figures of your generation saw the terror and the blood behind the political symbolism of the colour red. Sometimes I think you were inured to that because of your profession, which made you less sensitive to blood than philosophers and literary writers. Perhaps I should not compare you to Western intellectuals who lived in the same era as you. For you belonged to the future. You belonged to China. You did not see the darkness in the Soviet Union. You saw only the future of Red China, where you would become a star to light up the sky. Who was Gide? Who was Rousseau? Who was Hemingway? Who was Zweig? And who was Freud? At a time when all of us could recite your "spirit" by heart, none of us had heard any of these other names, intellectuals with ideas to contend with. In Red China, you ruled over all Western intellectuals to become a role model for an enormous number of Chinese people. Your image was pasted on both sides of our classrooms. You changed our thinking, and you inspired our thoughts. You took part in our daily lives.

And on top of all that, you left some important living fossils in various strata of the Chinese language. Certain terms have new meaning because of you. You are therefore one of the sources of meaning in modern Chinese. You are both the signifier and signified. Your relationship to Chinese is an issue historians of language have never discussed. I will discuss this in detail in your biography, if I ever pen it.

I seem to have gotten off topic again. Let us keep on discussing the former mayor of Montreal. I don't know whether this mayor—who was called the "people's mayor" —read in the paper the day after May Day about your return to Montreal from Spain. If he had read this news, would he have been jealous of your popularity?

And if he lived into the 1960s, his jealousy would

have been even more intense. Because your popularity as the "people's doctor" would have put his popularity as the "people's mayor" to shame. On the other side of the world, there are not only streets named after you, but also hospitals and schools and even an honorific, for at the time, our best doctors were described as "a good doctor in the mould of Dr. Bethune." Even more important, you had us, your hundred-million-strong posterity, Dr. Bethune's children.

However, the mayor knew what his people thought of him, while you didn't know what your people thought of you. The honour you received was posthumous. In 1939, the year that you left this world, George IV, king of England, the father of the present Queen Elizabeth II, came to Canada. He came to persuade Canadians to stand with the other citizens of his empire against fascism. In the company of Mayor Houde, he passed through the city of Montreal. People lined the streets. The king's self-absorption was deflated by a humorous remark from the mayor, who said, "Your Majesty, *some* of these people are here to see you." This was the mayor's witticism, which also reflected his self-confidence. He knew of the passion Montrealers felt for their mayor, "the people's mayor."

The king of England was unable to persuade the people of Montreal. More accurately, he was unable to persuade the "people's mayor." After war broke out, Camillien Houde appealed to Montrealers to resist the draft. He was not willing to send his constituents to foreign lands to save others, to kill and be killed. He just wanted to do his duty by his own people, not by other nations nor by "history." Is such a person to be labelled "a man who is of value to the people," like you?

Your situation was totally different, dear Dr. Bethune. You were a revolutionary, a man who wanted to do his duty by history. So, you went wherever a war was being fought. War was your home, your love, your true love. The First World War, the Spanish Civil War, the Sino-Japanese War. Your life's story could be divided into chapters by war. You might be able to defend your participation on the basis of your profession. You were a doctor after all. You could say that in every war you fought you were there to save people, not to kill. But if the "people's mayor" pointed out that the people you saved would go on to kill, what would you say in your defence?

The fate of Camillien Houde was a matter of "historical necessity." Because of his anti-war views, he was arrested by the federal government and spent the war that changed the world in jail. He was released towards the end of the war. The nations he had urged his own people not to go to war to save ended up winning the war. But he, too, ended up a winner, without having to fight—he was elected mayor of Montreal for a fourth term in 1944.

The end you met seems arbitrary, by contrast. You cut your finger accidentally during an operation. The wound got infected, and you died. At the time, it was an ordinary tragedy, until your great friend wrote that short eulogy for you—and described you as a noble-minded and pure man, a man who is of value to the people. Until he won the civil war (which we call the War of Liberation) and founded the new China. Until in 1966 he launched another unprecedented people's war, known as the Cultural Revolution. Only then was your immortality assured. That last revolution was the particular background against which your children grew up. That revolution gave you a place in our culture, our language, our consciousness. You became a political icon in China. You conquered the most populous people in the world.

A main road in my hometown was once named after you. It passed in front of the mayor's office. And the most intense military clash between different factions of the Red Guards at the climax of the Cultural Revolution happened in that same spot. Yangyang's father was an eyewitness. One day, he recreated the drama of the scene that day for us. "It was huge! Like it was happening in a movie," he said, in a state of nervous excitement. That particular clash led to the deaths of 168 people, including fifteen bystanders.

In order to prevent their blood from besmirching your name, dear Dr. Bethune, the road was renamed Harmony Boulevard. In the 1980s it was renamed again. Prosperity Boulevard.

A GREAT SAVIOUR

Dear Dr. Bethune, had you foreseen the tragedy that would befall him thirty-six years after you departed this world, would you have been so determined and in such high spirits when you came to China?

His name was Yangyang. His mother was our math teacher, who called her way of finding the lowest common denominator, which she was so proud of and which I could never understand, "the best method." And his father was "the least busy person in the world," as Yangyang put it the first time he ever took me to his home. He also told me his father had just come back from the May Seventh Cadre School and was waiting for his next work assignment. He said his father had been doing "labour training" at that school for the past four years. To Yangyang, his father was a stranger. Except for waiting every day for the Municipal Revolutionary Committee to send the work assignment notice, he had nothing else to do. He talked very seldom, Yangyang also told me, and he was very serious.

I was a transfer student to Class 3 of Grade 3. I had come with my mother from a small county seat in a hilly area in the south to the provincial capital to reunite with my father. My parents used their connections to get me into this particular elementary school. There were sixty-one students in our class, so the classroom was crowded. On my first day, I was assigned a seat in the last row. Ill at ease, I did not leave my seat at all. When I was called by the math teacher to stand up to compare fractions, everyone laughed at my accent. My classmates turned their heads to look back at me, I noticed, except for one boy sitting immediately in front of me.

The next day, after Chinese class, that boy turned and asked if I needed to go to the bathroom. When I nodded my head, the boy indicated I should go with him. "You didn't go to the bathroom the whole day yesterday," he said. His mention of yesterday made me very nervous. I worried that the next thing he was going to mention was my accent. I followed behind him, not saying a thing.

"How many times a day do you usually pee?" the boy asked me at the urinal.

I had never counted. Even if I had, I would never dare tell him, afraid that he would laugh at my accent.

The boy sneered at the urinal. "Look at all the maggots," he said.

This came as no shock. There had been even more maggots in the urinal of my previous school, and they would crawl out of the trough. What shocked me is what my classmate said next.

"To them, we humans must look ugly," he said with the utmost seriousness.

I found his comment provocative, but I still did not

speak. After I sat down the day before, I hadn't listened to the teacher's comments on my answer. I stared at your image on the wall of the classroom, dear Dr. Bethune. I imagined you heard my classmates' laughter, even that you were laughing at my accent along with everybody else. The thought made me unhappy. On the way home, I blamed myself for not listening to my mother's recommendation that I use Mandarin, the standard language, in the new school, because Mandarin was considered superior not only to my hillbilly dialect but also to the local provincial dialect. The reason I had not done so was that, with my accent, my Mandarin was not standard at all. Had I spoken Mandarin, my classmates would not only have laughed at me for being dumb. They would also have despised me for being pretentious.

The boy glanced over at me and said, "If you don't speak, you'll never . . ." He didn't finish, because he was peeing too hard.

I was grateful for his concern, but I did not express my gratitude. I had to be careful.

When we were leaving the bathroom, he told me that our math teacher was his mother. He also said that her method of finding the lowest common denominator was hardly the best. For him to criticize his mother in this way in front of a stranger made me uncomfortable. Right then the bell for class sounded. We ran to the classroom, stopping to catch our breath before going in. "My name is Yangyang," he said, panting.

From this first experience in the bathroom blossomed

our fateful friendship.

Two weeks later, when the class was divided into "Groups for Studying Chairman Mao's Works," Yang-yang asked me to join his group. At the end of term, every pupil had to pass a recitation test, reciting in Mandarin what were called the Old Three—three famous essays by your great friend: "Serve the People," "In Memory of Dr. Bethune," and "The Foolish Old Man Who Moved Mountains." The study groups were formed so we could help one another prepare.

Dear Dr. Bethune, while writing these essays, your friend was only the leader of the communists, whose future was far from certain. He had entertained you once in his cave at the communists' barren, isolated base in northwest China. You must have had a sense of his situation. But by the time we recited those essays, he had done away with all his enemies and was the supreme leader of China and a major player on the international stage. He was a key figure in the Cold War. Cold War? To you this must be another neologism. With your prodigious experience of war, dear Dr. Bethune, can you imagine what kind of war a cold war is?

In "The East Is Red," the most popular song of the time, your great friend was described as the great saviour of the people. This great saviour was a great strategist during the Cold War, dialectically turning our friends, especially the boss in Moscow, into enemies, and our enemies, like the Japanese and American imperialists, into our friends. As a result of these fundamental changes, he broke the stalemate of the Cold War and rebuilt the world order. So, in our hearts, he was not only the great saviour of all Chinese people, but also a saviour of people all over the world. Yangyang once noted that "The East Is Red" contradicts "The Internationale," which clearly says "there have never been any so-called saviours." His mother was not pleased with his discovery. She warned him to not always use logic to tackle such a sensitive matter.

When asked to recite in Mandarin—my Achilles heel—I could not distinguish between /n/ and /ng/, the two tricky phonemes, and often made embarrassing mistakes as a result. For instance, the pronunciation of *star* is /xing/ and the pronunciation of *new* is /xin/ without /g/. So the pronunciation of *new star*, as in a new Hollywood star, is /xinxing/. But I pronounced it as /xingxing/, which is the same as the pronunciation of *chimpanzee*. "How many chimpanzees live in Beverly Hills?" my classmates used to ask, making fun of my hick Mandarin.

In memorizing the three essays, the main problem for me was not actually pronunciation, because pronunciation was not what we were evaluated on. The problem wasn't the essay entitled "Serve the People," either. My problem was with the other two essays, starting with the first sentence of "In Memory of Dr. Bethune," which goes, "Comrade Norman Bethune, a member of the Communist Party of Canada, was more than fifty years old . . ." I now know that your great friend got your age wrong. When you made light of travelling thousands of miles, you were not yet forty-eight years old. This mistaken piece of information gave me the impression that you were already an old man when you came to China. So I imagined you being about the same age as the foolish old man who moved mountains. This seriously interfered with my recitation, because I always confused those two essays.

Yangyang had a nearly photographic memory. Memorizing these three essays was no sweat to him. "He can even recite it in reverse," our homeroom teacher once said, when she was praising his talents at the school assembly. He often represented the school at community or municipal recitation competitions, and he made the school proud every time.

In the month before the test, the four pupils who were the worst at recitation were compelled to stay in the classroom to receive "enhanced training." Naturally, I was one of the four. Our homeroom teacher—the Chinese teacher—monitored us, sitting sat on the podium and making us stand in front of her and recite, one by one. If we made a single error or got stuck, we had to stand at the back of the classroom, facing the wall, practicing the problematic sentence thirty times. Then we would wait for her to call us up to stand in front of her and start reciting all over again.

That was how it went the first three days, but on the fourth day there was a significant change. First the teacher called Big Eyes to the front. He had just recited the first two sentences from "In Memory of Dr. Bethune" without making a mistake when she lost her temper. She said she could not stand our obtuseness anymore and was no longer willing to waste her time on us. She said she had something "more important" to do. She would come back in two hours and check on our progress. Then she locked the classroom and went to do that something "more important."

It was the same every day after that. She would leave the classroom after our enhanced training started and came back to check on our progress two hours later.

This kind of enhanced training was seen as the concrete expression of a teacher's responsibility. And our teacher was praised by the principal and given the title of the "Most Responsible Homeroom Teacher." Our principal was a gallant looking man, a bit like the Minister of Foreign Affairs at that time, which inspired our nickname for him, Foreign Affairs. And of course we called his office the Office of Foreign Affairs.

The enhanced training ceased to be effective from the fourth day on, as we no longer focused our energy on recitation. Most of the time we spent arguing about why the teacher always had something more important to do at that time and what the hell it was. Our argument was put to rest by a discovery made by the boy we called Dumb Pig.

Dumb Pig was the naughtiest boy in the class and the worst at recitation. He was also the only pupil who had never passed the recitation test. The nickname Dumb Pig was the teacher's idea. We had never heard her use his real name, so we all called him by this same nickname. Anyway, Dumb Pig's discovery was that after locking the classroom door, the teacher would go to the Office of Foreign Affairs. He said he had discovered this through the crack over the back door to the classroom.

We found this extremely interesting. The next day, when the teacher walked out of the front door, we rushed to the back door, which was never opened and was blocked by the last row of desks. We stuck our eyes over the crack. We saw the teacher walk past, obviously headed towards the Office of Foreign Affairs. But the crack constricted our field of vision, not allowing us to see all the way to the office at the end of the hall. We all accused Dumb Pig of making up stories. But he rebuked us as our teachers did. The eyes are merely windows on the soul, he claimed. To find out the mysteries of the world, you have to rely on more than what you can see with your eyes; you have to use your imagination.

Dumb Pig was considered the most sexually knowledgeable pupil in our class. He often bragged that he had climbed the camphor tree located outside the public bath not far from his home to watch the women bathing. To prove his claim, he often shared the special discovery he had made. He said don't believe your eyes when you see a woman's bosom lifted up, because every breast sags in the bathroom. Every time I heard Dumb Pig talk about women, I wouldn't be able to get to sleep, impressed with how mysterious women were and chagrined that I had never witnessed anything like that. Another time Dumb Pig was dragged to the podium by our homeroom teacher because he had not heard her explanation of the beginning of the story entitled "A Chicken Clucked in the Night," which deals with the class struggle. Instead, he had been drawing a picture of a woman's genitalia in the textbook. And after class, he was even dragged down to the Office of Foreign Affairs. When Foreign Affairs asked him what he had drawn, Dumb Pig replied, "What my female classmates pee with." When Foreign Affairs asked him how he knew what it looked like, Dumb Pig replied that he had learned it from *The Barefoot Doctor's Manual*.

Dear Dr. Bethune, you probably have never heard of the barefoot doctors, but I don't think you would find the term hard to understand. They were like the medical personnel given rudimentary training in the makeshift medical school you helped build in the Wutai Mountains— doctors who wandered in rural villages, sometimes without any shoes, representatives of your great friend's concern for the health of hundreds of millions of Chinese peasants. *The Barefoot Doctor's Manual* was the only medical book available to them when he launched the Cultural Revolution.

The next day, we all seemed focused on memorization, pretending that we had lost interest in Dumb Pig's discovery. He opened his *Little Red Book* unenthusiastically, as if preparing to practise, just like the rest of us. But then he burst out laughing. He said he had just figured out why our teacher called what she had to do something "more important." "Her words are completely correct," he said. "Because she is going to 'serve the people.'"

To this day I don't know why the pupil the teacher

considered the stupidest in the class could be so smart as to know how to apply the title of Chairman Mao's essay to real life. From this incident, I also understood your great friend's remark that "the lowly are the most intelligent," and his mastery of dialectics. It was often said that Mao learned dialectics from Marx, but it's really in the essence of Chinese culture. For instance, we have a saying, "The great wisdom often appears foolish," and this certainly applied to Dumb Pig.

This reminds me that it is dialectics that allowed your great friend to "make a sound in the East and strike in the West" and to "turn bad things into good things." With such a strong intellectual weapon, he won all political struggles. He did not use dialectics in the essay about you, though. He highlighted your "utter devotion to others without any thought of self," thereby contrasting selfishness and altruism. Would you agree with this assessment?

As exam day got closer, I became more and more dissatisfied with you and the foolish old man who moved mountains. You two were always inseparable, and I mixed you up into a single person who did not care about my exam. But I was concerned about or, more accurately, worried about my test. One day in class the teacher said that an inability to recite the three essays reflected not a lack of intelligence but rather a moral problem. She said it was a sign of moral turpitude not to be able to do this. I didn't really know what moral turpitude meant, but I knew it was something very, very bad. I did not want my behaviour to be characterized as moral turpitude. In retrospect, it's odd that I never blamed you at the time. Dear Dr. Bethune, had you not chosen my country and, especially, had you not died in my country, "In Memory of Dr. Bethune" would not exist, and we would not have had to memorize so much. I would have only had to memorize one essay about an old man. Indeed, maybe I should blame you. Why did you make light of travelling thousands of miles to come to China, anyway?

Yangyang resolved to drag me out of the linguistic labyrinth that your great friend had constructed. Every time I was kept in school for enhanced training, he insisted on staying with me. The teacher did not disapprove. She even praised him as a model of serving the people and utter devotion to others.

Yangyang thought of a lot of different ways to help me avoid mixing up the two old men. The most useful method was a picture he drew of one tall old man and one short old man with serious expressions standing side by side. The tall one was twice as tall as the short one. When I was memorizing "In Memory of Dr. Bethune," he covered the lower half of the tall man's body with a piece of newspaper. In this way, he totally covered up the short old man. And when I read about the foolish old man, he covered up the tall old man's upper body. In this way, I could only see the short old man's body from head to toe. At the same time the lower half of the body of the tall one would accentuate the physical features of the short one.

This picture was a great help to me. I even discovered that the upper half of your body is unnecessary. All I needed was half of that picture—the lower half of your body—and the body of the foolish old man, and I could avoid mixing you up. To make sure it worked, Yangyang hid behind the teacher whenever she was testing me on my memorization. When I got stuck, he prompted me, exaggerating the shape of his mouth and his gestures in an effort to make his meaning clear. There was only one occasion when I nearly misunderstood.

The day that I passed the test, I said to Yangyang, "You are my great saviour."

My great saviour had saved me and ensured that I would not be guilty of moral turpitude. I will always be immeasurably grateful to him for this.

A MEMORABLE EVENING

Dear Dr. Bethune, our most responsible homeroom teacher failed one day to appear on time to let us out from our enhanced training. We were listening to Yangyang tell the thrilling story of an espionage network called the Plum Flower Party, not realizing that the two hours had already passed.

Then Dumb Pig heard his maternal grandmother calling him. Only then did we realize it had gotten dark without our teacher returning to check on our progress after doing whatever was more important.

The grandmother kept calling his name, and Dumb Pig ran to the window, yelling in response. Then it was our turn. We all crowded to the window and cried, "Help! Our teacher has locked us in the classroom!"

The old woman didn't know how to help us. She paced up and down in a state of agitation.

Dumb Pig placed his palms together, looked up at the sky, and declared, "Chairman Mao, you are the great saviour of the people. Please hurry up and save your poor people!"

His overacting amused us.

Soon we heard others' voices. First was the mother of Only Girl (she was the only girl in enhanced training). Then Big Eyes's older sister. Then I heard my father's voice. We were so excited that we started shouting to the people downstairs. Dumb Pig yelled himself hoarse. But he seemed to be the only one who wasn't really worried. Then he stopped yelling. He said he could crawl down the drainpipe outside the window. "And what about us?" cried Only Girl, as if Dumb Pig would really do as he had said. Then she cursed him. For a moment, Dumb Pig did not know how to respond. Yangyang started laughing. In the end, embarrassed, Dumb Pig sat on one of the desks. "In contrast to Dr. Bethune, our teacher's misconduct shows her utter devotion to self without any thought of others," he said angrily, once again displaying his talent for applying what he had learned from the Old Three. "Tomorrow we should go to the Office of Foreign Affairs to lodge a complaint."

On the way home, I sat on the back of the bicycle and listened to my father recount the complicated rescue operation. The parents had found the school caretaker, who had copies of all the classroom keys, but he said he was not allowed to open a classroom door without the teacher's permission. He said it was school policy. He lay on a wicker couch, uninterested in what had happened. Only when the parents demanded he take action did he get up and take a tattered old notebook out of a drawer. In it he found the homeroom teacher's address on the other side of the city.

My father rode forty minutes to get there, and only

when she opened the door and saw him did our home-room teacher realize she had forgotten to go back to the classroom to check on our progress after finishing something more important. She did not seem surprised or sorry. Quite the opposite. She blamed us for wasting so much of her time. She said we had better memorize the three essays before the weekend, or she would not let us into class the following week. She did not return to the school with my father, as he had hoped; she just gave him the classroom key. My father politely asked her whether he should ride back with the key after opening the door. While she was hesitating, her husband interrupted and said my father could take the key to school the next day. Our teacher gave him a look to tell him to butt out. Then she thought it over and ended up repeating what he had said.

So that's how we were rescued. When the door was unlocked, Only Girl's mother rushed in, stood in front of her, and slapped her twice on the cheek. Dumb Pig's grandmother grabbed him by the ear. Big Eyes's older sister shoved him twice from behind. My father didn't lay a finger on me, but he did blame me for wasting so much of his time. Then he warned me that if I couldn't memorize the essays by the weekend, I wouldn't be allowed home the following week.

When we came out, all the parents said we should be ashamed about what had happened that day. They all said the teacher had done right in locking us in the classroom after school for enhanced training, that it would benefit our studies. They all said that they should not have had to come to rescue us. They all said that our homeroom teacher was the most responsible in the school.

Only Yangyang's parents hadn't come. I was so envious!

The following morning, during our political study period between the second and third class, Foreign Affairs reported on the events of the previous evening. He criticized us harshly for not actively studying the works of Chairman Mao. He stressed that our passivity was the intellectual cause of this serious incident. His forceful voice shook the intercom over the front door of the classroom. We lowered our heads in shame.

The political study period was a most important activity in the school. In that half-hour, nobody could leave the classroom. We learned a lot in that period that we could not have learned in class. After criticizing us as "regressive elements," Foreign Affairs went on to assert that this was by no means an accident. It was no isolated event. In fact, it had exposed a serious problem, which was that pupils were less and less earnest in their study of the glorious works of Chairman Mao. This merited a high degree of vigilance among all pupils and teachers. In the long term, we were in danger of succumbing to moral turpitude. He even said that if we did not arm ourselves with the power of Mao Zedong Thought, our minds might be taken prisoner by capitalist ideology, and we might very well be hijacked by class enemies. At the end of the announcement, Foreign Affairs announced the unanimous decision of the Revolutionary Committee of our school:

the pupils who had been locked in the classroom would have to write a two-page "self-examination" within three days. He explained that our self-examinations should not have to waste ink on the incident as it happened. We should focus our attention on the intellectual cause of the incident. It would be up to Foreign Affairs to vet our examinations. If we did not write penetratingly enough, he would require us to revise or even rewrite.

In the Chinese class that followed, our homeroom teacher repeated the core of Foreign Affairs's announcement in her own words. She explained in particular that Yangyang had stayed on with us because of his noble nature of utter devotion to others. He did not belong with us regressive elements and did not need to write a self-examination. I looked up and saw Yangyang looking back at me, making a face. I took some small comfort from the fact that I had not incriminated my great saviour.

We never blamed you, dear Dr. Bethune, but later on I did formulate the following hypothesis: If you had not come to China, making light of travelling thousands of miles, that unforgettable evening would never have happened. I did not blame you. I knew you had any number of reasons to cite in defence of your fateful (and fatal) decision. For instance, you might say it was because of history, not because of you. Indeed, history! We were all victims of that mysterious history.

A couple of years later, two days before leaving me forever, Yangyang took me to an air-raid shelter beside the school field. In the past, I had only been there during air-raid drills, which were always held during political study time, and always impromptu. The alarm just went off, and Foreign Affairs interrupted his report to yell that Soviet Revisionist Elements had finally launched an attack. Sometimes he expressed himself metaphorically by saying the "Polar Bear" had come, which made the announcement even more dramatic. We flooded out of the classroom and lined up in the corridor, and then our teacher led us out of the school building, across the field, and into the air-raid shelter. These were the happiest moments in our elementary school life. I even hoped that the Polar Bear might change its proclivities and appear once a week, not just once a month.

On that spring evening in 1976, however, when Yangyang and I walked out of the air-raid shelter, I had a sense that something serious was about to happen. I was trembling, sensing that a familiar distance had become a long road. Even today, I sometimes imagine I am still on that road, that I haven't reached the end. This was the most painful evening of my life. I vowed I would never tell anyone about my experience. You are the only one who knows the secret that goes back almost thirty-two years. And, dear Dr. Bethune, it is a secret about you.

I don't know how long we stood there. It seemed like forever. When we walked out of the shelter, it was dark out. Yangyang asked if I still remembered the evening we were locked in the classroom during enhanced training. I said I would never forget. "I don't think you'll ever forget this evening, either," Yangyang said. "This is the last evening we will ever spend together."

I did not understand. But I was very afraid. I had already felt afraid when we were walking towards the air-raid shelter. Yangyang hadn't stopped talking. He even asked if I had heard any news about the martyr's bride. I was frightened. I didn't understand most of what he said.

Before we walked out of the shelter, Yangyang took a notebook out of his pocket and handed it to me. "You have to take care of it," he said, "forever."

I had known Yangyang had a secret notebook. He said it was his life. His giving me his notebook made me all the more afraid. "What do you mean by 'forever'?"

Yangyang smiled. "'Forever' means that it belongs to you from now on."

I felt even more afraid. "But I remember you said it was your life," I reminded him.

"Yes," he said. "Soon it will be all that's left of me."

The plastic red cover of Yangyang's notebook has become brittle, and the gold lettering of the quotation from your great friend has faded, but the words are still legible. Those are the most famous words from the memorial that your great friend wrote for you. Dear Dr. Bethune, every time I flip through Yangyang's "life," I have to pause at your "utter devotion to others without any thought of self." I have always treasured this notebook. Here it is in front of me now, beside my "typewriter." On a quiet North American night, I am gazing at your spirit. It's so far away, yet so near. There it was on that evening, here it is tonight. It confuses me and fills me with awe.

A SEPARATIST

Dear Dr. Bethune, I imagine you probably considered yourself a Canadian rather than a Québécois, when you were here in Montreal. Claude makes a distinction between Canada and Quebec. He's another neighbour of mine, one of my two close neighbours, Bob being the other. Claude and Bob have both lived in the building for nearly thirty years, but they don't really know each other. The reason is that they have different mother tongues. Claude's is French, and he believes that native English speakers like Bob are the progeny of invaders. Your great friend taught us to care about class struggle on a daily basis. In Quebec, in lieu of class struggle, language conflict has become the primary contradiction in social life.

Claude loves travel and women, just like you. He told me he'd made two round-the-world trips, and planned to make a third before he died. He also told me he had slept with fifty-three women from different places, of various ethnicities. His sex life is therefore characterized by "multiculturalism," an integral part of the Canadian identity since the 1970s. That may be the only thing Claude has in common with Canada. He was once married, for ten years, to a woman who was the thirty-first. She was a Hungarian who had moved to Montreal with her parents after the Hungarian Revolution of 1956 (another political event that you would find embarrassing). After he found out that she had had an "abnormal relationship" with one of his students, he divorced her. The divorce, however, did not lessen Claude's opinion of her. He always said she was the woman he was most obsessed with in the entire world.

Judging from the variety of his sex life, Claude could probably, like you, be called an "internationalist." But in Canada he's not even a "federalist." He not only refuses to admit he is a Canadian, but also refuses to admit that Quebec is a province in Canada. To him, Quebec is *mon pays*—my country. He is a separatist. You must have been familiar with this word when you plunged into the Spanish Civil War.

Back when I was in China, I heard about the separatist movement in Quebec and the referendum that almost made Quebec independent at the end of the last century. However, it was not until I met Claude that I myself ever experienced separatism.

Unlike most diehard separatists, Claude does not blindly oppose everything and everyone foreign; he's just hostile towards native English speakers. He is concerned about what is going on in the world. He often invites me to restaurants and is more generous even than most of my Chinese friends. For sure, I have to listen closely to his political opinions over the meal. In fact, listening to his analyses of political situations is a "necessary and sufficient condition" of his generosity. What he cares about most is, of course, the political situation in his country and in neighbouring Canada, or to be exact, in the "Great Cause" of Quebec independence. But he is also interested in the politics of other regions in the world, including China. When important congresses are held in Beijing, such as the National People's Congress, I get to enjoy feasts for lunch, so long as I can put up with his superficial understanding of the politics of my native country.

It is never easy to get along with Claude. His temper is the opposite of Bob's. When I talk to Bob, I can say anything I want, but I've learned to be tight-lipped with Claude. One time, I unthinkingly mentioned the former prime minister, Pierre Trudeau. I told Claude I had spotted something in the bookstore, a travelogue about China that Trudeau had written before he became prime minister. At this, Claude became restless and completely lost his appetite, pushing his plate away. "Why are you interested in a book written by that kind of person?" he asked in an accusatory tone, staring at me.

"Because I'm interested in how he saw China then," I replied calmly. "That is what China was like when I was a child."

Claude stared at me with a mixture of fury and pain in his eyes. "He was a dictator," he said. "Do you have any idea what he did to my country? He rolled his fucking Canadian tanks onto the streets of Montreal! That was the darkest day in the history of *mon pays*."

He was talking about the period of martial law in 1970 known as the October Crisis. "A man who grew up in Quebec, who was nurtured by Quebec," he continued. "He was a traitor to Quebec, a sinner who committed an unforgivable crime against Quebec." At that point, he walked angrily to the checkout counter, throwing the notes down and leaving the restaurant.

The reason I befriended Claude was not because of his generosity, but because of you, dear Dr. Bethune. The first time I met him was in the elevator of our building. He was accompanying a woman downstairs (I wonder now if she was one of the fifty-three), and from their conversation, I learned that they had just celebrated Claude's birthday. I was amazed. Staring at him, I took the initiative of wishing him a happy birthday and introducing myself. That was the start of our friendship.

Claude is the only peron I've ever met who shares a birthday with you. He doesn't know this and doesn't seem to have any interest in learning about it or about anything connected to you. What's more, I later found out that Claude is the same age as my mother, which means he was born in the same year you left Montreal for good. What a coincidence! But your lives in Montreal did not overlap. When Claude was born, you were heading from Hankou toward the communist base in Yan'an. That was your first birthday in China, the most ordinary (and thus the most extraordinary) birthday in your life. No friends, no celebrations, but you were full of yearning for life and longed for a conversation with your great friend in his historically significant cave dwelling. One year later, though, while Claude was celebrating his first birthday in his poor French-speaking family in Montreal, you had already tired of your legendary life in China. That day, you had performed an eleven-hour, non-stop surgery, without rest. By night-time, you were exhausted. After a short sleep, you got up from your cot, typed a long letter to a Canadian comrade whom you missed. You celebrated your birthday with memories as your only companions, not knowing it would be your last.

The fact that Claude is not interested in you has disappointed me from the outset. He does not even know that you lived in Montreal and did a lot of good things for his country. It is impossible for you to earn his respect, because you were a "fucking Canadian." In Claude's opinion, nothing that a fucking Canadian ever did for Quebec could be good. I respect his sentiment, and decided not to mention that your birthdays are on the same day. Such a coincidence would not be a happy surprise for a separatist.

A retired French teacher, Claude still loves teaching, always eager to impart his knowledge and skills to people around him. In addition to his "required course" on politics, he also taught me some "electives." The elective I benefited the most from was a skating course. One Christmas Day, he knocked on my door in the early morning, prodding me with a pair of skates and inviting me to go for a skate with him on Beaver Lake, at the top of Mount Royal. Then after the second time, the third time, it was no longer an invitation. It became an obligation. To be honest, he was too impatient to be a good teacher. I learned anyway. And after suffering his teaching for a whole winter, I was able to skate, which surprised me.

This experience slid me more deeply not only into life in Montreal but also into memories of my perplexing past. It was a mystical experience in some ways. One morning at five o'clock, not long after learning to skate, I was awakened by a nightmare about skating alone on Mount Royal for the first time. So I got up and went to Beaver Lake, as I had dreamed, and skated on the ice in the faint light of dawn. The tranquillity of the scene and my inner serenity were so in tune with each other that I experienced an absolute freedom I had never felt before.

But then my reverie was broken by a faint sound. Someone was calling me, just as in my nightmare, and it was a familiar voice, my wife's voice. I stopped in agitation, turning around, and saw my wife standing at the end of the lake. I waved at her, as though we were not separated by a decade. But just as I was about to skate toward her, she disappeared. I skated to where my wife had been standing. I took a deep breath of cold air, even though I could no longer sense her presence. On the ice, I saw a baby's glove, just like in the nightmare. I picked it up and saw the small red stain. Then, with the glove in my hand, I knelt down on the ice, trembling and sobbing.

Dear Dr. Bethune, Claude was not the first separatist I had met. The first separatist I met was Dumb Pig. In the night we spent locked in our classroom, he claimed he could go down the drainpipe and escape through the sewer, a claim for which Only Girl called him a separatist, just "like the Dalai Lama." Yangyang was so amused by her outburst that he shouted, "Unite, don't separate." This was your great friend's warning to his opponents inside the Communist Party, which we heard every day over the high-pitched loudspeaker. We children of Dr. Bethune lived with this warning every day we were in school.

Fifteen years later, Only Girl and Dumb Pig did unite, as expected. It can be said that their union was a result of their shared experience of memorizing the Old Three. At their wedding, Dumb Pig mentioned that night we were locked in. He said that he and his wife had had two matchmakers. One was Yangyang, and the other was you, Dr. Bethune. Their union gave birth to an enterprise that became renowned in the entire country, a business producing children's food. My mother once told me on the phone that their office is in a prime location on Prosperity Boulevard, in the highest building in the city. It is even iconic. My mother also told me that this couple are known as models of respect for teachers. When our homeroom teacher was still alive, they used to visit her every month. When she was hospitalized with cancer, they covered all her medical expenses. More interestingly, one day, when she was dying, she was suddenly unable to remember Dumb Pig, the nickname she herself invented—though she clearly remembered that he had failed that special examination on "In Memory of Dr. Bethune," and that because of his "sabotage," our class, Class 3 of Grade 3, failed to win the city title that year in the "Excellence in Mastering Chairman Mao's Writings" category. Not long before she passed away, our homeroom teacher said to Dumb Pig, "You're a Dr. Bethune in action now."

A NOTEBOOK

Dear Dr. Bethune, Yangyang begged me to go to the air-raid shelter with him. His expression and voice alerted me immediately that he had something very special to tell me. I had never been to the air-raid shelter on my own initiative and was extremely uncomfortable, but Yangyang's expression and voice made it impossible for me to refuse his request (or should I say his demand?).

The air-raid exercise was the most interesting activity in my third year of elementary school. When the alarm sounded, Foreign Affairs's voice came over the intercom, asking our teachers to protect us, "the flowers of the nation." He asked us to walk "calmly" out of the classroom, line up in the hallway "in an orderly fashion," walk downstairs "with composure," cross the field "in silence," and enter the air-raid shelter "in a disciplined way."

Foreign Affairs was the overseer of the air-raid drill. He always gave his orders over the intercom, always emphasizing certain words, which made his orders seem all the more forceful. However, the overseer himself never appeared in the air-raid shelter, as Only Girl pointed out. One time she asked our homeroom teacher why Foreign

Affairs always stayed in his office and never once hid with us in the shelter. She said the absence of the overseer made her feel that the exercise wasn't real.

Only Girl's question displeased the teacher, who clearly did not know how to explain Foreign Affairs's absence. We never imagined Dumb Pig would be the one to break the stalemate. He gave Only Girl a look. "You don't understand," he said. "This is called guarding the home front, and it is the expression of utter devotion to others." Dumb Pig's explanation made us a bit more respectful of Foreign Affairs. The facial expression of our home teacher relaxed. She took a long look at the boy who was supposed to be the stupidest pupil in her class, and with great satisfaction said, "Sometimes you're not as dumb as I think you are." At this unexpected praise, Dumb Pig lowered his head in embarrassment.

The atmosphere during the air-raid drill was a bit tense, but the times we actually spent in the shelter are happy memories. The day I walked there with Yangyan, however, I felt afraid and stifled. When we reached the shelter, I felt an intense antipathy to the place, which was cramped, damp, and cold. I had a strange new feeling, too. It was as though I had never been there before. I vowed never to tell anyone about my experience. In the investigation that took place over the weeks to come, I never once mentioned going to the shelter with Yangyang.

But now I'm telling you, dear Dr. Bethune. The last time I spent with Yangyang was in the air-raid shelter. We went soon after class ended. He begged me not to ask why. I was so scared, I started trembling. "Why?" I asked.

Yangyang laughed bitterly and said he was going somewhere far away.

"Where?" I asked uneasily.

Yangyang looked at me without answering my question.

"How far away?" I asked stubbornly.

Yangyang kept looking at me, but he did not answer my question.

"How far?" I asked again. "Farther than where Dr. Bethune came from?"

I don't know why I asked the question in that way. Maybe I had suddenly remembered that you had made light of travelling thousands of miles.

Yangyang looked alarmed, as if I knew something I shouldn't, and then he told me, "Much farther than that."

I did not dare ask the next question. I did not dare ask when he would be back.

"Nobody knows," Yangyang said. "Neither do you. If anybody asks you, you should say you don't know."

Yangyang's cold tone made me feel like we were conspiring to commit a crime.

I really did not know. Where was he going? What was he going to do?

Then, Yangyang started to remember some of the things we had experienced together over the three years we had known each other. He mentioned the two weeks he had spent with me in my hometown the previous summer. He mentioned that Dumb Pig was sweet on Only

Girl. He even mentioned the maggots in the urinal. "The first day you came to school I knew you would become my best friend," he said, with feeling.

"And you are my great saviour," I said.

But Yangyang did not mention going to Graveyard Hill to pick mulberry leaves. I don't think he overlooked it; I think he was refusing to talk about it. Moreover, I noticed that he did not use a flashlight to light the way in the shelter, but rather a candle. This was certainly a choice. Just like he avoided mentioning our most mysterious experience. His stubborn avoidance made me all the more uncomfortable.

Dear Dr. Bethune, thirty years have passed. My eyesight has started to go. I'm already near the age you were when you left the world. But I can still see Yangyang's final expression. I can hear his voice. That evening was a turning point in my relationship with you. My respect for you did not diminish, but my fear of you increased quite a bit. Yangyang did not end up coming to your home country, as I have done, but he did go to the place where you had gone. That is a place we will all go. But he went too suddenly, too violently, and too early. In retrospect, the loss seems all the more painful. If Yangyang could have been more patient, we would have entered high school together in the autumn of 1976. We would have learned about the Cartesian coordinate system. He had probably never heard the name Descartes. For a time in 1976, that name drew my attention away from the painful past.

The one who taught us about the coordinate plane

was an overseas Chinese from Indonesia. Oppressed under Suharto's anti-Chinese policy, he had left his homeland to return to "the embrace" of his fatherland. Everyone in the school thought he was strange. First, his attire and his manner were really odd. We all wore plain white and blue shirts in summer, while his shirts were always in bright colours with many different patterns. His hair was always combed extremely neatly, but he put a kind of cream in his hair that we found quite pungent. And he really liked to exercise. On holidays, he would take his family mountain climbing. After school, he enjoyed playing badminton with his ten-year-old son in the empty lot by the teachers' dormitory.

Even more important, he had a very particular way of teaching. Other teachers only talked about content; he liked to talk about the stories behind the content—which mathematician had what kind of weird habit, or which mathematician had marital troubles. From his class, we learned that mathematics was a bit like literature, and that it was also connected to daily life.

In explaining the coordinate plane, this strange teacher told us that Descartes had made mathematics simple and clear, but that he himself had been devoted to occult learning. I couldn't understand this, because we had learned from our politics teacher that the occult was a kind of idealism, while science was founded on materialism. "How can a person be a materialist and an idealist at the same time?" I wanted so much for Yangyang to be sitting in front of me so that we could discuss the contradiction of Descartes's life.

In addition to my incomprehension, I was little bit worried about our mathematics teacher. The distinction between materialism and idealism is a basic standard of right and wrong in Marxism. A Marxist should not only hate idealism but also fight it resolutely. Our teacher obviously had a great admiration for Descartes. When he discussed Descartes, he seemed, judging by his tone of voice, to be promoting idealism. Promoting idealism was counter-revolutionary. And we all knew that being counter-revolutionary was a capital crime. Anyone who was convicted of counter-revolutionary crimes would be sentenced to death.

Our odd teacher did not stop there. He started talking about something that Descartes had supposedly left behind for the world: a notebook. His choice of words made me extremely nervous. I felt he must know about Yangyang's notebook. I felt he was staring at me, at someone who was counter-revolutionary, just like him. Agonized, I lowered my head.

"Many people believe in the existence of Descartes's notebook. But nobody has ever seen it. That mysterious notebook may always remain a secret, like many details in daily life."

I was certain the teacher's gaze had settled on me. "Right," I told myself. "Just like Yangyang's notebook." This voice from inside my head suddenly gave me tremendous courage. I looked up and discovered our teacher was not staring at me at all. I was sure he could not have known Yangyang. Our teacher had returned to the embrace of his fatherland only after Yangyang left that embrace. Of all the flowers of our great fatherland, Yangyang was the one who had wilted the soonest. Dear Dr. Bethune, he was the earliest of your children to be lost.

A BEAM OF LIGHT

Dear Dr. Bethune, on the second last page of Yangyang's notebook, there is a drawing of a luxuriant mulberry tree. Two children crouch beneath it, both frightened. I know where that mulberry tree grew. I know those two children were Yangyang and me. The reason we were frightened does not appear in the drawing. There was an unexplained beam of light.

Silkworms were our common interest. I discovered we shared this interest on the day we became friends, on my second day at the new school. The first time he took me to his place, he told me on the way over that since his father had come back from the May Seventh Cadre School, he had had to reduce the number of silkworms he raised because his father found them disgusting. Yangyang had given some of his silkworms to the neighbour's children, and he gave me more than forty that day at his home,

Interestingly, the year we went into Grade 5, it was Yangyang's father who accidentally discovered the closest mulberry tree to our neighbourhood. I still remember the expression on Yangyang's face. There was a downpour that day. After early study period ended, Yangyang took me to the end of the hall and excitedly told me that he knew of a very big mulberry tree on the south side of Graveyard Hill. "Now we don't have to go so far to pick mulberry leaves to feed the silkworms." He looked around, as though afraid that someone might hear.

Graveyard Hill was only three or four kilometres from where we lived. Prior to that, we had had to take a bus to a mountain valley over ten kilometres away. I asked Yangyang how he knew about this mulberry tree. He told me that one day his father had gotten lost while out walking and happened upon it. His father even wrapped up some leaves with an old newspaper for Yangyang. He told Yangyang it was the most magnificent mulberry tree he had ever seen. Yangyang often told me that his father was like a stranger in his life, and that evening he seemed even more strange. Why would he bring his son mulberry leaves if he hated silkworms?

Yangyang looked back again and then asked me if I wanted to go with him on Saturday afternoon to look for the mulberry tree. He said his father wouldn't tell him exactly where it was. "He said it was difficult to find and that the vegetable farmer said the area wasn't too safe," Yangyang told me.

Of course, Yangyang's father's explanation made us yearn for adventure.

It was a rare day of fair weather in spring. The fresh air and the warm breeze put us in the mood to go exploring. We walked happily, stopping every so often to enjoy our leisure. Every time we came to a pond, we took the time to skip stones. Yangyang wasn't as good at this as I was—a kid from a small country town—but he insisted on competing with me, and wouldn't let me give him a break.

It was no longer early when we neared Graveyard Hill. We looked around without finding the mulberry tree until Yangyang suggested we climb to the highest point. The view was fantastic up there. In the cool of dusk, we soon saw a small grove and what had to be Yangyang's father's mulberry tree on the edge of the grove at the foot of the hill. "How could he lose his way and end up at a place like this?" I heard Yangyang mumble.

We did not immediately head toward the mulberry tree. "Let's rest a bit," Yangyang said and sat down on the ground.

I sat down most unwillingly beside Yangyang. I felt uncomfortable on the damp grass in the cool of dusk.

Graveyard Hill was not a formal cemetery. It was just a place where local residents buried their dead, ignoring the Municipal Revolutionary Committee's prohibition against ground burial. People usually buried the dead on the sly, but I did see one big burial parade. The pallbearers got into a fight with the police and militiamen who were waiting at the crossroads close to our home. In the end, the coffin was confiscated and pushed into the prison van parked at the side of the road. One bystander told me the deceased would be taken away for cremation.

The fight and the police van gave me the impression that cremation was the same as execution—a death sentence, something frightening. You never suffered the pain of fire, dear Dr. Bethune. You must be counting your lucky stars. Let me add that your great friend only stopped breathing thirty-seven years after you did. He didn't suffer the pain of fire, either. Nor did he break the prohibition on ground burial. In fact, he was not disposed of after death in any way, but was embalmed and placed in a mausoleum in Tiananmen Square, in the centre of Beijing, at what we call "the heart of our fatherland." His people can still see his dead visage there today.

Yangyang looked around. His ease and relaxed demeanour made me feel ashamed. "Sometimes I wonder what death is like," he said in an ordinary voice.

"Don't talk of such things," I said quietly. "It's scary."

"What's scary about death?" Yangyang asked. "The people in the Old Three are all dead."

"Can you please not use that word?" I begged him. I regretted coming with him to a dim, forbidding place. Think about it. If ghosts suddenly jumped out from behind a grave, where would we run? I doubted my great saviour would be able to save even himself in such circumstances.

"There's nothing scary about death at all," Yangyang said, patting my shoulder.

"Don't speak so loud," I continued to beseech him. "And don't touch me. I'm scared."

"Dead people won't hurt us," Yangyang said with certainty. But then his expression turned very serious. "Only the living can hurt us," he said.

Later, I often recalled this declaration of Yangyang's

on Graveyard Hill. It gave me the impression that, even though we were best friends, we were living in different worlds because we felt differently about so many things. At the time, though, my mind was occupied only by fear. I was not in the mood to understand the truth in Yangyang's statement. I just wished he would say as little as possible.

Yangyang seemed unable to stop. "Do you believe in an immortal soul?" he asked.

This question did elicit my interest. "I do," I replied. "But my mother always criticizes me. She's a Communist Party member. She says that Party members are materialists. They don't believe in souls. And we are Chairman Mao's Red Guards, the inheritors of the communist cause, so we should not believe in souls, either."

"My mom said the same thing," Yangyang said. "She's not only a Party member but also a mathematics teacher. She says math has nothing to do with the soul."

"I think it does," I said.

"I think so, too," Yangyang said. "Math is like the soul. It will continue to exist after we die."

"I don't want to die," I said. Only then did I realize I had uttered the word that made me so afraid.

"Neither do I," said Yangyang.

Then came what seemed like an endless silence. I believed Yangyang was contemplating the mystery of death as I was.

Suddenly a faint beam of light interrupted our silence. It was coming from the grove. "What is it?" asked Yangyang, pointing towards the source of the light. I was so scared I'd broken out in a cold sweat.

"What is what?" I asked anxiously, refusing to look where he was pointing.

Yangyang turned my face in the direction of the grove. "Look at the light, the beam of weak light," he said.

"What could it be?" I asked.

"Your voice is shaking," Yangyang said.

"So is yours," I retorted.

Yangyang looked at me in disbelief. "I'm not afraid of dead people," he said. But his voice was trembling.

It was like the light of a flashlight. That's what I thought, but I did not dare to speak. I remembered what Yangyang had just said. "You just mentioned living people," I said despairingly. "I don't want to get hurt."

"Maybe we're imagining it," Yangyang said, noticing my fear of the living.

"Why would we both be imagining the same thing?" I asked. I didn't think we were imagining it.

Yangyang's bravery was frightening. He recommended we go down immediately to find out what on earth the light was.

I was terrified. I didn't dare go down with him. But I wasn't willing to get separated from him, stuck all alone on Graveyard Hill amidst all the graves. I had no other choice but to stay by his side. We trotted down, bent over at the waist, and then crawled for bit. As we approached the grove, the light got clearer and clearer. It hadn't been our imagination.

But when we got about thirty metres from the grove,

the light disappeared.

Yangyang and I had just climbed behind a grave. We stopped there.

I had the feeling that disaster was upon us. I stuck my cheek to the grave mound, smelling the ground and the grass. At the same time, I reflected that a dead person was lying right under my body, and that made me all the more afraid. I put my hand on Yangyang's back, wanting to discuss countermeasures. Then a blood-curdling scream came from behind the grove of trees. I felt Yangyang shudder.

The scream was really strange. I couldn't tell whether it was a male or a female ghost, or whether it was a scream of pain or joy. Before I had time to react, the scream turned into the sound of panting. I still could not tell whether it was a male or female ghost, but it was panting harder and harder, more and more scary, as if the ghost were approaching us.

I pushed Yangyang hard. "What do we do?" I whispered.

"I don't know," Yangyang impatiently.

Then the panting stopped. We had obviously exposed our presence. After a frightening silence, the ghosts ran like lightning out of the grove. Yes, there was more than one. Ghosts! The shadows and the sounds of the footsteps clearly indicated that there was more than one. I was limp with fear. Then I felt Yangyang pull me hard. "Run!" he ordered. I ran with Yangyang, like crazy. We kept running until we reached a lighted road.

A FLASHLIGHT

Dear Dr. Bethune, Yangyang did not come to school on Monday. After mathematics class, which was taught by his mother, she called me to the front of the classroom. She asked me where I had gone with Yangyang on Saturday. According to our agreement when we parted that evening, I replied that we had gone to the reservoir. His mother stared at me for a long time and said, "You are not telling the truth." How could she tell that I was lying?

Then she also lied, saying that Yangyang was not in school because he had come down with a fever on Saturday night. That was not the case. The reason Yangyang missed class on Monday was not because of a fever, but because there was still a bruise on his face from when his father had beaten him on Saturday night.

The next day, when Yangyang came back to class, the bruise had not completely disappeared. After political study ended, he sat with me on a bench in the schoolyard and told me what had happened at his house on Saturday night. "Why was your father so rough with you?" I asked. He said he did not know. He said his father had never beaten him like that before.

When he got home that evening, Yangyang had not followed our agreement and said we had gone to the reservoir. He did not know why, but he fell apart as soon as he saw his mother and told her what had happened on Graveyard Hill. When his father got home, Yangyang was already in bed, not yet asleep. He heard his mother tell his father what had happened to us, and when she mentioned the two ghosts, he lost control. He dragged Yangyang out of bed, beat him savagely on the head, and kicked him to the ground. "I told you it's not safe there, why did you have to go?" he growled.

"That was nothing," Yangyang said to me. The worst thing was when his father dumped out all of the silkworms he was raising and stomped on them, crushing them to death. His mother was unprepared for this violence. "She started crying and yelling," he said, "but she didn't do anything else. She didn't know what to do."

After his parents had gone to sleep, Yangyang told me, he wrapped up all the crushed silkworms in smooth rice paper. Then he put the paper parcel in a little wooden box and hid the box in his satchel. He asked me whether I could go with him to Graveyard Hill after class.

I was taken aback, since we had vowed we wouldn't go back there. And I was still angry at Yangyang. He should not have put me in the position of lying to his mother. So I hesitated. Yangyang said he did not want to go back there again, either, but he wanted to bury his silkworms under the mulberry tree. Half-joking, he reminded me, "Don't forget, I'm your great saviour." His smile accentuated

XUE YIWEI

the bruise on his face. I ended up agreeing to his request.

So that's what we did after class, and this time we weren't interested in the scenery at all. We did not stop or dilly-dally. We did not say anything. We just rushed to the mulberry tree that we had not dared to approach on Saturday. We weren't interested in it, either. We just knelt down and started digging.

Before burying the wooden box, Yangyang opened the cover. He got me to pick a few mulberry leaves, which he gently placed on the top of the parcel. Then he very carefully closed the box and put it in the ground. "Goodbye, my little comrades," he said, covering the grave with earth. I saw tears trickling down his cheeks.

More than thirty years have passed, Dr. Bethune, and I can still clearly see Yangyang's tears. At that moment, I suddenly realized how truly distraught my great saviour was. It was he who now needed my help, but I did not know what to do. I was quite shaken. "Let's go home," I whispered in his ear, tugging his shoulder.

"Give me a minute, okay? I want to spend a little bit more time with them," he said, staring at the smallest and most recent grave on Graveyard Hill.

I went to the other side of the mulberry tree and wandered around. I was glad I had not broken the agreement I had made with Yangyang on Saturday evening. I had not told my parents what had happened to us. It was weak of him to tell his mother, I thought.

Then a reflection in the grass not far away caught my attention. I walked over, curious, and knelt down.

95

What I found surprised me. "Come and see," I yelled, rushing over to Yangyang. "There's a flashlight in the grass."

He remained kneeling. He didn't say anything.

I picked up the flashlight and waved it in front of him. "I found it over there," I said, indicating the other side of the mulberry tree. "Do you remember the light?"

Yangyang's expression changed. He didn't look surprised. He looked shocked. He grabbed the flashlight and looked it over furiously. "My mother was right," he said, his voice shaking.

"About what?" I asked. "What did she say?"

Yangyang was shaking. He told me that when his mother heard about our encounter on Graveyard Hill, she had laughed and said there was no such thing as ghosts.

"Are you alright?" I asked.

"I'll never raise silkworms again," Yangyang said gazing vacantly into the dark sky, furious. He didn't seem to have heard my question.

I didn't know what silkworms had to do with my find. "Are you alright?" I asked again.

Yangyang looked at me and made a strange request. "Can you take the flashlight home with you?"

"No," I said. "The ghosts will come looking."

"There's no such thing as ghosts," Yangyang said impatiently.

I looked down.

"What we encountered cannot possibly be a ghost," Yangyang said. "This flashlight is the best proof of that."

I had no idea how a flashlight could prove there were

no ghosts, and I took Yangyang's request as a sign of weakness. Then, on an impulse, I asked, "If there are no ghosts, why don't you dare to take it home?"

Yangyang looked at me with a terrified expression. Then he burst out crying. He covered his face with his hands, his body shaking as he lay on the ground. This was the first and last time I saw Yangyang so distraught. "Because, because . . . I've told you, the scariest thing is living people, because living people . . . I'm afraid of living people."

Dear Dr. Bethune, I still regret my question to this day. I know how much it hurt my best friend, my great saviour. I did not hurt him willingly. I would never have done that.

Dear Dr. Bethune, Yangyang's notebook had a long note entitled "A Flashlight." I have read it many times. After I read it the first time, I felt let down, because Yangyang didn't even mention the flashlight in the note. Instead, he wrote about his father. I couldn't understand why.

I have now finally figured out how apt the title of the note is. Dear Dr. Bethune, I record it below, to show you what an incredible impact you had on our lives. Please bear in mind it was written not long before Yangyang left this world. He was thirteen years old.

> *Who is my father? Maybe I should not ask in this way. But I really don't know. When he went to the May Seventh Cadre School, I was still in kindergarten. Last spring, after the visit to Graveyard Hill, he beat me. I don't know whether he regrets it now. To be honest, I don't hate him. He's just become a stranger. But I am a little afraid of him. He picked some mulberry leaves for me, which I found quite strange. One evening after he beat me, he announced, "Your mother has sacrificed*

everything for you. When you grow up, you have to take care of her." *It was like he was telling me what to do after he died. I found that strange, as well. His relationship with my mother was also weird, always fighting. When they fought, his voice was always softer than my mother's. He always said less than she did. One time, my mother accused him of always thinking of himself and of not being devoted to others. I knew she was deliberately misquoting "In Memory of Dr. Bethune" to belittle him, because in the May Seventh Cadre School he had always won the Old Three recitation competitions. The towels we used at home, the enamel cups, and the wash-basins are all prizes he won in these competitions. Sometimes, Mother cursed him long into the night. One time, she said she wanted to get a divorce. I was so anxious. At first, I sympathized with my father, because he said less than my mother. I don't sympathize with him anymore. And that's not because he beat me, but because I found out why he beat me. Sometimes, the less you know the better.*

Yangyang never told me why the flashlight upset him so much. On the way back from Graveyard Hill, that day after class, he repeated several times that he would never raise silkworms again. When we parted, he urged me to hide the flashlight and not tell anyone about it.

"I can't even tell your mom?" I asked on purpose.

"Especially not my mom." At the time I did not know what *especially* was supposed to mean. But I know Yang-yang never told anybody about the flashlight. He never even drew it in his notebook, just used it as the title of his note.

When I was walking with Yangyang to the air-raid shelter on the Saturday, I realized something serious was about to happen. When he gave me his notebook to take care of forever, I felt all the more apprehensive. But I didn't want to think about it. And I never could have imagined what did happen.

On Monday afternoon, I was in geography class. Our teacher, a tiny old woman with a submissive manner, had grey hair and a weak voice. She was the only teacher in the school we were not required to show respect for, because her husband, once the most famous physics teacher in the best high school in our city, was now a criminal counter-revolutionary and was serving his sentence in jail. Only when he was released a few years later did we learn of the two incidents that led to his conviction. One time he claimed in class that nature's laws were supreme, and that Chairman Mao's notion that "man will triumph over nature" was a kind of idealism. This was considered an open challenge to the authority of the Communist Party. Another time, during class break, he was chatting to a few keen students and described America, home to the great number of Nobel Prize laureates, as a great country. We all knew that the word *great* was only to be used to describe our own fatherland. How dare he use it to praise imperialist America, the Paper Tiger despised by your great friend? This was taken as a betrayal of socialism.

Our geography teacher had just written the word *Tibet* on the blackboard in preparation for a discussion of how much the enslaved Tibetans loved our great saviour—who was of course also their own great saviour—when our homeroom teacher opened the door. She had a serious expression on her face. She did not greet the geography teacher. She just walked to Yangyang's desk and searched through it, but did not discover anything except for the end of a pencil. Then she turned to me. "Come with me," she said.

I followed her to the Office of Foreign Affairs.

It was a very clear day, but the atmosphere in the office was stifling. A police officer was sitting by the desk. He looked less flustered than Foreign Affairs. Foreign Affairs did not introduce the police officer to me, and he did not indicate that I should sit down, either. I was starting to feel very nervous. Then I noticed my homeroom teacher sitting on the cot by the wall, which reminded me of the discovery Dumb Pig had made during enhanced training. I looked down and tried to contain my smile.

"When was the last time you saw your friend?" Foreign Affairs asked in a severe tone of voice. He said "your friend" and not "Yangyang," which took me aback. This cold substitute made me feel Yangyang had already gone somewhere far away.

I pretended I was trying to remember. "The day before yesterday," I said.

My answer displeased Foreign Affairs. He exchanged a look with my homeroom teacher and the police officer, and then asked another question, "What time two days ago?"

"In the afternoon," I replied.

"Where?" the policeman chipped in.

"Here," I replied. "At school." It was a reply I had rehearsed. I would never mention the air-raid shelter. They all exchanged another look. Then Foreign Affairs asked if I had noticed anything strange in my friend's conduct lately.

I pretended to really think it over, and said no.

Then he asked me whether my friend had told me where he was going.

Again, I pretended to think it over, and said no.

My terse negatives angered Foreign Affairs. He reminded me that as the inheritor of the revolutionary cause I should not lie to the Party.

"Do you know what that means?" my homeroom teacher butted in to ask.

I nodded. Of course I knew what Foreign Affairs meant. But I would not give in to his demand. If he kept on asking questions like what was the last thing that Yangyang said to me, I would lie to the Party. "I'm not lying," I assured him.

Foreign Affairs indicated that I could leave. But just as I was about to step out the door, he stopped me. "Don't tell anyone what we talked about here today," he said.

Getting ready to leave with me, my homeroom teacher patted me on the shoulder. "Do you understand what that means?" she asked.

But what if other people *ask* me what we talked about? I thought. I knew Foreign Affairs meant that I had to lie to other people. This was the Party's demand. "I won't say a thing," I said. I noticed my homeroom teacher nod at Foreign Affairs.

When we left the office, my teacher stopped and told me in a serious tone that Yangyang had gone missing on Saturday. She sounded upset and then she started sobbing. I didn't know what to do. I'd never imagined the homeroom teacher would get so emotional in front of me. I did not know how to reassure her. I looked up and down the hall, hoping some other teacher might happen to come to comfort her.

What a relief it was when she finally stopped sobbing. She wiped away the tears with a hanky and then repeated the very first question Foreign Affairs had asked. The only difference was that she used "he" instead of "your friend" to refer to Yangyang. Why didn't they refer to Yangyang by name? It was as if Yangyang had committed some sort of awful crime.

I replied in the same way as I had to Foreign Affairs.

She asked me the same follow-up questions, and I answered the same way.

Our homeroom teacher did not look disappointed. She patted me on the shoulder and praised me as an honest child. When we came to the geography classroom, her attitude hardened. She pointed a finger at me and said, "Don't tell anyone what we talked about today."

Then she pushed open the classroom door and motioned for me to enter.

I returned to my seat. I felt exhausted. I looked in a daze at the main point of the lesson that our geography teacher had just written on the blackboard: "Tibet is an inseparable part of China." She urged us to memorize it, because it would be on the final exam. Then she drew a map of China on the blackboard and said in a heuristic tone, "Look, our great fatherland looks like a fighting cock. If Tibet splits away, what would it look like?"

This was clearly a rhetorical question, but Dumb Pig couldn't resist. "Like a fighting cock without a butt," he said.

The whole class burst out laughing. Only I sat there expressionless and still.

The geography teacher's face went bright red, and she looked very uncomfortable. Mercifully, the bell sounded just then, and she hurried to gather up her lesson plan and teaching aids. Before leaving she said, "So we must never let the Dalai Lama's reactionary clique succeed!"

The class responded in unison, "Never!" Then everyone burst out laughing.

The geography teacher tore out of the classroom without announcing the end of class.

I seemed to hear Yangyang's laughter, as though he were still among us. I reached towards his empty seat. "Are you there?" I asked hopelessly. My tears dripped from my cheeks on to the textbook. For a moment, the whole world was drowning in my tears.

That evening, Yangyang's father came to our home. His manner was strange, and he was clearly agitated. My mother had been unwilling to let him in, but he walked right up to me and asked me the same questions as Foreign Affairs and our homeroom teacher. The strange thing was that he, too, used "he" instead of his son's name. I gave him the same replies. My replies saddened him. "I know my child," he said, shaking his head. "He couldn't have told you anything. He didn't trust anyone."

I didn't want to correct him. I didn't want to say anything.

When my father saw Yangyang's father to the door, he comforted him, saying that Yangyang would surely return soon, but then he went on to complain about Yangyang's immaturity. "Children should always tell their parents where they are going," he said in a loud voice, likely wanting to be sure I would hear.

My father's words were of no comfort to Yangyang's father. They made him even more agitated. "It's not his fault," he said, shaking his head. "It's my fault, all my fault."

The next day, our mathematics class was changed to a study period, because the teacher, Yangyang's mother, was absent. Our homeroom teacher had us copy your great friend's two most recent poems ten times each. I didn't copy a single word. All I could think about was Yangyang. I remembered a lot of details of the times we'd spent together. I hoped he would come back from the distant place to which he had gone and sit in front of me again.

The next day, a substitute teacher taught us mathematics. She told us that Yangyang's mother had something else to do and would not be able to teach us for the time being. This was obviously a lie. The truth was that Yangyang's mother would never teach again. She had lost her mind. She had become what my mother would forever afterwards call "that madwoman."

In the months that followed, I saw her twice, from a distance, but I never got close. I avoided her, in fact, until one afternoon, catching sight of me, she came over to me and touched me on the head. It was a moment in which life and death encountered one another in my life.

Yangyang's body was discovered two weeks after he disappeared, hanging from a rusty frame in an abandoned warehouse. My mother told me that the body had decomposed and smelled so bad that the security guards decided to go in and find the cause.

"What did it smell like?" I asked in terror. I thought of my discussion of death with Yangyang on Graveyard Hill.

My mother's face contorted in disgust. She glanced at me and said, "They said it smelled worse than shit."

A STATUE

Dear Dr. Bethune, if I told you I had just returned from Concordia, you would scratch your head, because Concordia is a name that does not exist in your memory of this city. What is it, where is it, and why would I go there? Concordia is the second English university in Montreal. Its main building is less than a kilometre from McGill, which you knew well. Just west of the main building of Concordia, there is a tiny park with a small statue. When I say I returned from Concordia, what I mean is that I returned from visiting the statue.

It is a statue of you, the only memorial to you in this city. The tiny park where it stands is just a few metres from an entrance to the green line of the Metro, so that thousands of people walk past your statue every day. Very few stop and look at you with a faraway expression on their faces, the way I do. And even fewer know about your legacy, about the millions of spiritual children you left behind in China.

Compared with the human passers-by, who mostly ignore you, the pigeons pay close attention, and I find that more upsetting. A battle rages among the birds vying for control of the top of the statue, and the temporary victor perches on your head. Its victory makes it so proud of itself, so relaxed, and your face is soon covered with shit.

Last night, I couldn't stop thinking about death. For a while, I even felt that my body was giving off an odour worse than shit. I could not get to sleep, as an intense cold wind beat against my window, against the darkness that surrounded me. I thought about your statue. On such a nasty evening, not even pigeons would want a place on your head. It must be so lonely. You must be so lonely. Death must be so lonely. Our bodies will all go rotten in the end. I cannot imagine that smell worse than shit. To me, the word is just a description that ensured that my mother's expression of disgust is stored in my memory for ever. Troubled by my mother's expression, I thought of death the whole night.

When I got up this morning, I had an intense urge to stand in front of your statue again. So I went to Concordia. I was disappointed, because the park is now a construction site, and I could not see your statue. I asked a construction worker, who told me that your statue was so dirty that it needed to be cleaned and restored. It would only be re-erected next spring. The word *restored* made me think of *revolution*, partly because both words start with the same letters, partly because in the lexicon of the communist culture I grew up with, *restoration* has almost the same meaning as *counter-revolutionary*, which is a word I'm sure you dislike.

Your statue was a present from the Chinese

government to the Canadian people, a symbol of the normalization of relations between China and Canada. The government of Pierre Elliott Trudeau—whom my neighbour Claude thinks of as a totalitarian ruler—restored your status by acknowledging your Canadian nationality. In addition to being an idol in a foreign country, you became a legend among your own people, too, thus becoming a bridge between the most populous country in the world and the country with the second largest area.

I've always thought it strange that I have no recollection of the normalization of relations between China and Canada. I only learned of Pierre Elliott Trudeau much later on. But I do have a vivid memory of the normalization of Sino-American relations, which happened soon after. In 1972, just after Nixon and his crafty secretary of state, Henry Kissinger, visited China, a lot of political jokes circulated in China. These jokes showed us the soft side of the American imperialists. It was a charming chapter in my childhood. We told those jokes again and again, finding them endlessly funny.

I remember talking to Yangyang about those jokes soon after we became friends, discovering that the versions we had heard were about the same as the versions circulating in the provincial capital. We all knew that Nixon had been interested in the basic means of transportation of the Chinese people, the bicycle, which we were sure was a Chinese invention—and we were confident he could never have seen such a vehicle before going to Beijing. The joke went that he made a request to Premier

Zhou Enlai, hoping to take a sample back to America so he could show it to his own people. Yes, the ignorance of the American president and his curiosity gave us a good feeling about American imperialism.

Another joke showed the wit of the Chinese leadership. At a state banquet one evening, Nixon suddenly had to go to the washroom, appearing as if he was suffering from indigestion. Dr. Kissinger, who understood what this visit to the washroom was really all about, made sure the president could go to the bathroom alone, with no bathroom staff in attendance. Remembering that Nixon had just read a CIA report saying that the wine glasses at the banquet table were made out of a special shatterproof material unknown to American science, Dr. Kissinger knew that Nixon had stuffed a glass up his sleeve.

In the bathroom, the American commander-in-chief racked his brains to work out the best plan of action. Even though that glass was supposedly as strong as stone, he still treated it as though it were fragile. In the end, he succeeded in finding a safe place for it, a place that not only offered privacy but was also as soft as a bird's nest.

When Nixon returned to his place at the banquet with a relieved look on his face, Dr. Kissinger got to his feet and clinked glasses with our premier, expressing the hope that relations between the United States of America and the People's Republic of China would always remain friendly.

When Nixon returned to his presidential suite, he rushed to the bathroom, unbuckled his belt, and was about to get out the Chinese national secret he had just stolen when he heard his wife exclaim in surprise. He buckled his belt again and rushed out of the bathroom to discover that the First Lady had found a single wine glass on the bed. Beside it was a note handwritten by our premier himself, which read: "Revered Mr. President, Sino-American relations must be built on a foundation of mutual trust. There should be no secrets between us. On behalf of Chairman Mao, I only hope that your digestion returns to normal as soon as possible, just as relations between our two great nations have now normalized. And this wine glass should go with another one — its 'brother.' Let the twin be a symbol of the friendship between our two great countries, never to be separated again."

Such jokes were passed around our cloistered world. They displayed not only the humour of the Chinese people but perhaps our excessive self-confidence as well. And they did give us a basic understanding of the American president, too, so we were hardly surprised by Watergate. Who could be surprised when a president who had stolen a wine glass was discovered to have wiretapped his opponents?

Many years later, I finally realized that the bicycle is in fact a Western invention. *The last Emperor*, a Bertolucci film, includes a scene of Puyi, the last emperor of China, as a teenager riding around the Forbidden City on what was supposedly the first bicycle ever imported to China— a present from his Scottish tutor. I also learned, later on, that Americans had produced unbreakable wine glasses long before their president's historic visit to China. These later realizations did not, however, detract from my appreciation of the jokes or of the Chinese confidence and wisdom that inspired them.

I feel sorry for Canadian politicians. They failed to stimulate our imagination and our creativity like their American counterparts. Now I think that one of the main reasons concerns you, dear Dr. Bethune, for you became a symbol of Canada. Your great spirit made us look upon Canada with great respect and tremendous seriousness, causing our wit to wilt.

I miss you, Dr. Bethune. I miss you the same way I miss my own childhood, the same way I miss my childhood companion, Yangyang. I hope your statue will be quickly restored and returned to the park. I don't know where the pigeons that usually surround you will winter. Sometimes they remind me of Oscar Wilde's famous children's story about a statue and a bird, "The Happy Prince"— even though I know that before you became a statue you weren't a prince, nor were you the least bit happy. When I learned from the archive just how unhappy your last few months in China were, I cried. I even felt our celebration of your life is a kind of insult to you. I know that what you really needed were women, coffee, correspondence, and news of the outside world. For instance, you should have known, before you cut your finger, that World War II had broken out. And you should have known who was awarded the Nobel Prize for literature in 1938, and why.

On the way back from Concordia, I thought of a story

Yangyang told me. His father had given a plaster statue of Chairman Mao to his mother as an engagement gift. It always sat on the desk in their one-room home. On the morning of Yangyang's eighth birthday, when he was arranging his pencil case, he accidentally knocked it over, and it shattered on the red tile floor. His mother rushed over and, seeing the shards, slapped Yangyang on the face, yelling, "How dare you! This is an counter-revolutionary act!"

That afternoon, when Yangyang returned from school, his mother was waiting for him. She had gone and bought a portrait of Chairman Mao to hang on the wall, and she ordered Yangyang to kneel in front of it, making "the most sincere" apology to the great saviour and begging for his forgiveness. Yangyang remained kneeling a total of two hours, humiliated and hungry. He knew he wouldn't get anything to eat later on, either, for his mother had dumped the birthday dinner she had prepared the day before down the toilet. He also knew he could not, as a counter-revolutionary, ask for anything to eat. After two hours of repentance, Yangyang went right to bed, still feeling humiliated and hungry. He told me he learned two things from this incident. First, that hunger isn't as scary as he had imagined. Second, that our most fearsome enemy was not the Soviet revisionists—the Polar Bear—or the American imperialists—the Paper Tiger. The fiercest enemy we had was time—the torture of hours, minutes, and seconds.

Yangyang recorded the details of his life in different ways in his notebook. He did not mention how he was punished on his eighth birthday, but he did add a mysterious ending to the story. He wrote that he lay awake the most of the night and saw his mother take the fragments of the plaster statue out of the drawer where she had put them, and wrap them in a cloth. He thought she was going to throw them out, but instead she started hammering on the cloth until the fragments turned to dust.

Yangyang never asked his mother why. He did not know if she did it out of fear or out of hate. In fact, he didn't let his mother know he saw anything that night. He didn't mention the ending when he told me this story, either.

Dr. Bethune, this little story might give you an idea of the environment in which your spiritual children grew up. After you died, your great friend became God for us, all the Chinese people. In every Chinese city, there were many statues of him. Unlike your statue, his were always huge. And, interestingly enough, I never saw pigeons dare to shit on the top of his statues. This showed the wisdom of Chinese pigeons. They knew the consequence of counter-revolutionary crime: "The criminal is sentenced to execution, to be carried out immediately!" This was the frightening announcement we all heard at the public trials we participated as part of the school curriculum.

Dear Dr. Bethune, I have a question for you. Had you read any books about China before you read Edgar Snow's bestselling book, *Red Star Over China*? Or, to put it another way, besides communists like Mao, did you ever develop any interest in other Chinese people, such as Cixi, the Empress Dowager; Puyi, the last Emperor; Sun Yat-sen, the father of modern China; the rebels of the Boxer Rebellion; or the fake foreign devil who was a xenophile in Lu Xun's story, "The True Story of Ah Q."

When I read your Canadian archive, I discovered that your interest in China was narrow. I could not see any sign that you were influenced by Pearl S. Buck, for instance. Her view of China was totally different from Edgar Snow's. Both were partial views of China. In fact, there are countless such partial views of China, including your China, my China, Snow's China, Buck's China, and on and on. There is always another China, a different China, or even the opposite China. And what you must know is that the China you experienced is strikingly different from the China that thinks of you as an icon.

In 1938, while you were isolated in war-stricken

China, Pearl Buck's bestselling book from the early 1930s, *The Good Earth*, was still fascinating Western readers. By that time, she had left China and returned to the United States for good, but she was a bridge connecting China and the world, and her support for the Chinese struggle had attracted a lot of attention in the West. In October, 1938, she was awarded the Nobel Prize in Literature. This has since been considered one of the worst decisions the Swedish Academy ever made. Western colleagues made fun of it, while Chinese intellectuals condemned it, criticizing Buck for having had a shallow understanding of the Chinese situation.

On the very day that Pearl Buck received the prize in Stockholm, you were operating on the injured in a village that had just been ravaged. Both Buck's reception speech and her Nobel lecture focused on China. In the reception speech, she predicted that China would win the war against the Japanese invaders, a victory for which you, dear Dr. Bethune, were devotedly working on the frontier. What a contrast! The prophet was fêted with applause and flowers, while the practitioner was plagued by boredom and loneliness. How lonely you were, in that mountainous area in north China! Every day the same— no news, no newspapers, no letters. You didn't know if Roosevelt was still the president of United States. You didn't know that Hitler was *Time*'s "Man of the Year." Not to mention who won the Nobel Prize in Literature. You didn't know whether your comrades in Montreal and in Yan'an still remembered you. You didn't know whether your lovers were still missing you or still complaining about you.

The same war that brought you loneliness brought honour to Pearl Buck, but her good fortune wouldn't last. After the communists seized power in 1949, she was accused of being a "slanderer" and "a running dog of American imperialism," and was tossed into the dustbin of history, while you became a rising star over Mao's new China.

Dr. Bethune, the difference between your two fates in China is rooted in the contrast between the two Chinas you each knew. She had lived in cultural and urban China, and you, in revolutionary and rural China. Your China emerged victorious. More ironically, Buck had lived in China for more than four decades and had put in many good words for China in English and in her fluent Chinese, while you lived in China for less than two years, and your letters to your comrades in Canada included many complaints. You once criticized the "too strong curiosity" of the Chinese, for all the packages you received had been opened.

But Buck ended up being a slanderer, while you became a man of moral integrity and above vulgar interests, a man who is of value to the people. This is the irony of history.

Because of you, dear Dr. Bethune, we felt great respect for Canada. Also because of you, we had great admiration for doctors. And it was because of you that we held internationalism in high esteem. You left the world in 1939, but in the 1970s you were still living in our hearts and our lives. Though Pearl Buck outlived you, by the 1970s she had not only been abandoned by China, her second homeland, but was also ignored in her own motherland, the United States. In 1972, she was eager to join the delegation of President Nixon's historic mission to China, but her request was refused.

The elderly Sinophiles I have met in Montreal were all devoted readers of Pearl Buck. And their knowledge of China was mostly derived from her work. Even Bob, who sees you as an icon, has praised Buck as an extraordinary writer. He says that the China she portrayed was more authentic than the China he actually saw. He couldn't imagine how it happened that she now has such lowly status and has left no traces behind.

The year 1938 was deeply meaningful for both of you. You began the last part of your life's journey, and she reached the peak of her literary career. In your imagination, war-torn China was a paradise, where the pain in your individual life could in some measure be assuaged. But did you know of Proust's pessimism about paradise? "The only true paradise is a paradise we have lost," he wrote. Such a sentiment might have comforted you in the hell of suffering that your personal paradise had turned out to be. Both of you, you and Pearl Buck, endured the ironies of history, which is what makes the contrast between your fate and hers so endlessly fascinating to me.

A HERO

Dear Dr. Bethune, you have heard me say that my neighbour's moans during sex excited and perturbed me. Sometimes, I heard the moans in summertime, when her boyfriend could not have been in the city. Sometimes I heard my neighbour fighting violently with a man and crying hysterically. The conflict soon subsided, however, and the pleasure of lovemaking cancelled out the violence of the fights.

When trapped in barren Chinese or foreign or alien villages, lonely and anxious, I wonder if you ever comforted yourself by masturbating. If so, who did you think about? Your first lover? Your last lover? Or the "impossible lover" you married and divorced twice? Perhaps it was one of the merry female students you amazed at what you called "the most unique university in the world"— the revolution university in Yan'an? Or some mirthless widow living on the other side of the village? Forgive me for asking you such a personal question. Your answer either way would not affect my opinion of you. It might reflect a little on your noble-mindedness, but it would not stain your purity too much.

Your affirmative answer to this question would be a breakthrough, breaking a taboo in the Chinese father-son relationship. It would bring us closer. Because I would like to tell you that hearing my neighbour's moans, I could not help but imagine a body shape to match those moans. I was enticed by that ever-changing body shape. My hands would follow my imagination around my body. I would start to touch myself. My hands would start from my chest, fall passionately into the two sides of my body and meet between the legs. Ah! I still remember the first time I strove to move my wife's hands onto my private parts. She was resistant, and her hands were sweaty. She hesitated, fearful, but soon I could just let go, because she no longer needed my guidance. She understood herself, and me. I felt the freedom she had just granted her fingers with the whole of my being. Now, only my hands are left. Lonely hands. It feels strange. I have to imagine them as someone else's, like my neighbour's. Time begins to flow in reverse. Oh, my fearless youth!

History will not care how masturbation has affected the progress of civilization. History has no interest in the travails of the flesh. Thank goodness for that. So your loneliness can be forgotten. Your reputation can remain scandal-free and unblemished. In our collective memory, you are a hero, pure and noble-minded, without the frailties and foibles that plague the rest of humanity. We idolized your spirit so much that we've forgotten that you had a body, that you were still a man of flesh and blood.

In the second year of high school, we had a class called

Physiological Hygiene once a week for forty-five minutes. In this class, we were supposed to learn the basics about the various parts of the body, including the male and female genitalia. This was a chance to learn about our bodies and those of other people, the only such chance that we children of Dr. Bethune had during our elementary and high school years. Only Dumb Pig had no need for this class. He had already learned all that needed from the pictures in *The Barefoot Doctor's Manual* and his practice of peeping into the women's area of the public bath.

The school did not, however, manage to find a willing teacher for this class until the week after midterms. He was a retired politics teacher with a very strong accent. Coming from his mouth, *sheng* sounded like *xin*, and *zhi* sounded like *ji*. When he pronounced *shengzhiqi* (genitalia), therefore, it sounded like *xinjiqi* (new machines). He was a dedicated teacher, following the textbook faithfully, starting at the head. Once he'd explained the digestive system to us, however, he split the class into two. He brought the boys to the teacher's conference room, where he explained the structure and partial functions of our "new machines" (skipping their most important role, of course), while the girls stayed in the classroom to study on their own, without discussion.

Even though this teacher's lectures were not offensive in any way, the school received many complaints from parents. The parents thought that this extraneous class distracted us from our proper studies. Some parents even went so far as to threaten to transfer their children to schools that did not require this "immoral" class. The pressure was such that the school cancelled the class and didn't arrange for a final exam. In the end, we all received full marks on our report cards for this class, which satisfied all the parents.

I found it strange that my neighbour's sounds of pleasure never made me think of the girlfriend I lived with a few years ago. Unlike my wife, my girlfriend would shriek in satisfaction when she reached orgasm. However, her cries didn't excite me the way my neighbour's moans excited me, and they didn't move me the way my wife's silence had moved me. We lived together for nearly four years. It was a haphazard and alienated lifestyle, though, and often made me yearn for life in another city, an imaginary city, or a remembered city.

I missed my wife more and more. After so many years without her, I was increasingly aware of her significance in my life, even though her silence had made me unable, when she was alive, to ascertain how she felt about our lovemaking. I asked her over and over again if it felt good. She would shake her head or nod her head. So, sex with her was like a soliloquy, with only my monologue pushing the plot. When she did orgasm, she bit her lower lip hard, refusing to make any sound. I had to track the changes in her expression carefully. She would frown and shake her head forcefully, as though undergoing unspeakable torture. This was the peak of her pleasure.

"If you could guide me with your voice," I said to her once, "I would be able to focus better, and we would have more pleasure."

"I can't," my wife said.

"But we need to communicate," I insisted.

"This in itself is communication," my wife said.

"I mean verbal communication," I said. "You should allow me to hear your pleasure and let me derive a deeper pleasure from yours."

"I cannot," my wife said.

"Why not?" I asked, feeling uneasy.

My wife looked at me, at a loss. She didn't answer my question, but her eyes suddenly grew wet, which flustered me.

I never dared ask her again. I grew used to that sort of silent lovemaking. In truth, the first time I was in bed with my girlfriend, I wasn't at all used to the sounds she made. Those weren't the sounds of guidance, but of warning. They warned me that my future would be lonelier than before.

That night, when I had finished reading my wife's story, we made love more passionately than we ever had before. After that, my wife told me the reason she couldn't say anything in the story about our lovemaking. She said that she did include some hints originally, in the first versions of her novel, but in the end, she decided to strike them out.

I never thought that her silence would have anything to do with her tortuous memoir. She began to explain, recalling the night of the earthquake.

"It was really hot that evening," my wife said. "I slept fitfully." Her fingers caressed my chest.

I rubbed her shoulders with my palms, waiting for her to continue.

"I heard my parents making love. It was the first time I'd heard that, and I didn't know what the sounds meant," my wife said. "Actually, the sounds my mother made caused me to shudder in terror. I was afraid she would die. And then, the entire world shook, and I don't remember what came after. When I woke, I was caught between two prefabricated panels, unable to move. All I could smell was blood and dust. Tortured moans came from all around me. I tried my best to listen, wanting to hear my mother's voice, even making the sounds that had made me shudder. But the sounds around me grew weaker and weaker. And I myself became weaker and weaker. I fainted again. When I woke, I was surrounded by soldiers of the People's Liberation Army."

I held her tightly. "You were right to delete it from your work," I said.

My wife curled in my embrace, her face glowing with satisfaction. "I'm very happy I could tell you," she said.

"And hereafter, one climax after another," I teased.

My wife caressed the what she called "the little hero"—her term of endearment—that had so bravely ventured into her depths just before. "Don't hide," she said naughtily. "Just once more?"

Neither of us could have imagined it would be our last time.

A BRIDE

Dear Dr. Bethune, Yangyang and I spent the last summer vacation of his short life together when I took him to my hometown. Since moving to the provincial capital I hadn't been back, and I missed my relatives and the scenery there.

Yangyang had a special mission on this trip, and he told me to bring the flashlight I had kept for several months by this time. He said he wanted to take it so far away from our city that it could never come back. The first evening in my hometown, we bound the flashlight to a brick and drowned it in the historic river that flows through the town. And before letting go, Yangyang said in a seemingly careless tone, "This is the way some people commit suicide."

I didn't feel surprised at the time by his mention of suicide, but it did make me feel that the flashlight was something with a soul.

"From now on nobody will know it ever existed," he said.

We were staying at my aunt's house. When we came in, her family called on Yangyang to recite "In Memory of Dr. Bethune," because they had heard from me about

125

his extraordinary gift. Yangyang's exemplary performance won a round of applause, and I felt proud of my great saviour and best friend.

Every evening during those two weeks, we went to the fields outside the town to catch frogs, and during the day our main activity was swimming in the river. Dear Dr. Bethune, did you know your great friend was a great poet? We would swim and recite his stirring lines, which all your children know:

> *Remember still*
> *How, venturing midstream, we struck the waters*
> *And waves stayed the speeding boats?*

What a delightful moment! We had totally forgotten about the flashlight that had sunk to the bottom of this same river.

We had a fun time. We talked a lot, every day, about our parents, teachers, and classmates. One day we talked about you. We were tired of swimming and were resting on the riverbank. "Do you believe Dr. Bethune was a real person?" Yangyang suddenly asked. He was staring at the sand that was slowly flowing through his fingers.

I looked at him. "Why ask such a strange question?" I asked. "If he wasn't, why would Chairman Mao write a memorial to him?"

"Is everything you write true?" Yangyang asked. "Like the things in your diary?"

I looked down in shame. The only way to avoid a lie

was not to reply.

"Nothing in my diary is true," Yangyang said.

This shocked me. Writing a diary was homework in Chinese class. Our homeroom teacher asked us to turn our diaries in every Friday. Then, on Monday afternoon, she would note who had written well, who had improved, and who had not. The worst was always Dumb Pig. And Yangyang's was always the best. The most improved pupil varied.

"There's nothing true in my diary, either," I admitted. But why, I wondered, did the teacher admonish the rest of us for writing untruthfully, but not him?

"Because I write well," Yangyang said. "If you write well you won't give the impression you're lying."

I didn't want to argue with him. "Chairman Mao would never lie," I said firmly.

"Everyone lies," said Yangyang, just as firmly. "Our parents and teachers lie to us."

"You mean Chairman Mao would also lie to us?" I asked this warily.

"That's not what I meant," Yangyang said. "I just see how selfish people around us are, and sometimes I doubt that there are really people like Dr. Bethune."

I looked at him in amazement, not knowing how to react.

"Why isn't there anyone noble-minded around us?" Yangyang asked. "Or anyone pure?"

I'd never thought about this before.

If the conversation had continued, Yangyang might

have even spoken of his notebook, his secret notebook, in which he wrote things that were true. But we were interrupted when a scantily clad, filthy-looking woman passed us, then suddenly stopped, as if she had discovered something. She looked back, surprised, then bounded right up to us and stared at me. After a few seconds, she reached out, pointing at me and said, "The singer!"

Yangyang nudged me with his elbow. "She seems to know you," he said in a low voice.

"But who is she?" I asked. I didn't know her at all. She looked like a madwoman. How could she know me?

The woman started jumping around and clapping. "Encore! Encore!" she shouted, giggling.

Yangyang gave me a signal, and we grabbed our dry clothes and ran off.

The woman did not come after us. She just kept giggling, then shouted again, "You're a singer, not a sprinter."

We ran all the way home and, out of breath, I told my aunt what had happened. "You must have met the martyr's bride," she said calmly. "You must remember her. You sang at her wedding ceremony."

I was shocked. I couldn't connect that scruffy woman by the river with my mother's prettiest colleague. "How could she end up the way she looks now?" I asked. Just three years ago, she had lived next door. And she was the first woman that had ever left me feeling sexually excited.

My aunt nodded and sighed. "That poor woman," she mumbled.

That evening, lying in bed, I told Yangyang how I

became a singer. That woman had lived in the same row of houses as us, behind the building in which my mother worked. One day, she came to our room in a brand-new Lenin suit and told my mother she was getting married. The groom was a platoon leader in an army unit garrisoned on the border of China and the Soviet Union in Heilongjiang province. I particularly remember he was a decorated war hero, a man of many victories. Like all kids at the time, I was familiar with all the battles he had fought in as I had a lot of *lianhuanhua*—picture books—of those battles. I was familiar with how our brave People's Liberation Army had repulsed the armed provocations of the Soviet Revisionists. And our war heroes filled me with reverence. So I wasn't jealous of him for stealing away the first woman I had ever longed for. When I glanced at our beautiful neighbour, I even felt that the news that she was getting married made her all the prettier.

Our neighbour told my mother that this woman had been introduced to the war hero at the previous Spring Festival by her uncle's widow. Chaperoned by their parents, they had had their first meeting at her uncle's widow's house, and each made a good impression on the other. They made a date to meet in the park a week later to go rowing. Then they went to see the movie *The Legend of the Red Lantern*, which was adapted from the "Eight model plays"—the only works permitted to be performed during the Cultural Revolution—and tells the saga of a revolutionary family. But the night before their second meeting, the war hero got an express telegram telling him to come back early, so their relationship could only continue through letters. Every week, each would write the other two letters. A year had passed, and they were so satisfied with the progress of their relationship that they arranged to get married during the following Spring Festival, when the war hero would have a ten-day holiday. Subtracting the days he would have to spend travelling, he would only be able to spend about a week with his bride.

"A war hero and a beautiful woman," my mother said, when she heard the neighbour's account. "What a perfect match!"

Our pretty neighbour blushed, and I trembled happily.

Our neighbour invited us to her wedding. She would decorate her room as the bridal chamber, she said. It would have to serve for the wedding ceremony, too. It would be a revolutionary wedding, with an atmosphere of unity, anxiety, gravity, and energy, qualities your great friend thought should characterize any solemn occasion. The newlyweds would host the guests with candies, cookies, pumpkin and sunflower seeds, and other snacks, and entertain them with speeches and performances.

Then our neighbour turned toward me. She said she often heard me singing and liked my bright boyish voice very much. She asked if I would like to sing a revolutionary song at the wedding. My mother said of course I would before I had the chance to reply. Our neighbour was delighted. She said that would be the most illustrious event next to the speech by the leader of her work unit. Her fiancé knew all about the plans, she told my mother, from "the last letter I wrote to him." I still remember the way she pronounced the word "him." She looked so shy and so proud, which added to my reverence for the war hero.

I was so excited to be able to sing for this match made in heaven, and I racked my brains trying to think of what song to sing. My choice should show my voice to best effect and should inspire the people at the wedding, especially the bride and groom. In the end, I decided to sing a song from *The Legend of the Red Lantern*, "The Wine Fills Me with Courage and Strength," sung by the protagonist, Li Yuhe, a revolutionary martyr. This choice would meet both requirements.

But what if people wanted an encore? I should prepare a second song. I thought it over and in the end was torn between "Five-Star Red Flags Fluttering in the Wind"— then a substitute for the national anthem which was abandoned when the lyricist was convicted as a counter-revolutionary—and "Follow Lei Feng's Good Example"—a song about a People's Liberation Army soldier and another role model for the children of Dr. Bethune. I was still undecided when I walked into the bridal chamber.

The wedding was held on a Saturday night and lasted almost five hours. It was hosted by the director of the Revolutionary Committee at my mother's work unit. In his opening remarks, he said that this wedding was a great honour for their work unit, because the groom was a war hero who protected our great fatherland. He quoted your great friend's words by describing the groom as both politically red and professionally able, and praised him for not only repulsing the advances of the enemy but also for conquering the tender heart of one of *our* female comrades. He was a hero in every way, a role model for everyone. The director's sincere, warm-hearted remarks were interrupted by applause several times.

After the director had made his remarks, the guests clamoured for the bride and groom to recount the history of their love. The groom's account did not leave the guests satisfied, and they demanded that the bride fill in some significant details. But lowering her head and twisting her body, the bride said nothing.

Then the guests started to ask questions of the bride and groom at the same time. Most of the questions filled the room with happy laughter, though I didn't understand many of them. The two questions I did understand had to do with their correspondence. One was how they referred to each other in their letters. The hero did not have to think about his answer. He said that they addressed one another as "Revolutionary Comrade." The bride glanced at the groom and nodded her agreement, smiling. The other question I understood was whether they had discussed having children, and whether they were hoping to have a boy or a girl. Neither the groom nor the bride replied to this question. They looked at one another, both blushing, then looked shyly down in unison.

So, the wedding proceeded. Just when everybody was feeling a little bit tired, the bride turned everyone's attention towards me. She introduced me as a member of my school's Propaganda Team of Mao Zedong Thought, a nationwide grass-roots unit to spread your great friend's words through artistic performances. She also said that I had a golden voice and that I was going to sing a revolutionary song to celebrate their revolutionary marriage.

The guests started clapping happily. I was pushed into the middle of the room, where the bride and groom had been standing awkwardly a little earlier. As planned, I sang the song from *The Legend of the Red Lantern*, staring at the ceiling the whole time out of nervousness. I gave it my all, though I had the distinct impression that nobody, not even the bride and groom, was listening. I could hear the sound of chirping whispers and popping pumpkin seeds. This hurt my feelings.

When I finished, the director led the applause, and the other guests followed along, but no one called for an encore, as I had imagined so many times in my dreams. I was disappointed.

Then the director stood up clapping and walked to the centre of the room. Gesturing for everyone to quiet down, he reminded everyone that the wedding should not go on too long, because tomorrow, which was to say Sunday, they were going to take part in a big parade organized by the County Revolutionary Committee, starting in the morning. The parade was to show the staunch support of all the people in the county for the continued revolution during the historical stage of the proletarian dictatorship, a great theory your great friend had just put forward, Dr. Bethune. "Everyone has to take part in the parade," the director emphasized. "This is our political obligation." Then he turned towards the groom and the bride. "Of course our beautiful bride does not have to be there, because she has an even more important political duty to fulfill," he said. "She has to attend to our war hero, a glorious revolutionary duty." All the guests burst out laughing at his remark.

But the next day, when my mother was preparing to leave, the bride appeared in our doorway. She said she had to go to participate in the parade with my mother.

My mother looked her over. "You don't have to go," she reminded her.

"But I don't want to miss it," the bride said. "It's a revolutionary duty."

"But the director said that attending to the war hero was also a revolutionary duty," my mother reminded her.

"A hero doesn't need attending to," the bride said.

Her cold way of referring to the war hero surprised my mother.

"You seem a little bit tired. You should stay at home and rest," my mother insisted.

"I can't get any rest at home," the bride said.

"What you mean?" my mother asked in disbelief.

The bride hesitated then said angrily, "I didn't get any sleep last night."

Again, my mother looked her over. "How lucky you are," she said. "Not getting any sleep the whole night long!"

The bride did not seem to hear. Her expression was full of confusion and sadness. Again she insisted on attending the parade.

Dear Dr. Bethune, the story I told Yangyang wasn't as complete as the one you have just heard. But it was enough to enchant my great saviour and friend. He liked the story so much that when I went outside to go to the bathroom, he followed me so I could keep telling him what happened next.

The evening after the parade, I was woken up by a loud noise. It was the bride knocking on our window. Her low and impulsive voice was calling for us to save her. My mother leapt out of bed and opened the door. I opened my eyes a little and saw our neighbour shivering in the doorway, wearing only a flimsy nightgown. That was the first time I had ever seen her wear so little clothing. I felt a kind of happy agitation when my mother let the bride in and wrapped her up in a towel. "What happened?" she asked.

The bride looked at my mother hopelessly and started crying.

My mother patted her lightly on the back. "Tell me what happened," she said.

"He," the bride said, in a wounded voice. "He tried to rape me." Then she cried even more brokenheartedly.

What the bride said flabbergasted my mother. Then she started laughing. She couldn't stop laughing until she suddenly remembered I was there. She covered up her mouth and tiptoed to the side of my bed. She bent down and checked to see whether I was sleeping or not. I pretended to be sleeping soundly and breathing evenly. She returned to the bride and kept patting her on the back.

"But," she asked curiously, "didn't you say yesterday that you didn't get any sleep that night?"

"Yes, I kept my eyes open the whole night," the bride said. "I repulsed innumerable enemy advances."

"It sounds like you, too, are a war hero," my mother said, laughing.

"But tonight he is fiercer," the bride said. "I can barely resist."

"He is your husband now, and you are his wife," my mother said. "When a husband is with his wife they can do anything together. You should not resist him. He is not your enemy. You should open up the gate and let him in, like you are welcoming a comrade."

"But he's completely changed," the bride said. "I'm scared of him."

I did not understand what she meant at the time, but my mother obviously understood completely. "That's normal," she said with certainty. And she again patted the bride on the back.

"It's not normal at all," the bride retorted. Then, gesturing, she said, "That's how big it is, and how long, and it's extremely . . . You don't know how hard it is. It's as hard as a rolling pin."

"Of course I don't know how hard *it* is," my mother said impatiently. "But I do know it's totally normal."

"It's not normal at all," the bride insisted. "It's frightening."

My mother was growing weary of their conversation, and she advised the bride to go back to her bridal chamber.

The bride stood there unmoving. "It wants to hurt me," she kept repeating. "I don't want to let it succeed."

"Quite the opposite, it wants to make you happy," my mother said, wanting to move the bride a few steps towards the door. You will get used to it. And you will want to ride it," she continued.

The bride refused to budge. "It really wants to hurt me," she repeated. "I can't let it succeed." Then she begged my mother to permit her to spend the night at our house. "Tonight I can only fight a guerrilla battle against it," she said in earnest.

My mother hesitated before agreeing to the bride's request. She walked to the side of my bed, took me in her arms to her bed, and directed the bride to lie down in my bed. "This bed is quite small," she said sarcastically. "I'm sure it won't hurt you."

I was so flustered about the pretty bride curled up in my little bed the whole night that I couldn't get any sleep.

The next evening, I heard the groom and the bride in a heated argument. Soon the bride came over and knocked on our window. She begged my mother to save her life. My mother didn't respond as quickly as she had the previous night, but she did open the door. This time the bride did not wait for my mother to agree to let her in. She rushed in and hid behind my mother. She was wearing just as little as the night before. She stood there shivering, staring at the open door. A while later, the war hero appeared. He was wearing even less, only a pair of military green underpants. He pointed at his bride and shouted like he was giving in order. "Come out right this instant!" he roared.

My mother indicated that the groom should restrain himself. Then she tried to persuade the bride to go back with the groom. But the bride started crying again. She told her that the war hero had just hit her in the face. "He was just yelling that he wanted to go *in*, and now he's shouting that he wants me to come *out*," the bride said brokenheartedly. "Now in, now out. Is there something wrong with him?"

My mother finally lost her temper. She put on a robe and said all she could do was go find the director and let him handle the dispute. She persuaded the groom to go back to his room and wait. "It's too cold outside," she reminded him.

The groom kept standing there. He said he wouldn't give up that easily. "I guarded a sentry post at forty below. You call this cold?" he said disdainfully.

"If that's how you're going to be, our doorway will be a Demilitarized Zone—the 38th parallel," Mom said, pointing to the groom and bride in turn. "You two have to restrain yourselves." Then she went to find the director, who lived at the end of the compound. Just to be safe, she locked our door, keeping the bride in and the groom out.

My mother soon came back with the director. She must have told the director what had happened, because he didn't ask any questions, just criticized the bride for lacking common sense and the groom for lacking patience. "Patience is essential," he said in an even tone of voice. "Of course, flexible and responsive tactics are also decisive." Then he accompanied the groom home to the bridal chamber.

Coming back to talk to his subordinate, the director's tone of voice was totally different. He not only repeated his criticism but also ordered her to go back unconditionally to the bridal chamber. "To you, the bridal chamber is the front line," he said with the force of justice. "Didn't you submit an application to join the Party? This is a moment of truth for you. A qualified Party member would never go AWOL, no matter what."

"Hurry back to the front line," my mother advised in response. With her hand of the bride's shoulder, my mother helped her walk out the door with heavy steps.

"You face a proud revolutionary duty," the director said behind them with a stern tone. "No matter how hard, you have to accept this duty courageously and complete it with flying colours."

Over the next three days, we heard no argument from the bride and groom. And nobody saw them come out from the room. "The door hasn't opened in three days," my mother reported when the director came to say goodbye to the groom.

"It just goes to demonstrate that from practice comes genuine knowledge," the director said.

"And that combat shows true talent," my mother chimed in.

Once again, they both were making vital use of your great friend's famous lines. My mother's response delighted the director. He nodded and said he could not bother the newlyweds, who were on their final sprint. He entrusted my mother with the task of seeing off the groom and sending his regards.

At dusk, the bride and groom appeared in our doorway. They'd come to say goodbye. The bride's bruise, located over her left eye, had not totally disappeared, the result of the fight with the groom three days before. The groom patted my head and said, "Next time I come back I want to hear you sing the majestic song again." The bride stared at him, infinite love flashing in her eyes. "I'm going to the train station right away to send him off," the bride told my mother. When she said "him" there was only pride in her voice, no shyness or shame. She leaned over to my mother's ear, mumbling a few sentences. My mother pushed her away jokingly when she was done.

Watching them walking away, I asked my mother what the bride had just said. "She said he is a true hero," my mother said without thinking. Then I asked her a question that had puzzled me for a few days in a low voice, "What does *rape* mean?"

My mother looked at me with a fearsome expression. She didn't ask me where I'd heard the word. She made as if to slap me as a warning and said, "You're not allowed to use that dirty word again."

Dear Dr. Bethune, I didn't have the chance to sing for the war hero a second time. A month later, late one night, I was woken up by the heart-wrenching cries of the bride. My eyes looked out into the lonely night. "What happened?" I asked my mother uneasily.

"The war hero gave his young life to the fatherland yesterday," my mother said calmly. "He will never come back again."

I found the calm in my mother's voice frightening. I looked at the darkness and said in my mind that I wasn't willing to give up my life for anything.

"The martyr's bride is a widow now," my mother sighed a long sigh and murmured. "Poor woman."

I couldn't get back to sleep at all that night. The wedding of just a month before stayed in my mind. Standing in the centre of the empty bridal chamber, I was singing the song over and over again, the song the war hero would ask me to sing if he could come back.

A FORMER ACTRESS

Dear Dr. Bethune, when we moved to the city to re-unite with my father, the bride had been given the title of Householder of a Revolutionary Martyr's Family. It was not only a rare honour but it also came with a number of practical perks. For instance, her monthly rice allowance was more than other adult city dwellers. Same for white sugar. And she got almost twice the monthly coal. When I passed by, I saw the certificate issued by the provincial government hanging beside the marriage certificate. I re-call the director personally delivering the certificate on a dismal afternoon. He told my mother to show concern for our tragic and lonely neighbour, and he himself also visited often to encourage her to turn her sorrow into something positive. The bride treasured the honorary title so much that she preferred her colleagues to call her the martyr's bride rather than just the bride.

Yangyang was keenly interested in her story. The next morning over breakfast, he asked my aunt what had hap-pened. How had the pretty bride turned into the raggedy lady we saw by the river? My aunt mumbled something about how she'd made a dumb mistake, as a result of which she'd lost the honorary title and the accompanying perks. She'd even been fired from her job.

Yangyang then asked why the director who'd shown her such concern had not protected her.

A look of disgust appeared on my aunt's face. "He made the same mistake," she said, disgusted. "He had assigned her too many revolutionary duties."

For that reason the director, too, had been relieved of his duties and had been assigned to a forestry centre in a distant mountain region for *laogai*—reform through labour.

The county put on a variety show every year on New Year's Eve, and the martyr's bride served as the announcer. I knew her dream was to join a song and dance troupe and work as a professional dancer. I also knew she loved films and thought she might also have wanted to become an actress. She told me she had seen *The Legend of the Red Lantern* thirty-two times. This was a blow to my self-esteem for I'd been proud of my own record. Now, almost forty years later, I still remember her pleased-with-herself expression when she told me this.

After breakfast, Yangyang insisted on my taking him to the auditorium in which the variety show was held. He said he'd had a strange dream the night before. He had dreamed of the martyr's bride and said he now knew where she lived.

The auditorium was being renovated, and Yangyang rushed backstage when we got there. I followed, not knowing what he wanted to do.

He found the ladies' make-up room, which was locked.

We peeked inside, and saw there were a couple of beat-up tables and chairs. Yangyang looked for a long time, sad to see nothing else. "My dream told me this was her home."

Yangyang's dream made me tremble from head to toe. Even if there was no trace of the martyr's bride or anyone else inside, I still thought we'd better leave. But Yangyang did not want to go. Instead, he pulled me onto the dusty stage, where he performed a highlight from *The Legend of the Red Lantern*, a piece by Wang Lianju, the traitor who leads to Li Yuhe's arrest.

It was a stylized rendering. "How many times have you seen *The Legend of the Red Lantern*?" I asked, when he was done.

"Twenty-five times!" Yangyang replied without thinking, as if he got asked this question all the time. Then he asked me how many times I had seen it.

"Thirty times," I replied without enthusiasm.

My demeanour surprised Yangyang. He stopped performing and looked at me. "Why that tone of voice?" he said. "You won!"

"But . . . ," I didn't finish. I didn't want to tell him I'd lost to the martyr's bride. Yangyang seemed uninterested in the explanation I hadn't given. He asked me to be the announcer. He asked me to announce the next number, the even more notable highlight of Hatoyama, the captain of the Japanese gendarmerie who kills Li Yuhe, the hero.

Standing in the announcer's place, which is where the martyr's bride stood, I could see how the auditorium must have looked from her perspective. The past and present were suddenly superimposed, and so were she and I. I was sad for that woman who had flustered me so profoundly. I was sad, too, that I couldn't compete with her in the number of times I'd seen *The Legend of the Red Lantern*.

Dear Dr. Bethune, you may find it hard to understand how important movies were in your children's world. At the time, there were only eight movies, which were adapted from the eight model plays. We watched those movies over and over again, in crude theatres or more often at outdoor screenings. We were familiar with all the characters, not only the stars but all the supporting roles, as well. We knew all the dialogue, whether humorous or serious. And we liked negative characters much more than positive characters. We liked to imitate the negative characters, because they were comical and very human. They came in two extreme body types: either obese or skinny. They had other physical features, too, such as narrow, shifty eyes or eyes that protruded so much they looked like they might burst out of their sockets. Stuttering was another common feature of negative characters. They stuttered especially when they were doomed. These negative characters turned the era of the Cultural Revolution, which has come to be called a catastrophe, into a heaven for your children. While we couldn't change the size of our eyes or the shape of our bodies in order to imitate these characters, it was easy to imitate the stuttering. And not surprisingly, the pupils who did the most imitating ended up with their own stutters.

The eight model plays were the political triumph of

the most influential woman of the era of catastrophe. Despite how nasty she herself was, the eight films derived from those model stage dramas opened up a miraculous world to your children. They were the popular culture of our time. They satisfied our children's curiosity and they inspired our imagination.

In fact, revolution itself was a kind of entertainment, a kind of popular culture, as Lenin himself knew. He said that revolution is "a great festival" for the oppressed; this festive metaphor was painted on the massive poster outside the entrance to the factory I passed every day. It reminded me that your great friend had said that "Revolution is *not* a dinner party." Discussing this metaphor with Yangyang one day, we both thought it contradicted Lenin's. In dealing with revolution, your great friend seemed so much more serious than his revolutionary mentor.

Dear Dr. Bethune, before I started writing your biography, some odd associations had occurred to me, and I made some peculiar discoveries. For instance, I assumed you didn't know who won the Best Actress award in 1938 at the Tenth Academy Awards or why she got the award—for the award was announced in March, when you were already in China on your way to the barren northwest. I was certain, though, that you knew the actress's name, Luise Rainer, because she also had won Best Actress the previous year. She got the second award because of China, like Pearl Buck. She even got the award because of Pearl Buck. Rainer played O Lan, the farmer's wife, in the film adaptation of *The Good Earth*. Did you read the book, which was published in 1931? If so, I have a few other questions for you. Did you watch the 1937 film adaptation before you left for China? If so, what was your impression of the German actress that played the O Lan? After you came to China, did you meet peasant women like that? Was the appearance of an actual Chinese peasant village at all similar to the one in the Hollywood film?

Another thing I find quite interesting is that the Tenth Academy Awards ceremony was originally supposed to take place on March 4, 1938. Your birthday! But because of a flood, the ceremony was delayed one week. You were on the way to Yan'an at the time, so this had no effect on you. By the time Luise Rainer won the award for playing O Lan, you had finished the most difficult part of your journey. You were already near the Yellow River. Two weeks later, you reached the "revolutionary Jerusalem" you had dreamed about. The evening you got there, you walked into the cave of our great saviour. For you, this was a great leap on the way to becoming our father. A print of an oil painting of that momentous encounter was pinned up on both sides of our fourth-grade classroom.

One day, in the Bibliothèque et archives nationales du Québec, I read a long article you sent to a newspaper in Toronto from Yan'an, expressing your deep dissatisfaction with North American women. You said that all they think about is dancing and watching movies and other decadent diversions. In contrast, the Chinese women you met in Yan'an had opened your eyes. Their lives were difficult but also happy, filled with revolutionary fervour.

The one who impressed you the most was a famous actress from Shanghai. You praised her in your article for giving up her lavish lifestyle and throwing herself into the torrent of revolution. Her choice was exactly the same as yours. "Is she happy?" you wrote. "She must be, she's as gay and as mischievous as a squirrel."

You must surely be interested in what happened to this squirrel. Like you, she made her way to the cave of our great saviour. She became a frequent visitor and eventually made a nest in there. Your great friend's comrades tended to underestimate the power of people's sex drive. Thinking that it would damage the revolutionary cause, they tried to stop the union of the squirrel and the great saviour. At this key moment, our great saviour displayed his revolutionary resolution. Ignoring his comrades' disapproval, he liberated himself from the net of morality and took the former actress to be his fourth wife. Then, riding from victory to victory, he liberated all of China!

Dear Dr. Bethune, your impression of this particular squirrel suggests that you had the same taste in women as your great friend. I wonder if he viewed you as a threat, an adversary on the battlefield of love? I've always found it hard to understand why he did not approve your request to stay in Yan'an with all those revolutionary maidens running around, full of ardour for the cause, and with the squirrel there, too, putting in gay and mischievous appearances. You were sent to the front line, where your life became so lonely and monotonous. The front line needed you even more than Yan'an—this was the reason your great friend gave you, but, in fact, he kept a lot of good doctors in Yan'an. So why did he deny your request to stay in the revolutionary Jerusalem? As a historian, I'm getting a whiff of mistrust.

Your article mentions that there were quite a few beautiful young women in Yan'an, but your great friend had eyes only for the actress from Shanghai. Why? This is another question I have been curious about. In traditional Chinese society, which did not respect women very highly, actresses got no respect at all. I believe that the new film industry might be the reason. Just like revolution itself, films were modern, exciting, and more than a bit disruptive of old ways of doing things. When your great friend was involved in revolutionary activities in some of the big cities—Beijing, Shanghai, Wuhan, and Guangzhou, for example—he must have been attracted by this new art form and noticed its compatibility with his revolution. To conquer a screen idol must have seemed a solid step along the way to conquering the world and a symbol of success for a leader such as he, a man of humble origins but with grand ambitions.

Dear Dr. Bethune, the gay and mischievous squirrel that you praised in your essay later became the evil Madame Mao. She was hailed as the standard-bearer for the Cultural Revolution, but she used her immense power not only to destroy culture but also to mangle life. She became a public enemy of the people and was arrested soon after her husband's funeral. The evidence against her was later circulated across China, purportedly proving in great detail that she had not been a true revolutionary. Her career as a decadent film star had been kept in the shadows and was now exposed for all to see. The incriminating evidence included photographs that had never been seen before, including provocative film posters. Scores of essays exposed her corrupt and debased life as an actress in Shanghai. She seemed to have lived in moral turpitude ever since she came into the world.

The tumult surrounding the death of your great friend and the arrest of his wife delayed our entry into high school by a month. All regular classes were cancelled, but we went to the school auditorium every day to hear the incensed school party secretary read out the incriminating evidence against Madame Mao. When she read the dialogues in the 1930s between special agents of the *Kuomintang*—the KMT, the party of Mao's enemy, Chiang-kai-shek—I remember the fury in her voice. "To think that they could talk about a mole on her thigh!" She slapped the desk, and in the severest tone of voice, asked, "What does this illustrate? What was the relationship of that wretched woman to those KMT reactionaries?"

Back in the classroom, we had to discuss the evidence. I remember my female classmates had intense debates about the actress. Some thought she was beautiful, others thought she was ugly, and their hatred of her was unanimous.

After three weeks, we had to deliver a reflection expressing our hatred for the squirrel you praised, dear Dr. Bethune. She was now public enemy number one.

This was how our high school careers began.

If you had lived to 1976, and if your praise of that nasty woman had been unearthed, you yourself might well have been taken as a conspirator. Your judgment was faulty. You did not see that the squirrel was in fact a vampire.

But let me return to film. Film was our main childhood entertainment. Before a film was shown, there would usually be fifteen minutes of political propaganda. The slide projector would project political slogans we knew well onto the screen. The first three were of course those with *wansui* (may you live ten thousand years)— "*Wansui*, Chairman Mao!," "*Wansui*, the Great Chinese Communist Party!," "*Wansui*, the Great People's Republic of China!" Next came "Never Forget Class Struggle!", "Down with the American Imperialists!," or "Our People's Armies are a Great Wall made of Steel and Iron!" Sometimes "Utter Devotion to Others without Any Thought of Self"—a sentence from the memorial your great friend wrote for you—appeared on the screen. After the propaganda, there was "extra programming"—a newsreel lasting thirty minutes. In the early 1970s, so we had had no television yet, the newsreel was the only media through which we could see living foreigners walking around. No foreigners could be seen in our provincial cities, aside from you and the four illustrious, but long-dead, revolutionary mentors whose pictures were pasted on the walls of our classroom.

Then, one particular newsreel changed our relationship

with the world. In it, a group of Red Guards at an airfield were welcoming the commander-in-chief of those lily-livered American soldiers represented in our films.

"Welcome! Welcome! A Warm Welcome!" they shouted, waving garlands and dancing. And then we saw our great saviour receive his American guest in his study! What an honour for an American imperialist! We were all proud of the great diplomatic victory of our great social-ist country.

I remember that we did not hear either the voice of our great saviour or the voice of his American guest. All we heard was the voice of the narrator. Thirty years later, I was in Montreal flipping channels one evening when I chanced on Larry King interviewing Nixon. That was the first time I had ever heard the voice of the American president we told jokes about. His voice made me feel that our jokes were on the mark.

We were in the theatre when my mother told me we were going to move to the provincial capital to reunite with my father. This news took away my interest in the political slogans, the newsreel, and the film itself. I felt agitated at the idea of a new school and new classmates. My new life started in the theatre, in a way, and I am still agitated about it today.

Dear Dr. Bethune, your great friend, our great leader, and the great saviour of all the world's peoples left us forever on September 9, 1976.

It was a hot afternoon. My father had taken me to the hospital not far from the compound where we lived, to get my eyes checked. A couple of months before this, on the afternoon of Yangyang's thirteenth birthday—his first birthday since his death—I had felt a throbbing pain in my right eye and then everything went blurry. It had taken me two months to tell my parents, and it was September 9th when my father took me to the hospital for tests. He was impatient, telling me not to dawdle, because he had to go to his office at three o'clock to listen to an important broadcast.

A voluble old woman was sitting beside us in the waiting room, her left eye covered in cotton, while her right eye was very active, peering around everywhere. The picture of Chairman Mao on my father's bag upset her, and she started to enumerate the bad things in the old regime and the good things in the new society, concluding that her life had been worse than a dog's under the vicious old regime and that it was only thanks to our great saviour that she had managed to survive and live the life of a human being. The reason she was so upset is that her son had mentioned that recently his colleagues had been wondering why the great saviour had not made a public appearance for such a long time. He said the rumour was being spread that our Chairman Mao, who was to live for ten thousand years, might have health problems, and this made the old woman very angry. She cursed her son and wondered how someone who had already become a father could be so immature, spouting such nonsense. She said there was no chance that our great saviour was in poor health. She said he would live forever.

We didn't pay much attention to what she was saying, but she kept on repeating it, over and over again. Her gravelly voice and persistent cough soon got on my nerves, so I was relieved when my name was called. My father and I followed the nurse to the doctor's office and sat down. When handing my my chart to the doctor, the nurse covered her mouth with her hand and yawned a big yawn. Then she smiled awkwardly at us. I felt that a young woman's yawn was a lot more pleasant than an old woman's chattering.

The doctor was really easy-going, meaning he wasn't too focused on what he was doing. He had no sooner started checking my eyes than he began to talk to my father. He asked where my father was from and where he was working and what his monthly salary was. Then they changed topics. The doctor's face was so close to me that

I could not only smell his bad breath but also see spittle flying out of his mouth. I found the irregular opening and closing of his lips a bit scary.

When my father mentioned that he was going to listen to "an important broadcast," the doctor sighed deeply. He said that 1976 had really been a year of calamities. He mentioned our beloved Premier Zhou Enlai's death in January, the counter-revolutionary gathering known as the Tiananmen Square Incident in April, the flooding of the Yellow River in June, the death of General Zhu De, once our army's commander-in-chief, and the Tangshan earthquake, the most disastrous earthquake in Chinese history, in July. "How can a country withstand so many disasters in one year?" The doctor sighed.

And Yangyang's death, I said in my heart. That was the disaster that had had the biggest impact on me.

Then the doctor mentioned the ironwood tree that had blossomed in the only park in the city, Hero Park, in December. In our culture, the rare blooming of such a tree is a bad sign, meaning that the following year would be unlucky. Many people went to see the tree, and worry about the future enveloped the entire city. "Who knows what's going to happen next?" the doctor said, and again sighed deeply.

My father looked back. Then he leaned down to the doctor, asking in a low voice whether he could guess at the content of the important broadcast.

The doctor, too, nervously looked around. Then he put his head close to my father's and said, "This is no time for wild speculation," he said in a voice almost too quiet for me to hear.

My father nodded thoughtfully. "The old woman in the waiting room said that her son had guessed," he said pointing at the doorway. But he did not finish his sentence.

"Guessed what?" the doctor asked.

My father shook his head and sighed but did not reply.

I'm sure the doctor understood what my father's head-shaking, sighing, and silence meant. When he was making notes on my chart, he was shaking his head and sighing, too. "This boy needs glasses," he said.

I was sad at the irreversible decline in my vision. I don't know why it had happened so suddenly.

My father was lost in thought and seemed not to have heard.

"This boy needs glasses," the doctor repeated in a louder voice.

This time my father heard. "My vision and his mother's vision are both good," he complained. "What's wrong with him?"

"There are many mysteries in our lives," the doctor said. He walked us to the door. When he shook my father's hand to say goodbye, he once again reminded him to take me to get glasses as soon as possible. "The sooner the better," he said.

After leaving the doctor's office, my father didn't say anything. He wasn't the way I expected, reprimanding me for my incorrect posture while reading or doing homework, causing my vision to deteriorate. He didn't say anything until when we reached the entrance to the hospital. "Don't hang around outside," he said coldly. "Go home immediately."

"Is the important broadcast about Chairman Mao?" I asked carefully when my father got on his bicycle.

He looked at me for a moment and said I should not talk nonsense.

But I couldn't help asking another question. "If Chairman Mao . . . ," I started to ask, pausing. "What will happen then?"

My father looked back at me and said in a low voice, "That isn't something that you kids should worry about." Then he set off for his office.

Watching my father ride away, I saw myself as a bystander at a turning point of history and felt an overwhelming loneliness. If only Yangyang were by my side now. I could not bear to hear about the bad health of our great saviour any more than the old woman at the hospital could. Let alone something more serious. Those guesses about his health contradicted our ingrained belief that your great friend would live an eternal life. "*Wansui*, Chairman Mao!" was the first thing my classmates and I had ever written down in our writing books. We had all copied it out innumerable times. It was not only the first motto we had ever learned but also the first truth. This truth told us that we would all die before Chairman Mao would.

I rushed home with a heavy heart. I did not know

what would happen in the world after the important broadcast. When I got to our apartment complex, I heard someone calling my name. A woman's voice, but not a voice I recognized. I stopped and looked in the direction the voice was coming from. In the blinding sunlight, I narrowed my eyes and saw Yangyang's mother. I hadn't seen her since his death. My mother had warned me to avoid meeting or talking to his parents. She said it would be better for me and for them that way. But this time there was no avoiding her.

I waited for Yangyang's mother to approach. I felt that my body was sweating uncomfortably. At the same time, I noticed that it wasn't just one person walking toward me. By her side was a little girl. I narrowed my eyes and looked at them. My heart was pounding. "How long it's been since I last saw you!" Yangyang's mother declared in a loud voice, when we were still some distance apart. Her voice had completely changed.

"Ever since...," I was about to reply but then I stopped. I should not mention Yangyang's death, I reminded myself. "It's been a while," I said unhappily.

Yangyang's mother changed the subject, just as she used to do in math class. She pulled the little girl in front of her. "This is Yangyang's little sister," she said.

I'd already heard that Yangyang's parents had adopted a little girl, one in the first batch of orphans from the Tangshan earthquake sent to our city. I had also heard that his parents had had a difference of opinion about whether to adopt a child. His father felt that adopting a child could help them through the mourning process, but his mother had thought it would only add to her pain. In the end the father won the argument, but he had to make a concession. He had originally hoped to adopt a boy.

"Her name is Yinyin," Yangyang's mother said. "I chose her because she has the same birthday as Yangyang. And she can also recite 'In Memory of Dr. Bethune.'"

That was the first time I saw Yinyin. She looked sprightly, but also dazed. There was a scar on her chin, a small scar. It had been mentioned, but it was much smaller than I had imagined.

Yangyang's mother put her hand on my head and patted it. I winced. "This is your elder brother's best friend," she said to Yinyin. "He doesn't even know how to find the lowest common denominator." She stroked my hair, which made me feel even more uncomfortable.

Yinyin did not look up at me.

"If your older brother were still with us, he would be taller," she said proudly.

I was terrified to hear her comparing me with Yangyang. I did not want to keep talking to her. "Why aren't you at home?" I asked, trying to change the subject and get away as soon as possible. "There's going to be an important broadcast."

Yangyang's mother kept on patting my head and looking over my face, as if she had not heard what I just said. But she suddenly started mumbling, "Nothing important, don't you know? Nothing at all, nothing at all, nothing at all."

In the past, when I used to hear her call my name in class to work out a problem on the blackboard, I trembled from head to toe. But that was nothing compared with this. I felt my blood go cold at this mad repetition.

Solemn music started playing through the loudspeaker on the power lines beside us. It was the music used for announcing a death. Hearing it, Yangyang's mother seemed literally shocked. Her hand jumped from my head and hung in midair. Her mumbling came to a stop. She stiffened like a statue, but a statue whose head could move, and she slowly turned her head towards the loudspeaker. Her lips were moving, and I could just hear a whisper that was even quieter than her mumbling. "Another boy has died," she said. "Another boy has died."

Thanks to the great saviour of all the world's people, I was finally liberated! The sound of the funeral music gave me a chance to break away from Yangyang's mother. I rushed into our doorway. I stumbled up the stairs. When I put the key in the keyhole, my hands started to tremble violently, and my tears began to fall.

It was two months before our wedding when Yinyin and I went to bed together for the first time. We squeezed onto a single bed in my bachelor's dormitory. After we made love, we held each other tight. Yinyin mentioned the first time we had seen each other. She could clearly recall all the details of that historic moment, which surprised me. I asked her about her first impression of her future husband. And she admitted that at the time she thought that I was kind of ugly. She said that my small eyes made her think of her little brother, who had big bright eyes. He was not yet eight years old when he and his parents were killed in the earthquake.

Then we talked about her second life, her life as Yangyang's little sister. I was sad that she had been selected by that household, because this choice meant to me that she had been chosen by death. Yangyang's parents should not have told her the true reason why they were adopting her. They should not have called her Yangyang's little sister. Still less should they have chosen her because she was born on the same day as Yangyang. I never told her that my right eye started to throb with pain on Yangyang's first posthumous birthday. Yangyang never knew he had a younger sister, so it was not necessary for Yinyin to know she had an elder brother.

I understood the causal relation between the disappearance of Yangyang and the appearance of Yinyin. But, unlike Yangyang's parents, I did not love Yinyin because she was Yangyang's little sister. And likewise, the reason she loved me was not that I was Yangyang's best friend. In fact, Yinyin never asked me about Yangyang. And I never felt I should let her share my friendship with him and my secrets with him. Our silence about Yangyang was a kind of unspoken understanding. Call it chemistry. I was not willing that our love should be shadowed by death. After reading her first composition, however, I decided that one day in the future, perhaps when we were old, I would tell her about Yangyang's notebook. But I never thought that she would leave me so soon, without warning.

Dear Dr. Bethune, that day, when they came home from work, my parents' eyes were swollen from crying. Over dinner, they said nothing. Neither did I. I kept my questions to myself. But when we were almost done, I couldn't stand it anymore. I needed to break that stifling silence. So I told them about seeing Yangyang's mother on the way home from the hospital. My mother was upset. "How many times have I told you," she said angrily. "Don't talk to that madwoman." Then she asked what the madwoman had said. I had decided not to tell anyone about Yangyang's mother's reaction when the funeral music began playing over the loudspeaker. From her reaction, especially from what she murmured, I had known how hard she was hit by the news. Her words were far more intense than my parents' tears, than anybody's tears. I looked down and finished my rice. "She didn't say anything," I said.

In the middle of the night, I heard my parents talking in their room. I heard them talk about a seizure of power. That stunned me. I sat lonely on the foot of my bed, suffering hot and cold flashes. When my mom came out to tell me to turn off the light and go to sleep, I asked her the question I'd been wanting to ask her ever since I heard the sad music. "Is it the end of the world?" I asked. "Maybe worse," my mother said coldly. Then she reminded me that, according to the decision of the funeral committee, all entertainment activities would be forbidden for the next ten days. "You must not sing. Do you understand?" she said. "If anyone hears you singing . . . ." She didn't finish, but I could well imagine how serious the repercussions would be.

I felt jealous of Yangyang, because he had left the world before it ended. I remembered the note in the notebook, the note to his mother. I don't know how many times I'd read it. It was etched in my brain. Dear Dr. Bethune, I'm hesitating as to whether I should let you know what was in that note. I worry that you, too, might feel guilty about Yangyang's death.

> Mom, I'm going to try to find Dr. Bethune. I once doubted he was real, because in the real world I've never seen a noble-minded person, a pure person. In the real world there are only selfish people. Now I believe. I believe he is greater than all the people we have ever known. I want to go find him.
>
> I am sorry, Mom. Please forgive me. Please do not say that I am a person who only thinks of himself.
>
> Mom, I'm telling this only to you. You won't blame me, will you? I don't hate Dad, not even a little bit. He is just a stranger. I forgave him

for hitting me. Now I know why he lost his temper that day. But I don't know why such a thing would happen to me. Mom, don't ask what I know, because I don't want to lie. Don't ask me.

Mom, please forgive me and forget me. Don't worry about me. Dr. Bethune will take good care of me.

Those were Yangyang's last words. But I've always wondered why he stuck the note in the cover of his notebook, leaving it for me rather than for his mother. Maybe he thought that such words would make his mother angry at his father or at you, dear Dr. Bethune. Maybe he worried that such words would make her blame herself? I've never figured it out.

I had turned off the light and lain down, but I hadn't closed my eyes. I looked up at the trembling shadows on the ceiling. Yangyang's mother's expression at that historic moment came back to me. "Another boy has died."

I'm curious about the world she inhabits. In that world, all deaths are the deaths of boys. She did not have to worry about the end of the world. Her world was a world without an end. Or perhaps you could say that her world had already ended, when the first child, her child, her only child, died. Even after all these years, that hot afternoon replays over and over again in my mind. It gave me the most memorable and moving phrase. Every time death appears in my life, I use that phrase: "Another boy has died." Yangyang's mother turned that solemn, historic afternoon into the most poetic moment of my life.

If Yangyang's mother were to read her son's last words, how would she react?

I know Yangyang really loved his mother. Perhaps that is why he was not willing to lie to her when he came back from Graveyard Hill. I still remember many of the stories he told me about her. The story about the plaster statue of Mao is one. Another story took place when he was six years old, soon after his father went to the May Seventh Cadre School. At the time, his mother was going to the office every night to take part in political study and to do criticism and self-criticism. Each night, she locked Yangyang in his room before she went. Alone in the locked room, Yangyang felt very bored and moved all the furniture around to make the time go faster. One day, he stood on the chair and went through the top drawer of the chest of drawers. Under some old underwear, at the back of the drawer, he found a precious book, *Selected Poems of the Revolutionary Martyrs*. The title page had his father's dedication on it, from which Yangyang saw it was a present his father had given to his mother on their wedding anniversary.

Yangyang never knew there was such a book at his home. Apart from *The Little Red Book* and a few other works by the revolutionary mentors, households were not allowed books. All other books were poison weeds that were supposed to be burnt or sent to the recycling station and sold. Yangyang did not know why this book was there. He sat on the chair and flipped through it, discovering some notations his mother had made in the margins beside some of the poems. Beside a couplet, "On the ground where my skeleton lies, the flowers of love will bloom," his mother had noted, "Revolutionary romanticism." Yangyang did not know what this meant. He read the lines many times and still did not know the meaning of the notation. But the word *love* in the couplet unsettled him. In the past, his understanding was that *love* was a verb, and had to be connected to a great object, like Chairman Mao, the Chinese Communist Party or the People's Republic of China. He never imagined that *love* would be a noun—a thing. What kind of thing was it? He instinctively felt that it was a secret he should not know. The secret made him feel nervous. But why did he not feel nervous at all when love was directed at a great object?

After Yangyang had put the book back where he found it and was lying in bed, he still felt unsettled and embarrassed and was unable to sleep. He was still awake when his mother got home from the office at ten o'clock. As soon as his mother had turned off the lamp and lain down, he asked, "Mom, what is revolutionary romanticism?"

After a long silence, his mother in replied, "Revolutionary romanticism means that romanticism is revolutionary."

This reply confused Yangyang even more. "Then what is romanticism?" he asked.

This time, the period of silence was longer. "It's a kind of positive or optimistic attitude towards life," she said finally.

This reply did nothing to clear up Yangyang's confusion. He wanted to ask more questions, but his mother told him that it was late, that he should not say anything more.

The next evening, when his mother went out for political study, Yangyang opened the drawer again. To his surprise, the book that he had flipped through the previous night was no longer there. He never saw the book again. And he never dared to ask his mother about it until the last birthday he spent on this earth. That day, he asked his mother what had happened to the book. His mother looked at him and said she had never heard of a book like that.

Dear Dr. Bethune, as I've told you, soon after your children witnessed Chairman Mao's funeral—that most solemn memorial ceremony—the squirrel you had met in Yan'an was arrested. She was charged as the leader of the counter-revolutionary clique and sentenced to execution, the sentence to be carried out after a period of two years. When the two years were up, she was then sentenced again, this time to life in prison. The judgement was the first in China's history to be televised, and modern technology gave the former actress a final opportunity to act on the stage of life. She could no longer be described as gay and mischievous. On television, she was presumptuous and insolent. Over ten years later, she went mad and eventually killed herself while she was under house arrest. I don't know whether she left a note. The news of her death was not released until three weeks afterwards, in a news bulletin consisting only of a single sentence. The report, which was not coloured by feigned emotion, nevertheless made me think of the indignant look on the face of our school's Party secretary when she was reading out the scandalous contents of the book of incriminating evidence against the former actress.

This woman, whom you found so charming, had been pitiless with her enemies. We learned that she had been responsible for the deaths of innumerable people during the Cultural Revolution, while you were becoming an icon. But you were a surgeon, not a psychiatrist. You saw her bright appearance, not the darkness in the depths of her soul. You could not, from her beauty and liveliness, predict the disastrous effect she would have on the future of China. In fact, you did not know anything about China's future. You couldn't. And you could not know the fatal relationship between your decision to come to China—which you described as a matter of *must*—and Yangyang's death and the tragedy of his family.

Yangyang's death was a curse. It pushed his entire family towards ineluctable tragedy. Not even Yinyin could escape its clutches. That last evening, I begged her to stay in the apartment, because the situation outside was explosive. But she insisted on going out for a walk. She said she wanted some fresh air. She said the baby needed some fresh air. She said she would be back right away. She did not come back. She never came back. Even today, I don't know how I should describe her death. Was she murdered or did she commit suicide? Was it an accident or a twist of fate?

No matter what, I still believe that Yangyang's and Yinyin's deaths are two sides of the same coin, inseparable. They left the world in the classic way for Dr. Bethune's children. It was a matter of *must*.

A CELEBRATION

Dear Dr. Bethune, let us return to Montreal.

Eight years after Yinyin and I parted forever, I started to live with a Vietnamese woman. She had come to Montreal a few years before I did. Like Yinyin, she was an orphan. Her mother had died on the evening they fled, and her father died on a boat in the South China Sea. It happened in the middle of the night. The refugees had carried out a simple funeral after he breathed his last and had thrown his body into the ocean. Nobody had woken her up. Several days later, their refugee boat was discovered by the Hong Kong Coast Guard. They were saved and sent to a refugee camp.

My girlfriend told me that she had never gotten a good night's sleep since her father's death. Night-time for her was always a time of panic, of despair, and of guilt.

The first time we met was an odd coincidence. It happened in her office, which was about four metres square. Her job was organizing government-subsidized French classes for immigrants. I went there asking for help filling out the form to apply for student support. To be honest, that was the first time I had been with a woman in such a small space since Yinyin's disappearance. We were separated by a very small desk, on which there was a computer and a pile of paper. When she checked the form, our heads were each inclined toward the other, almost touching. A long-forgotten intimacy suddenly caught me. I smelled a woman, a smell I had for so many years stubbornly refused. I looked at her hair. My lips felt dry in that familiar way. Even more amazingly, I immediately felt that she was an orphan, like Yinyin. This intuition made me sentimental, but it also excited me.

She checked my form, line by line. She paused at my marital status and looked up at me. Maybe she had never seen such a young widower. I explained that I had had a brief marriage, that my wife had died in an accident. She did not ask what kind of accident it was. She just looked at me and said she was sorry to hear it.

We had our first date when my French course was about to end. Two months after our first date, we started living together.

Unlike Yinyin, she was a perfectionist and very emotional. The first day we started living together, I noticed I had lost the most basic freedom, the freedom of expression. She used a negative tone in response to whatever I said. If I said that the weather was pretty good at a certain time of year in some Chinese city, her response was that I should go back if I liked the weather there so much. Such immediate and absurd associations left me with fewer and fewer things to say. Another way she limited my freedom of speech was by monitoring other people's responses to my statements. When I was paying the bill in a café where I knew the owner well, I made a joke, and he laughed. But she got angry and didn't talk to me the entire week. "Do you know what he really thought?" she finally said, adding that laughing at a joke doesn't meant the person really thinks it's funny. Another time, I had said a few things too many to a taxi driver, and she got out in the middle of the ride, which made me and the taxi driver feel extremely awkward. Even my attempts to endear myself to her always had the opposite effect. There are too many incidents to list, and some were so absurd that I can't bear to describe them. In the end, being with her made me even more lonely than when I was alone. Our relationship changed me quite a lot. I became more and more afraid of other people's reactions to what I said. And I dared less and less to say what I really wanted to say.

Many topics of conversation were absolutely forbidden zones. Except for that first time we met, I never mentioned Yinyin again. I never told her about my intuition that first day that she was also an orphan. I do not know if that intuition was the reason I never let myself get close to her. I never mentioned Yinyin or you, dear Dr. Bethune. Maybe she doesn't even know who you are. And I always avoided walking past your statue with her, for fear that she would direct her sarcasm at my esteem for you. All in all, our relationship had no future, just as it had no connection with the past.

Even so, it lasted almost four years. Then she left me. Her goodbye was not an attack on me, but it was an insult. She said the reason she had accepted my offer to go on our first date was that she had just broken up with her boyfriend, because she had discovered that he was still in contact with his previous girlfriend. She said that was the darkest time in her life. It left her listless and depressed. And this emotional tumult on dry land was more painful than when she was a refugee getting sloshed around on the ocean. She decided to start a new relationship in order to drag herself out of this sorry state and also to get even with her ex-boyfriend. That's why she chose me. "That doesn't mean I don't like you," she explained kindly. "Actually, the first time you came to my office, I had a good feeling about you."

Dear Dr. Bethune, I know that you had relationships with a lot of different women in your life. And I know that quite a few of those relationships brought you humiliation. So you must understand my reaction when I heard her farewell. I was not one of the people whose feelings and opinions she cared about. I was nothing. I was nothing. Of course, my reaction was not important to her in the least. I quietly accepted her decision and politely wished her happiness. I think that what I said to her in the end might make her feel good. This time I wasn't wrong, for once. It was one of the few times in our relationship where we had some kind of chemistry. Then she left. She did not want me to see her out. She said her ex-boyfriend was waiting for her downstairs. He had returned to her. She said she loved him too much, and that she could forgive the hurt. She left with expectations for the future based on the past. And the only mark she left on me with was my new love for Vietnamese noodle soup.

Soon after that relationship ended, I invited my parents to visit me. We had not seen each other in almost twelve years. I had hoped that time would have healed the wounds and allowed us to forgive the harm we did one another in a series of incidents, because of my marriage to Yinyin. My parents accepted my invitation and made plans to spend at least three months with me in Montreal.

But, what happened was the opposite of what I had hoped. Their visit brought us nothing but unhappiness.

From the day they set foot in Montreal, they began to complain about the city, the people, and the country. They didn't like anything. The city was too quiet, too dark. The buildings were too old, too weird. And there were too many potholes in the roads. The things my father found hardest to tolerate were the television programs. "Besides hockey, there's nothing to watch on television." He did not understand why people here were so fond of hockey, "ice ball" in Chinese, a ball game in which there isn't even a ball. He had not even gotten over his jet lag when he started thinking about going back. "It's only when I got here that I realized how good China is," he said. "China is the best place in the world. It's so lively. I never feel lonely there." And when I took him to see your statue, he said that he only truly understood now, after coming to Canada, why you had wanted to go to China. "Dr. Bethune was a passionate person. How could he stand living in such a dismal place?"

Dear Dr. Bethune, I did not want to correct my father. I did not want to tell him what terrible loneliness and solitude you had to bear in China. You, my spiritual father, did not have books or newspapers. You did not have female companionship or coffee. You did not receive the letters you dreamed of receiving. I did not interrupt my biological father's endless complaints.

Unlike my father, my mother was so limited by the way she lived on the other side of the planet that she behaved as if she were still in China. Every day, she talked about their little world back home. She said that the madwoman was getting crazier and crazier. One time, she even put urine in her husband's lunchbox. Another time, she went to the police to accuse her husband of wanting to use DDVP to poison her. The police investigation reached the opposite conclusion—that the one who was trying to poison the other was the madwoman herself, who had laced the honey with DDVP. After the poisoning incident, the madwoman was sent to the mental hospital for the second time. My mother also mentioned the neighbours' sympathy for Yangyang's father. They all thought he should get a divorce, but he was not willing to do so. My mother kept on repeating these stories. Sometimes she would remember other things that happened long before, such as when the martyr's bride knocked on our window asking us to save her life. "I never imagined she could be so ignorant," she sighed.

I found my mother's *Schadenfreude* towards Yangyang's family tragedy particularly disagreeable. I always attempted to find a way to interrupt her. Once, in the middle of her monologue, I reminded her that Canada is a wonderful country. "There are lots of interesting things here," I said.

She stopped and stared. She knew what I meant, of course, but she just carried on with her tirade. "Who knows what that madwoman might do next?" she said. "Sometimes I wonder whether she's really mad, or whether she's just acting mad."

I knew that this was just a prelude, that the real drama was still to come.

The drama played out in a Vietnamese restaurant in my neighbourhood. I took my parents there to celebrate their fortieth wedding anniversary. But there was nothing to celebrate. My father started to complain about Canadian restaurant service as soon as he sat down, and my mother kept repeating the same stories she had been telling on the way to the restaurant. "That madwoman accused a neighbour of sexual harassment!" I looked at my parents. I found their dedication to their respective pet peeves extremely annoying. But I tried to tamp down my own emotions. "Can we please talk about something else?" I asked quietly.

I never imagined what a violent reaction this would provoke in my mother. "Our family was almost destroyed by that madwoman," she said furiously, pointing her finger in my face.

Her body language and her rough words hurt me deeply. "How can you spout such nonsense?" I yelled. This was the angriest I had ever been at my mother.

My father was shocked at my outburst. He shook his head and said in a low voice, "Life here is even worse than I thought."

His words seemed to encourage my mother, and she

started yelling. "If it hadn't been for that little vixen she adopted, our family wouldn't have ended up like this!" She was screaming even louder now. "It's been twelve years since you left us."

I could not bear the way she referred to Yinyin. But again, I tried to restrain myself. "You should not mix everything up," I said, calm on the surface.

My mother kept on criticizing Yinyin. "If it hadn't been for that vixen, who crawled out of her den, you wouldn't have ended up like this." She paused, and looked at my father, and then kept on speaking. "Your stupid marriage ruined us, and it ruined you, too. Look at the kind of life you are leading!"

"You never tried to understand us," I said. "We loved each other. I still love her."

"That was the reason why your marriage was so stupid," my mother said. "That little vixen was not worthy of my son's love."

"Please do not refer to Yinyin in that way," I beseeched her.

"That word isn't my invention. That's what that madwoman calls her," my mother said. "That's about the only thing we agree on."

"I never thought you would be so unfeeling," I said. "Yinyin died so many years ago, and here you are, still complaining about her."

"I may be more heartless than you think," my mother said. "I'm very happy that she died the way she did, without the chance to explain herself."

I was totally unprepared for my mother saying such a thing. This was way beyond what I could bear. I immediately stood up and stared at her, livid.

My mother seemed prepared for my reaction. She remained sitting calmly, not the least flustered. Then she finished what she had to say. "If she hadn't died, we would never have had a chance for a family reunion."

Her heartlessness sent me over the edge. I was apoplectic. But she just looked out the window as if nothing were the matter. After a moment, I ran out of the restaurant.

For the first time in my life, I felt like an orphan. I was sad about the way my mother had insulted Yinyin. I felt like I had lost my parents forever. I walked over to Place du 6 décembre. I was crying so hard that my tears had wetted my shirt.

This small park is a memorial to the most frightening night in the history of Montreal, even Canada. In the same year that Yinyin died in the shadows on the streets of Beijing, fourteen female students at the École Polytechnique de Montréal—the engineering faculty of the University of Montreal—were killed by a gun-wielding man who blamed women for his troubles. Two of the victims were born in the same year as Yinyin. The man left a note in which he expressed his hatred of feminists, of women. In contrast to Yinyin's death, there at least seemed to be an explanation for the December 6th tragedy.

I sat down on a bench in the square. Scenes from my life with Yinyin kept on appearing in my mind. "Now, I too have become an orphan," I said quietly. In my mind, she very tenderly touched my cheeks. I felt a kind of healing intimacy.

It was very late when I finally went home. I hoped my parents would already be asleep, but they weren't. I had just sat down in my room when my father walked in. He said I should not have treated my mother like that in the restaurant. He said I should go and say I was sorry. I said I would not do so. I said that she should apologize to me. And to Yinyin.

"Yǒu know how difficult what you did is for your mother to bear?" my father asked.

"Does she know how difficult it is for me to bear what she said?" I replied.

My father looked at me sadly. "We used to be such a tight-knit family," he said. "Now I feel like your mother is right. That girl disrupted everything."

I looked out the window. I did not want to have another argument.

"We have already decided," my father said. "We're going to go back early, the sooner the better."

I also felt no wish for them to stay any longer. The next morning, I changed their tickets. Three days later, they left. We had spent less than two months together.

I took them to the airport and helped them check in. I watched them go through security without a hitch. I did not say anything to them. I did not even say goodbye.

Because of Yinyin, my family, which had reunited after so many years, was once again split up.

Dear Dr. Bethune, I was estranged from my parents for almost two years after that. But on the day of my mother's sixty-fifth birthday, I got back in touch with them. It was a strange day. In the morning, I left my bank card in the ATM machine, which had never happened before. At noon, I was almost hit by a car at an intersection not far from my home, when I mistook a green light facing a different direction for the one that allowed me to cross the street. That evening, I sat alone at the same table in the Vietnamese restaurant where my parents and I had eaten dinner the evening of the argument. When I was almost finished, I realized that the next day was my mother's sixty-fifth birthday, and that it was already the next day in China.

The two years since I parted with them had been full. I had resumed contact with a lot of friends in Chinese academic circles. With their encouragement, I had started to write articles for Chinese newspapers, and I got a lot of good feedback. To be honest, I did not really want to resume contact with my parents. Had these incidents not happened that day, I probably would not have made the telephone call to my mother. Warning me that I might suddenly lose my memory or even my life, the day's incidents served as fateful reminders.

At ten o'clock in the evening, I placed a call to my parents' home. I had hoped it would be my father who picked up, which would have been less awkward. But the voice I heard was my mother's. She seemed to know who I was before I even said anything. "I just got back from the hospital," she said, as if the two years of silence between us did not exist. I was a bit disappointed that my phone call did not surprise her. "I had a feeling you would call me today," she continued, her tone of voice still extremely calm. I asked what she went to the hospital for. She said she went to discuss some recent blood sugar results with her doctor. She said she had been diagnosed with diabetes soon after she got back from Montreal, and the doctor had asked her to monitor her blood sugar regularly. "My situation is very stable," she said. "There's nothing to worry about."

I felt a bit guilty that I hadn't known about her health situation over the past two years. "Diabetes is no big deal," I said, not knowing whether I was comforting myself or comforting my mother.

"I am not the least bit worried," my mother said. "I believe in my genes, that they're genes of longevity. Look at your grandmother, almost ninety years old now, but she still insists on living by herself and is still doing well."

Dear Dr. Bethune, maybe I should tell you a bit about my grandmother's experience. Not just because she took care of me for a time when I was a child, but also because her life had a connection with yours. Born in the same year as the squirrel, she had no opportunity to become a liberated "new woman." She was married off by her parents just after she celebrated her fifteenth birthday. Her parents took a liking to the future son-in-law who, as the only son, stood to inherit the family fortune. In comparison with the squirrel, who made her way into the great cave of her own free will, my grandmother had no choice. She had never seen her future husband before she got married.

My grandmother gave birth to my mother when she was twenty-four years of age. I remember the first time I asked my mother what year she was born, her reply was she was born in the year that you arrived in China. That's probably why I'm so sensitive about the year 1938. It was much later that I found out Claude was born in that same year.

Dear Dr. Bethune, my grandmother enjoyed the life of a rich wife for only twenty years, because, after taking power in 1949, your great friend carried out a number of land reforms, under which her husband, who was a gentleman of leisure, was convicted as an oppressor and executed. His public trial took place on a stage erected in their yard. My grandmother and all four of her children, including my mother, witnessed the execution. At the age of thirty-five, my grandmother became a widow with four children, deprived of any means of livelihood. For the first few months, she had to beg to make ends meet.

All right, let's return to that call I made to my mother. My mother told me she had just read a magazine article about you written by someone who also lived in

Montreal. After finishing the article, my mother said she realized that you weren't so noble-minded or pure after all. "He wasn't even good to his wife," she said. "What do they mean about his devotion to others?"

I was delighted to hear there was another Chinese person living in Montreal who had a deep interest in you. Dear Dr. Bethune, he must also be your child. I know there must be many such children of yours living in this city. "What kind of person Dr. Bethune was doesn't matter," I said. "The main thing is that we all were shaped by the spirit of his noble-mindedness."

"But if he himself was not noble-minded, weren't we lied to?" my mother insisted.

"No matter whether we were fooled or lied to, we were shaped by our Dr. Bethune," I said impatiently. "The real Dr. Bethune is not important. The important person is the one who shaped us."

"I don't accept that," my mother said.

I did not want to continue talking to her. I wished her happy birthday and good health. Then I prepared myself to put down the phone.

Just as I was about to hang up, though, I heard my mother's voice call my name. I put the receiver to my ear again. My mother said she forgot the most important thing. I guessed that it was going to be about that mad-woman, but it was about her husband. "Yangyang's father has been missing for over two weeks," my mother said.

Dear Dr. Bethune, only then did I understand why I had to make this phone call to my mother. It was not to thaw the ice, but to hear that item of bad news.

"Where have they looked for him?" I asked, my voice urgent.

"Everywhere!" my mother said.

"Even Graveyard Hill?" I asked.

"Why there?" my mother asked. Then she started laughing. She told me that Graveyard Hill no longer existed. The government had reclaimed the land and established a high technology zone, what the local media was calling "our Silicon Valley." But my mother had sensed something in my question. "Why would you think of that place?" she asked, warily.

I hesitated before replying. "Because other people would not think of it," I said.

My mother was no longer curious. She laughed and then asked me to guess what the madwoman's reaction to her husband's disappearance had been. My mother's tone of voice put me off. I said I would not guess.

"She told everyone not to go looking. She said they would never find him. She said that only *she* knew where her husband had gone."

My mother paused, as if waiting for my reaction. But I didn't say anything. I knew her patience would run out soon.

As I expected, she soon continued. "The police were suspicious, of course. They interrogated her for two days and two nights."

She paused again, but I still didn't say anything. "Are you listening to what I am saying?" she asked, impatiently.

"Yes," I said.

"Do you want to know what she said to the police?"

"I'm listening."

"She said he went to hell," my mother said.

I felt a spasm in my heart. But I did not know who I was unhappy for.

"I don't know if she is really mad or if she is just pretending," my mother said. She coughed a few times before continuing. "What a scary woman she is! How could she reward her husband with this?" She coughed again and then said, "Everybody knows he has cared for her for over thirty years, ever since the first time she went to the mental hospital." My mother then sighed.

My mother's sigh made me very anxious about Yangyang's mother's situation. How would she cope without her husband? But I did not dare express my worry. My worry about Yangyang's mother would only make my mother very unhappy.

All I could hear was my mother's coughing. She was clearly agitated. "I want to see how she'll cope by herself," she said, apparently gladdened by the madwoman's misfortune. Then our conversation got cut off.

A STAGE

Dear Dr. Bethune, I've never understood why my mother hated Yangyang's mother. They used to get on well, starting soon after Yangyang and I became friends. I recall my mother sympathized with his mother, because her husband had gone to the May Seventh Cadre School, and it couldn't be easy for her, raising her son on her own. "We are basically in the same boat, like sisters," she said, recalling that she, too, had had to live apart from her man with a child to raise. Even after Yangyang went missing, she continued to express sympathy for this "sister." Yes, she did tell me to avoid his parents, but I thought this was because she was trying to make their loss easier to bear. And then, all of sudden, she changed completely.

Why the change? I have never asked her. But now I figure it must have been her intuition that caused the change. An intuition about the love between Yinyin and me.

My high school was on the other side of the city, and I spent most of my years there living in the school dormitory, so I did not see Yangyang's parents for several years. I did occasionally ask my mother about them, and she was always very cold, saying she had not seen them, either.

In Montreal, she once commented on this reticence, saying that she didn't mention Yangyang's family because she didn't want such news to have an impact on my studies.

It was only when I was at university, home from Beijing for my second summer vacation, that I had any contact with Yangyang's family again. I was at the market with my mother, close to the high school and our community compound, when a quiet, friendly girl walked towards us. She and my mother exchanged greetings, and my mother told me that she was the orphan that Yangyang's parents had adopted. I did remember the dazed little girl I had seen seven years before, on that momentous afternoon, and was amazed at the changes that time had wrought. My mother said Yinyin was a student at the high school. She had just taken the *gaokao*, the highly competitive national university entrance exam, and was considering attending university in Beijing.

"An ill-fated girl," my mother said with a sigh, and then told me about the family. Yangyang's mother was in a mental hospital again, mostly on account of that girl. Calling her "that vixen who crawled up out of the rubble," Yangyang's mother had accused her adoptive daughter of trying to seduce her husband. She threatened to return the girl to the government agency responsible for transferring her from the earthquake zone eight years before. She also threatened to divorce her husband and kill herself. "There are no waves without wind," she told everyone she met. She promised that one day she would "catch them in the act." Everyone thought both the waves and the wind were in her imagination.

There was one time when she thought she had proof of their guilt. After Yinyin finished evening study, Yangyang's father went to get her on his bike. Like all parents, he let his adopted daughter sit on the rear bike rack. Yangyang's mother was hiding beneath the old camphor tree close to the community compound, and they came past, she jumped out, grabbed the handlebars, and screamed that she had finally caught them in the act. Yangyang's father explained that all parents let their children ride on their bicycles. This explanation enraged her. "That's their own flesh and blood? Who's riding on *your* bike rack?" Before Yangyang's father could respond, she added, "She's just some little vixen that crawled out of the rubble! It's totally different."

Soon thereafter something more serious happened, when Yangyang's father bought Yinyin a bilingual Chinese-English dictionary as a birthday present. According to my mother, the madwoman insisted that the birthday should not be a celebration but a memorial, because it was also Yangyang's birthday. Moreover, like all Dr. Bethune's children, his mother said, Yangyang had never gotten a birthday present. Birthday presents are for petty bourgeois, symbols of a corrupt lifestyle. And Yangyang, she said, had always spent his birthday doing something meaningful—cleaning elderly neighbours' windows, for example, returning screws he had found in the road to the factory, and—let's not forget—kneeling in front of Chairman Mao's picture to beg his forgiveness.

She ordered Yinyin to rip up the dictionary and flush the pieces down the toilet.

Before going to sleep that night, Yangyang's mother sat washing her feet in a porcelain basin next to her adoptive daughter's bed. Humming a popular song, she stared at Yinyin, who had just lain down. All of sudden, her expression changed. She reminded Yinyin that she had yet to do something meaningful to celebrate her birthday. Yinyin sat up, and then, to her astonishment, the madwoman started crying. Yangyang's father rushed over, but he did not know what had happened and did not know what to do. A little later, he reminded Yinyin that there was a mock exam the next day. Finally, Yangyang's mother stopped crying. She reminded them that the meaningful thing Yangyang had done on his last birthday was to recite the Old Three before going to bed. And she asked Yinyin to do the same. "This is the best way to commemorate your older brother on this special day," she said.

Yangyang's father got angry before Yinyin had the chance to react. He said that memorizing those "red" texts was no longer the thing to do. "You can get her to memorize something classical," he said. "Like 'The Old Drunkard's Pavilion' or 'Ode to Yueyang Tower.'"

These suggestions enraged Yangyang's mother. "I said that your relationship is abnormal, didn't I?" she shouted. "I only want her to commemorate Yangyang's birthday. What's wrong with that?" She picked up the basin and dumped the water over her husband and Yinyin. Then she smashed the basin on the floor and grabbed a pair of scissors on the desk, threatening to stab herself in the throat.

Yangyang's father subdued her in time. Then, with the help of a few neighbours, he stopped a truck at the entrance of the community compound and took her to the mental hospital.

When he returned, afraid the neighbours might believe what his wife had said, he sent Yinyin to a relative's home. She stayed there for three weeks, including the days when she was taking the university entrance exam, until Yangyang's mother was released from hospital.

That was the first news in years that my mother had given me about Yangyang's family. The stories she told made me feel very sad, and I had trouble getting to sleep that night. A little girl I had met on that historic afternoon had grown up, but the environment in which she lived was so dark. Seven years earlier, she had been saved from the edge of hell only to fall into another hell. I thought I had a kind of responsibility, one I could not shirk. I knew I was the only one who could help this girl escape the hell of her life.

If she really chose to go to Beijing to study, I felt she would be choosing me. I kept imagining us sitting on the train to Beijing. I imagined her sitting by my side, leaning softly against me. "You are my life," I said in my heart. Tender is the night, I thought, for the first time in my life.

Two weeks later, Yangyang's father came to see us. When he knocked on the door, my mother's intuition kicked in, and she motioned for me to hide. Confused, I sat in my room, at my desk, listening to the conversation outside. Yangyang's father told my mother that Yinyin had received her acceptance letter to Beijing Normal University. My mother praised her, saying that she had always felt that she was a good child and had a bright future. Yangyang's father then said that the reason he came was to ask whether Yinyin could travel with me to Beijing. My father thought it was a good idea, but my mother's tone of voice was not encouraging. This was the first time I noticed my mother's negativity towards Yinyin.

My mother did not actually veto Yangyang's father's request. She came up with an excuse, saying that, given how difficult it was to buy train tickets nowadays, she had already asked a friend working in the provincial government to help get me a ticket. I knew this was a lie, but Yangyang's father seemed not to have noticed that my mother was trying to put him off. He asked what day we had gotten the ticket for. My mother hemmed and hawed and in the end told him the day. My father must have known she was making it up as she went along, but he did not dare say anything. Yangyang's father said before leaving that he would try to get a ticket on the same date for Yinyin.

The next evening, my mother took me to the home of a friend who worked in the provincial government and asked him to help buy me a ticket to Beijing either for the day before the date she'd told Yangyang's father, or the day after. On the way home, I asked her whether I could just go on the same day. My mother said my father did not have time to take me to the station that day. I was astonished at her determination to prevent me from taking the same train as Yinyin.

Her intuition was another source of astonishment. She had a premonition about my relationship with Yinyin long before I did—and about the way it would end. At the time, she was not willing to tell me the secret in her heart. It was only on the evening when I returned Yinyin's ashes to our home city that I asked her why she had been so determined to prevent Yinyin and me from getting together. My mother's reply was simple. "I just did not want you to be cursed by association with that family," she said calmly. "Now you have seen the power of my premonition, and it's a shame you yourself didn't see it." She shook her head and did not finish her sentence, but I knew she was going to add, "before it was too late."

Yes, perhaps she did anticipate it all. But she had no way to prevent any of it from happening. This must be the meaning of *yuanfen*, the Chinese Buddhist idea of a predestined affinity between people. Maybe it had its source in Yangyang, or maybe even in you, dear Dr. Bethune. On the day I was travelling back to Beijing, we ran into Yangyang's family on the railway platform. His father saw us first and walked over to us to say, "We could not get a ticket yesterday," he explained. My mother responded with her excuse, saying, "We were going to leave yesterday, but his father wouldn't have been able to...." Yangyang's father cut her off, exclaiming, "What a coincidence!" And my father followed up with, "It's *yuanfen*." My mother stared at him angrily.

Yangyang's father greeted me. He said that the last time he had seen me, I was still a kid. Kids grow up fast, and now I was a young whippersnapper. When he mentioned the last time he saw me, I felt nervous. Did he mean seeing me at the entrance to the neighbourhood movie theatre? That was the last time I remembered seeing him. I had never told my parents about this encounter, but I had never forgotten about it. I never will.

Yinyin was standing to one side with Yangyang's mother. "She wants to come to send off the child," he said to my parents, "but she does not want to see anyone she knows. This is the first time she has been out of the house since she came out of hospital." My parents looked at her. "She is much better now," he said, adding that he was still worried about her, and especially worried that this send-off might cause a relapse.

Before leaving, Yangyang's father asked me what carriage I was in and told me where Yinyin was sitting. He said he hoped I would take care of her. "Should I call her over to introduce you?" he asked.

"No need," my mother said. "They have met before."

I did not know whether she meant seven years before or recently in the street. I could feel that Yangyang's father's wish that I take care of her made my mother unhappy. Before we parted, she whispered in my ear not to pay too much attention to that little vixen who had crawled up out of the rubble.

I did not follow my mother's advice. Soon after the train left, I went along to Yinyin's carriage. Noting that my forwardness did not make Yinyin uneasy, I asked the middle-aged woman sitting beside her whether we could change seats. "She is my cousin," I said. "I want to sit with her." The woman was pleased to comply.

I will never forget that trip. In fact, from the day I saw Yinyin near the entrance to the high school, I realized that my life was on the cusp of a major change. Yinyin replied to my questions during the trip, but barely said anything else. She was a good listener, and she was also curious about the scenery outside the window. When the train was getting close to our destination, she told me this was not the first time she had been to Beijing. Seven years previously, after the earthquake, she and some of the other orphans were first taken to Beijing before being sent to other parts of China. "But that time, I arrived in Beijing from the opposite direction," she sighed. "The city seems to be a kind of stage for a few scenes in my life."

Dear Dr. Bethune, soon after the start of Grade 5, Yang-yang asked me whether I had seen the announcement posted up by the Municipal Revolutionary Committee. Every two weeks, such an announcement was pasted on all the important bulletin boards in the city and one of them was by the entrance to our school. The announcement was about the latest bunch of criminals to be sentenced, with their names, birthdates, birthplaces, details of their crimes (we found these the most exciting parts), and sentences. The announcement was called "the latest fruit" of the Cultural Revolution. The names of the convicted were arranged in order of the seriousness of the crimes they had committed. Capital crimes were listed first, and the names of those guilty were identified with red crosses. Then came those who were not to be executed immediately, followed by those sentenced to life in prison. The more red crosses an announcement had, the more people paid attention.

Every term, we were brought to a public trial. The criminals were tied up and dragged onto the stage. When they heard that they were sentenced to death, some would just collapse while others would stand up even straighter than they had before. These two opposite reactions inspired me with terror over the death penalty. After the trial was over, those condemned to immediate execution were dragged onto a truck and taken to the execution grounds.

Most of the audience at such public trials had come with a collective, as many units made attendance at a public trial a form of political study for their members. I remember the one we attended with our school in Grade 3 vividly. On the bus back to school after the trial, Foreign Affairs was relating his experience as the commander of an execution squad to our homeroom teacher in the row in front of me. He spoke really loudly, as if he wanted us all to hear about his glorious past, five years earlier, when he was a platoon leader in a factory militia. One day, he got a special mission, shooting live targets. There were six men to execute that day—two current counter-revolutionaries, one historical counter-revolutionary, one rapist-murderer, and two burglar-murderers. Describing this as a rare opportunity, the commander insisted that every bullet strike its target, just as on the firing range. Foreign Affairs's platoon was known as the "platoon of sharpshooters," and this was why they had been chosen for this glorious revolutionary task. "So you were a sharp-shooter!" our homeroom teacher commented contemptuously. Foreign Affairs leaned over to her and said, "Do you even have to ask?" I did not know what he meant, but our homeroom teacher evidently did. She laughed broadly and pushed Foreign Affairs away.

The person in our class who had the most experience of such public trials was Dumb Pig. In addition to being in the audience once every semester with our school, he often went alone. He had even followed the execution truck to the execution grounds a couple of times. At first, we thought he was bragging, but when we heard the details during enhanced training, we had to believe him. After the criminals were dragged off of the truck at the execution grounds, he said they were split into two groups. One group was untied so they could start digging their own graves. After they had each finished, they were bound up again and ordered to kneel down by their respective graves. The members of the execution squad prodded the backs of their heads with their rifles and pulled the trigger. The other group of criminals was then untied so they could fill in the graves and they, too, dug their own graves before being bound up again and shot in the back of the head. Their graves were filled in by the execution ground personnel.

Dumb Pig's account made my hair stand on end. "Why don't those criminals try to escape when they are untied?" I asked him. Dumb Pig looked at me with contempt. "Where are they going to run to?" he asked. "Each one's leg is roped to another's!" Only Girl came up with a good way to die. She said that if she were a criminal sentenced to death, she would intentionally dig her grave as slowly as possible. "See how well that works for you!" Dumb Pig said mockingly. "You'd have the opposite effect." He said that once he had seen a dumb ass do just that. (Dumb Pig's use of the term "dumb ass" to refer to such a person amused us). A couple of the people on the execution squad beat that dumb ass with a rifle and let his groupmates dig his grave—which they did almost immediately, so that that dumb ass was the first one executed.

Those details opened our eyes and were passed around class next day. Not a few pupils regretted that they had recited the Old Three too quickly and lost the chance at enhanced training, because that meant passing up the chance to hear Dumb Pig's amazing experiences. A few pupils even felt that the school should arrange for us to go and witness an execution, which would have a better pedagogical effect than just attending a public trial. Yangyang did not agree with this suggestion. He was more interested in death itself, not execution. One day during enhanced training, he asked us to imagine we knew we were going to die the next day. What would we do with the last hours of our lives? Dumb Pig retorted that he'd thought about that a lot. He would go and kill people, he said, as many as possible. I had never thought about it before. When Yangyang was waiting for my reply, I thought I would rather kill myself to end the torture of waiting. For a long time after Yangyang's death, I regretted having said that. Once again, Only Girl surprised us with her choice. She said that she'd finally memorize "In Memory of Dr. Bethune" once and for all, so this shadow wouldn't follow her to the next world.

Yangyang laughed out loud. "What a great idea for delaying death," he said ironically.

Then he told us a story about delaying death, which he had just read in a book called *A Thousand and One Nights*. This was a book about a vicious king who would kill the woman he had just spent the night with, until one day the woman he chose told him an interesting story. The king was hooked, and he decided to delay her execution until she finished the story. But the next day there was another story, and then another. She kept on telling these endless stories to put off her own death. She saved many women's lives because, a thousand and one nights later, the king had changed completely. He married the woman who could tell the great stories and became a good king.

"What a great book!" Dumb Pig said. "Bring it us next time."

"I can't," Yangyang said. "It's a poisonous weed."

Dear Dr. Bethune, like you in a barren, mountainous area in China in the late 1930s, your children in China in the early 1970s had no access to any books except those that were labeled one-hundred-percent revolutionary. Burned to ashes, smashed to a pulp, or sealed in a warehouse, all those great books were labelled "poisonous weeds."

"Why is it a poisonous weed?" Dumb Pig asked, displeased.

Yangyang shook his head and said he did not know.

"Maybe because there is a king in the story." I said. "Communism sees all kings as nasty people, so of course a book about one of them is a poisonous weed."

"But we have Chairman Mao," Only Girl said. "Isn't a

chairman equal to a king?"

Dumb Pig rolled his eyes. "No wonder you're not only bad at Chinese, your mathematics is also a problem," he said, disgusted. "How can a chairman be *equal* to a king?"

"I think Chairman Mao would hate this book for sure," I said. I don't know where the idea came from, but I was quite proud of myself for coming up with it.

"What do you mean?" Yangyang took the idea and ran. "Do you mean it's a poisonous weed *so* Chairman Mao wouldn't like it, or that it became a poisonous week *because* Chairman Mao wouldn't like it?"

There was a certain logic to this, but I didn't mean either, and the way he used what I said to connect Chairman Mao with a poisonous weed frightened me.

Dear Dr. Bethune, please let me return to where I started. Hearing that I had not yet seen the announcement, Yangyang dragged me off to the new announcement at the school entrance. "I've got something important to tell you," he said.

When we had caught our breath, he pointed at a name in the middle of the list and asked: "Do you know who that is?"

"How should I know?" I said annoyed. But I immediately reflected that maybe it was something I should know or something worth knowing. So I asked him, "Do you?"

Yangyang whispered that it was Dumb Pig's father. His words shocked me. This is the first time that someone I knew had been related to a criminal. I started to read his father's crime word by word. I was terrified. "What crime did he commit?" I looked at the strange crime and asked Yangyang. Yangyang shook his head to say he didn't know, either. But he said he would ask his mother.

The next day, after self-study, I asked Yangyang if he had found out what *sodomy* meant. He paled and did not reply, and I did not dare to ask again. The conversation between Yangyang and his mother about that crime was in his notebook. I read it soon after her son's death. When he asked what Dumb Pig's father's crime was, his mother seemed very uncomfortable. Yangyang's mother said that it was a kind of reprehensible crime. Dissatisfied with this response, Yangyang annoyed his mother by saying that all crimes were reprehensible. Provoked by Yangyang's words, she said people who commit that particular kind of crime are not human. "They're even worse than homosexuals!"

This made Yangyang tremble from head to toe. This was the first time he had ever heard his mother use the word *homosexuals*. He asked her what that meant. He had been waiting such a long time for this opportunity. And what he mostly wanted to know was whether homosexuality was a crime, or whether the names of homosexuals might appear in an announcement. "Of course it's a crime," his mother said firmly. "Sending that kind of person to prison is really too good for them." She paused, coughed, and added, "That kind of person deserves to go to hell."

Dumb Pig's father was sentenced to ten years in prison for sodomy. Yangyang expressed his sympathy for the son in his notebook, and he claimed he could fully understand his shame and pain. "It can't be easy to be the son of a criminal," he wrote, at the end of this notebook entry.

Before going to the May Seventh Cadre School, Yangyang's father had gone to the kindergarten to say goodbye to him. Yangyang had never told his mother this. It was a sunny day, around noon, and he was taking his nap. A teacher at the kindergarten woke him up and took him to the entrance, where his dad stood with his luggage, waiting. Taking a handful of candy out of his pocket, he crouched down and held Yangyang's hand flat, wanting to put the candy in it. But Yangyang did not accept them, saying he wasn't allowed candy or snacks in the kindergarten. After a long silence, tapping at his shoulder, his father told Yangyang he was going somewhere far, far away and might not see him for a long, long time. Glancing at the luggage and at his father, Yangyang felt frightened, especially at his father's repetition of the words *far* and *long*. Not knowing how to express himself, he looked down. And he could feel his father looking him over with sad eyes.

When he was leaving, his father told Yangyang that he had come to say goodbye against his mother's wishes. "This is our secret," he said. "A secret between two men." he said. These last words made Yangyang all the more afraid. He was afraid of secrets.

And Yangyang never told his mother about the second time we went to Graveyard Hill and about the flashlight we found. That, too, was a secret between two men. A secret between him and me. Now I am telling you, so you have become the third man to know. Dear Dr. Bethune, you were our common father. You should share in all of our secrets.

I was sad when my mother told me over the phone from Montreal about Yangyang's father's disappearance. Over the next week, I called my mother another couple of times. In the end, she told me that the investigation into his disappearance had been closed. "Everyone says he's more amazing than his son," she said. "Because he disappeared into thin air."

She also told me that Yangyang's father's disappearance was mainly the result of his relationship with the man who had been the projectionist at the neighbourhood movie theatre. Their relationship had been discovered by accident not long before. About ten years younger than Yangyang's father, the projectionist had taken early retirement when the movie theatre stopped operating. One day, not long ago, he was standing in the entrance of the movie theatre, which was now a restaurant called Real Sichuan Food, when he was hit be a speeding motorcycle and killed.

Going through his personal effects, the projectionist's wife discovered a sealed envelope in which she found some photographs of her husband with Yangyang's father. The photographs had been taken soon after Yangyang's father had returned from the May Seventh Cadre School, about thirty years ago now. They enraged the projectionist's wife, who found them "disgusting." She rushed to Yangyang's home to confront Yangyang's father, but he was not there. The furious wife handed the envelop to Yangyang's mother, expecting that she would react strongly to the photographs.

But she was wrong. Yangyang's mother looked through the photographs one by one and seemed to appreciate them. Her expression was calm. Her voice was calm. "Everyone considered your man handsome. He looks even more handsome in photos than he did in real life," she said slowly. "If that little vixen who crawled up out of the rubble were still alive, she would finally know why she never succeeded in seducing her adoptive father."

In the end, she stuffed the photographs into the envelope and returned it to the projectionist's wife. "You should take good care of your man's personal effects," she said. "You can count yourself happy to have spent your life with such a handsome man."

His relationship with the projectionist and the madwoman's abnormal response to the projectionist's wife soon spread around our little community. Yangyang's father never showed himself in public again.

Dear Dr. Bethune, five years after our first trip together, Yinyin and I got married in the autumn of 1988. Our union caused our families, or more accurately our mothers, irreparable harm. Yinyin and I were no match, they both agreed, and neither were our families. But each thought it was the child of the other family that did not match her own.

The news that we would register our marriage infuriated Yangyang's mother. She rushed to our home and attacked our door with a brick she had just picked up off the road. At the time my parents did not know what had happened, as they had not yet received my letter. Hastily blocking the door with furniture, they too were livid.

"I knew this would happen sooner or later," Yangyang's mother yelled, bashing on our door. "I knew you had your eye on my daughter."

At her yells and the sound of the brick hitting the door, a number of neighbours came round to see what was happening.

Unable to bash the door down, Yangyang's mother sat down on the ground. "That retard son of yours! He can't even memorize 'In Memory of Dr. Bethune'!" she yelled, crying. "He's got some nerve, seducing *my* daughter like that. As if he deserves her!"

I don't know whether my mother's account was true or not. When Yangyang's father rushed over, she said "that madwoman" was surrounded by the neighbours. Yes, that was the first time she described Yangyang's mother as "that madwoman." And she has never referred to her in any other way since that day. Her hostility to her was now out in the open. According to my mother, Yangyang's father pushed through the human wall to stand in front of his wife. He tried to pull her up and away, but she pushed his hands away. "I want compensation!" she screamed, hitting the ground with the brick. "I want my daughter back!"

With the help of the neighbours, Yangyang's father finally succeeded in getting the brick out of her hands, then they pulled her up off the ground and took her away.

Yangyang's mother kept struggling and yelling at Yangyang's father, calling him "a traitor" and "an insider," all the while hollering for compensation. As all your children knew, "traitor" and "insider" were labels your great friend applied to Liu Shaoqi, his major rival in the Communist Party, whom he launched the Cultural Revolution to destroy, politically and physically. Yangyang's mother also shouted that she was going to Beijing to stop us from consummating the marriage. "I swear I'll get your retard son for ruining my dear daughter."

She was unable to set out, however, because that's

when she was committed to hospital again.

That evening, my mother went to the post office to call me long distance. She asked me if I really planned to get married. Yes, I replied. My firm answer agitated her. I told her I'd written to let her know about this about a week ago, but evidently my letter had not yet arrived. She said a lot, giving me no chance to interrupt. She yelled at me for not seeing what that little vixen had up her sleeve and what she likely had in store for me. She told me what the madwoman did that afternoon. She said that even without such a scandal, she would still ask me to change my mind. "Nobody knows what's gone on in that family," she said.

This was a sentence I had heard many times before. My mother had been repeating this ever since that first time I went to Beijing with Yinyin and every single time I mentioned her or Yangyang's parents after that. She knew my relationship with Yinyin became more and more intimate after that trip, and she did everything she could to put a stop to it. Our marriage told her all her efforts had been in vain. "You should not have gotten married so soon," she continued coldly. I knew, by the way she said "you," that she meant only me, not Yinyin. She had never used the second-person plural pronoun *nimen* to refer and Yinyin and me. "You have to end the relationship with that little vixen," she said with certainty. That was her ultimatum as a parent. "Otherwise I will cut off *our* relationship," she said in a resolute tone of voice.

I never told Yinyin about my mother's attitude

towards our marriage, though I'm sure she knew. After we got married, my mother never got in touch with us. Our parents did not attend our wedding, which was simple and frugal, even though the two fathers were not opposed to our union. In fact, the day of the wedding, I got a telegram from my father, wishing us happiness. And two days later, I got a letter from Yangyang's father, a letter to me personally, in which he explained that he could not come to Beijing to attend our wedding because he had to take care of Yangyang's mother. He said that it was "right" for us to be together, a simple but moving choice of words. He said that from the first time Yangyang brought me to their house to play, he had always felt that I was a good boy. He also said that he believed I would take good care of Yangyang's little sister. At the end of the letter, just like my father in the telegram, he wished us happiness.

I reread Yangyang's father's letter many times, trying to discover some trace of psychological abnormality, but I never found any such thing. During my mother's stay in Montreal I interrupted her at one point and asked her what she meant when she said, "Nobody knows what's gone on in that family." My mother looked at me, surprised. "Isn't that obvious?" she said, contemptuously. I mentioned the letter I'd received from Yangyang's father on my marriage and said I could not see any abnormality. "The letter itself was abnormal," my mother said. "Of course, he was grateful to you, because he had lost interest in that little vixen, and you helped him out." Her nasty tone made me feel uncomfortable.

"Nobody believes Yangyang's mother's overactive imagination," I said, dissatisfied. "At first you didn't believe, either. When did you change your mind?"

My mother paid no attention to my question. "I bet that the little vixen never told you about the sick relationship she had with her adoptive father," she said. "Of course she wouldn't. How could she? She had so many things up her sleeve."

I never told Yinyin about the letter from Yangyang's father or asked her how she felt about Yangyang's mother's accusation. This was not only because I knew Yangyang's father was a homosexual, but also because I had no interest in the accusation. Even if it had been true, I would still have continued my relationship with Yinyin. My feelings for her and my need for her were greater than those rumours about her family. I believed I could build a new home for her that would remove the curse. In this way, besides being our fate, our marriage was also a kind of responsibility. Dear Dr. Bethune, my attitude towards my wife was the opposite from your attitude towards the woman you married and divorced twice, the woman you promised you would never "bore," even though you knew you could make her life "a misery." I was like so many ordinary men who think it normal never to make their bride's life miserable and never to let marriage become stale and boring.

On the telephone, my mother said that the projectionist's accidental death exposed the secret that shocked everyone except "that madwoman." She did not know that it hadn't been a secret to Yangyang and me for almost three decades. I did not want to mention my experience with Yangyang on Graveyard Hill. Still less did I want to mention Yangyang's notebook. "Here in Canada, gay marriage is legal," I told her calmly.

Chinese people's attitude toward homosexuals has now changed but, my mother said, many people still believe that it is abnormal. "But you know their relationship started in the 1970s," she said, interrupting herself with a fit of coughing. "Had he been caught at that time, he might have died before his son."

Her tone of voice in mentioning Yangyang I found equally distasteful. "Imagine if his son knew of his behaviour, how ashamed he would feel," she added with great enthusiasm.

"Maybe he knew," I said deliberately.

My mother thought I was kidding. "Be serious, okay?" she said in a disapproving tone of voice.

"I'm completely serious," I said.

She seemed to think about this for a while, before going on, first denying that Yangyang could have known, and then adding that what I'd said reminded her that his mother once told her that her husband had lost interest in her, ever since he went to the May Seventh Cadre School. "Now I know the reason she did not show any surprise when she saw those photos," my mother said. "It wasn't because she had lost her sanity. On the contrary, it was because she was very rational." She coughed again, then said, "She must have known all along."

Whether Yangyang's mother knew about the secret before Yangyang or not, I had no idea. This might be an eternal secret, just like Descartes's notebook.

"One day, recalling a visit to her husband at the May Seventh Cadre School," my mother continued, "she said that her husband, though enthusiastic when he was reciting the Old Three with their son, had become an indifferent lover. He was unwilling to touch her and to be touched by her. He said he was afraid of being heard by their son, who slept on the same bunk, or by his comrades, whose bunks were in the same bunkhouse, separated from them only by linen curtains."

I had never heard this before.

"That was the reason I broke off contact with her," my mother said. "A middle-aged woman who doesn't get any love from a man is too dangerous. I've met a lot of cases like this." She looked toward the kitchen, where my father was cooking, and continued in a low voice, "That madwoman, her eyes were full of temptation. Even with an honest and respectable man like your father, her eyes were full of temptation."

I never thought my mother would tell me so much, but doing so failed to result in any improvement to our relationship. The problem was her attitude towards Yinyin. The secret revealed by the projectionist's sudden death had made my mother realize her assumption about Yinyin was completely wrong. But she still refused to say sorry to me or to us.

I think she never will.

Dear Dr. Bethune, soon after I broke up with my girlfriend, I moved to the tower that I live in now. What you
might call the "cultural environment" here is multi-lay-
ered, which I like very much. Among the local neighbours,
who are mostly retirees, about a fifth are separatists, and
two fifths are federalists. The rest are, of course, opportunists. And the immigrants living here can also be divided,
for instance, into new and old. The new immigrants have
been here for a couple of days, weeks, or months. They're
still looking around for a good school for their kids and
for a nice supermarket where they can get the cheapest
green onions. They have a lot of hopes and dreams for the
future. The old immigrants are those who have been here
for a couple of years at least. They have gotten tired of all
of the votes and elections, of the game of "true democra-
cy." They've even gotten used to the social safety net that
attracted them to Canada in the first place. And, more
significantly, they've discovered that having a passport
from a free country does not guarantee absolute freedom.
Freedom might have a more direct relationship to wealth.

Various wars are fought between the neighbours—

the war between the new and old immigrants, the war between the separatists and the federalists, the war between the opportunists and the opportunists. Attitudes towards China can also split the neighbours into different camps. Bob, a federalist, and Claude, a separatist, are both Sinophiles. Allied with each other on this issue, they fought against the Sinophobes who enjoy calculating how much harm those poisonous made-in-China toys have been causing *our* Canadian children, just as back, in 1970s, we children of Dr. Bethune were appalled by capitalist ideology that was poisoning the flowers of *our* socialist nation.

War has been a profound part of my immigrant experience. In addition to those bloodless wars between my neighbours in this building, I have witnessed two bloody wars against the same country led by our neighbour to the south. The first, launched by Bush Sr., was swiftly fought and resolved and is generally seen as just. The second, also launched in the name of justice by Bush Jr., ended up messy, nasty, and seemingly endless.

During that summer vacation I spent with Yangyang in my home town, we talked about justice and war. We were sure no man would think that the war he launched was unjust, just as no man would think that the war his enemy launched against him was just. Every war, therefore, was both just and unjust. This clearly contradicted the law of the excluded middle, which we had learned at school from Yangyang's mother, who was our mathematics teacher, so we reached the further conclusion that all wars were illogical.

On a related topic, Yangyang wondered whether you, dear Dr. Bethune, would consent to treat a wounded Japanese soldier. Yangyang said he'd thought about this for a long time. In those days, there was a huge sign at the entrances of all the hospitals in our city which read "Uphold the Revolutionary Humanitarianism!" a famous "highest instruction" from your great friend. We all knew that revolution required us to be heartless towards our enemies, while humanitarianism meant that we should treat everybody as a human being, not divide people into friends and enemies. In other words, we should help everyone without prejudice. Again, according to the law of the excluded middle, your great friend's instruction was also illogical.

Later on, we discovered that the law of the excluded middle did not have the last word on many things. There is also the law of dialectics, which enables us to find a hidden unity in opposites by mastering the negation of the negation. Your children were all brainwashed with these dialectics. But would you save a wounded Japanese soldier? We never resolved the problem to our satisfaction.

Yangyang always approached such questions skeptically and critically. One time, after an air-raid exercise, he told me that even if we described the Soviet Union as revisionist, they themselves would never think of themselves as revisionist. Which is to say that something one side thought was wrong, the other side might not think of in the same way. Yangyang also challenged your great friend's claim that we have to be opposed to anything our enemies possess. This time, he used common sense. If our enemies believe that people need to eat to survive, does that mean we should not eat? Does the fact that our enemies love life mean that we should relinquish it? And, if our enemies refuse to eat shit, does that mean that we should relish it? Following this kind of logic, Yangyang even doubted the most famous sentence in "In Memory of Dr. Bethune." Was it possible that a lack of any thought of self was a cunning way of advancing personal interest? These continuous challenges often left me feeling mentally exhausted.

Dear Dr. Bethune, all the paintings of you that I saw when I was growing up showed you dressed in a military uniform. Yes, you were a warrior. And your life was inseparable from war. As a young man, you were injured in the First World War. In middle age, you risked your life in the Spanish Civil War. And, in the end, you sacrificed yourself to the Chinese people's war of resistance against the Japanese invasion, which was in fact a part of the Second World War, though you did not know that at the time. If any of those three wars in the first half of the twentieth century had not broken out, your own life would have been illogical. It was war that made your life logical.

You may claim that your reason for participating in war was that you were a pacifist. But when I delved deeper and deeper into your archives I felt more and more that your motivation was to justify your own painful individual life. If, one day, I happened to come across a copy of Filippo Tommaso Marinetti's *Futurist Manifesto* in your archives, I would not be the least surprised. Marinetti declared war on any fixed form, not just the class war between proletariat and capitalist. To Marinetti, war was a source of inspiration. Your own life is proof of that. You were both a Communist Party member and a futurist artist. Perhaps communism is a kind of futurism? The murals you created when you were recovering from tuberculosis in the Trudeau Sanatorium were futurist documents. If we can borrow some words from Marinetti, "who hurls the lance of his spirit across the Earth" showed "the love of danger" in the murals.

Marinetti claimed that beauty only exists in struggle, and war is the only cure. This could be a quotation from your great friend's *Little Red Book*. I remember the loud-speaker broadcasting his highest instructions every morn-ing—"Never Forget Class Struggle!," "From Practice Comes Genuine Knowledge," "Combat Shows True Tal-ent!" and "Struggle with Heaven, Struggle with Earth, Struggle with Man—It's Endlessly Fascinating!" I still remember those instructions—and others. Like the Old Three, they nourished our lives and created the founda-tions of our thought.

Like you, your great friend needed war to justify his life. Peace was a disaster for him. When there was no war, his health deteriorated. So, in the last decade of his life he put on his military uniform once again and stood on the rostrum of Tiananmen, waving at his Red Guards as their commander-in-chief. The name of the war he launched was the Cultural Revolution. He wanted to crush the old world and create a new one. Then Chinese people were divided into two opposing camps. Unlike the opposing sides in any other war, the sides in this war had common ground. They both were "infinitely loyal to Chairman Mao." And they had all memorized the Old Three.

The sauna in my building is the main battleground for the wars between my neighbours. Claude, Simon, and three other old men are the most active debaters. These last are two Romanian Jews, both Holocaust survivors, and one sculptor from Hungary who escaped after the Hungarian Revolution of 1956. These old men are waging more and more complex wars. Claude detests people whose native language is English. He hates their pride. Simon detests or looks down on people whose native language is French, thinking them limited. These two are civil enemies who are allies in their view of foreign affairs. Both are anti-Semites and fervently opposed to America's protection of Israel. The two survivors of the Holocaust have no interest in your great friend, because they suffered greatly under totalitarianism, while the sculptor, who also fled from a totalitarian regime, is the opposite. The first time he saw me, he said that he really liked your great friend. He said Mao had a very handsome face. He also said that, at the beginning of the 1950s, in large-scale demonstrations in Budapest, he was one of the students that held up the largest placard with your great friend's portrait on it. He did not agree that your great friend should be considered a dictator.

These three old men were ardent supporters of Bush Jr.'s war at first, because no price is too much to pay for the removal of a dictator, and all means are justifiable. Claude would hit back by saying, "The American president is himself a dictator." Simon would provide reinforcements by saying, "The United States itself is a fascist country." Their opponents would heap ridicule on these two native Canadians, two naïve Canadians. They said the Canadians had never suffered under a dictatorship, let alone a fascist dictatorship, which is the only explanation for why they clung to such infantile ideas. "The world would have gone to hell without a great America," they yelled.

I playfully refer to the sauna as the place where history gets naked, because these old men remember and discuss history there in the nude. But the thing that makes me most curious is not these bellicose old men, but rather another fellow who sits in the corner and never says anything. He looks the most like you of anyone in my daily life. Dear Dr. Bethune, the first time I saw him I found his appearance arresting. Later I found out Bob was of the same opinion. "He knows he looks like Dr. Bethune," he said.

He also told me that this silent neighbour had once been very talkative, and had once participated in the wars between the neighbours. He had a beautiful voice. He was once a member of the most famous amateur choir in the city, singing tenor. But in the winter before I moved into the building, two tragedies befell him. First his eighteen-year-old daughter committed suicide two years after running off with a drug addict who was even older than he was at the time. Then, the day after her funeral, his wife and his son were hit by a car when they were crossing the street. His son died instantly, and his wife died after a week in a coma. After handling the funeral, this once talk-ative man went to Miami and lived with his elder sister for a year. Nobody had heard him speak since he came back.

This man's story brings back a lot of memories for me. I don't know why your life was surrounded by so much death and insanity, or how you got involved with so many suicides and madmen. Dear Dr. Bethune, I would really like to know why and how. Only if could I find this out might I be able to finish writing your biography. But it's all so hard to believe, that readers would assume I'd written a novel.

One day I found a letter to one of your lovers, a fare-well letter, among your papers. It struck me that your ac-cidental death might have been suicide, that you might have cut your own finger intentionally, prematurely end-ing your life. This absurd idea made me feel uncomfort-able, even guilty. But from your letter I knew how much you hated your life, how lonely you were, how tired of the most ancient war in human life, the war of the sex-es, which you found tedious. To escape this tedium was probably part of the reason you threw yourself into the Chinese war of resistance against Japan. But the last war of your life brought you even more tedium. You were un-happy with your life. You were unhappy with your body. You were unhappy with your solitude. You had various reasons to commit suicide. I wonder, had you not died in 1939 at the age of forty-nine, what would you have become? Maybe a taciturn and morose old man like the neighbour who looks so much like you?

Dear Dr. Bethune, you must have heard of Bertrand Russell, a philosopher, a liberal, and a British aristocrat. A travelogue of his I happened to read yesterday allowed me to compare your different experiences in China. During his one-year sojourn in China, in the early 1920s, he lectured in quite a few cities and exerted considerable influence on some Chinese intellectuals. It is said that your great friend went to one of his lectures, but he could hardly have found Russell's ideas compelling. At that time, inspired by the success of the Bolshevik revolution in our neighbour to the north, radical young Chinese minds like your great friend chose communism over liberalism. Yes, compared with the explosions of the October Revolution, Russell's wisdom and sympathy seemed to lack vitality. But after three decades of communist dictatorship, especially after the end of the catastrophic Cultural Revolution, liberalism became popular in China in the late 1970s. The children of Dr. Bethune had grown up. We rebelled against the old order, smashing former idols and ripping down the pictures of the great mentors from the classroom walls. We discovered that Marx and

Engels had their weaknesses, that Lenin was paranoid and Stalin a mass-murderer. Dear Dr. Bethune, you were not as big a target as these great mentors, so you were spared. We were gentler with you. All we did is take *The Little Red Book* and throw it away or recycle it like so much scrap paper. After smashing the old idols, we started an insane pursuit of new ones. The spectres of the West flooded in: after Lord Russell came Sartre, Freud, Wittgenstein, and Chomsky, to name only a few. These new Western stars started to reshape our intellects, which had been formed by you and our revolutionary mentors.

What these new idols brought was a long way from "without any thought of self" and a long way from "utter devotion to others." Freud taught us about the Oedipus complex, according to which we, the children of Dr. Bethune, were full of instinctual hostility for our spiritual father. So remember, one day we might usurp you. And Sartre told us something even more provocative, that Hell is other people. So wait, why should we devote ourselves to others? And Wittgenstein claimed that language is a game. If so, why should we bother taking "In Memory of Dr. Bethune" so seriously?

In the travelogue I read yesterday, Russell discusses his visit with Lenin in Moscow, the only time they saw one another. Lenin affirmed the violence of the poor peasants against the kulaks—the rich peasants. His idea that such violence was delightful smashed Russell's delusion about the first socialist country in human history. Yes, in Lenin's eyes, revolution is a festival of the oppressed, in other words, a kind of entertainment. From then on, Russell was circumspect about the new totalitarian regime.

We were not so circumspect. We saw Lenin as a lantern, lighting the way in the night. "The explosions of the October Revolution brought us Marxism and Leninism!" your great friend declared. Yangyang and I liked the metaphor in this quotation. Our great revolutionary mentors were good at creating metaphors to light up our young hearts.

I remember that, on the way to Graveyard Hill, Yangyang shared with me the metaphors that he had committed to memory. He said that I had only to name a revolutionary mentor, and he would immediately cite the metaphor that great mind had created. Yes, it was Marx who wrote that religion was the opium of the people. And, with Engels, they announced that the spectre of communism was haunting Europe in *The Communist Manifesto*. Yes, Lenin had said that revolution is the locomotive of history as well as describing the revolution as a festival. Your great friend's metaphors were even richer and more numerous. All counter-revolutionaries are paper tigers. Revolution is not a dinner party. And so on and so forth. Yangyang's desire for knowledge was extremely strong. Had he lived to the 1980s, how eager would he have been to read Sartre, Freud, and Wittgenstein as well as Russell and other Western writers.

What your great friend actually learned from the explosions of the October Revolution was terror. Like Lenin, he was ruthless with his enemies. He knew that denying his enemies space to breathe was the only way to ensure the victory of the revolution. And he had a lot of terrible inventions, such as the public trials. As early as the first soviet in the Jinggang Mountains, long before setting off on the Long March, he was strenuously practicing the public trial as an opportunity to disseminate Red Terror. He knew terror made politics simple. Dear Dr. Bethune, haunted by the Red Terror that your great friend invented, your children had a most peculiar childhood.

Your great friend was not only ruthless to his enemies but also kept turning friends into enemies. If you had known this, would you have dared befriend him? Had you lived to the years of the Cultural Revolution, your great friend might have turned you overnight from an idol into a spy. You would have been arrested, sent for labour reformation—or even executed. Every revolution is full of turning points, fissures, and surprises. Who knows how the next metaphor might change your status?

Dear Dr. Bethune, forgive me for writing in such a convoluted way. My mind right now is a bit of a mess. This afternoon, I went to the biggest English bookstore here, because I knew from a book review that a new biography of your great friend had just been published. The favourable review predicted that the new revelations in the biography would shock the world. At first, I did not believe it, but after flipping through the chapters, I was indeed shocked. Our great saviour had been turned into the twentieth century's cruellest tyrant, equal to Hitler and Stalin! Can you accept this version of the truth? I did not buy the book eventually because, disillusioned though I am by the history we lived through, I was still frightened by this version of the truth.

On the bus home, I noticed that the construction in the park has not been completed. Your statue has not been returned to its place. My cheek resting against the glass, I was in a daze at the changes in the world. Seventy years ago, it was *Red Star Over China*, Edgar Snow's work of propaganda for your great friend, which shocked the world with its truth. Now the world needed to experience the opposite view and be shocked in a negative way. The truth you discovered in Edgar Snow's book brought you, a Canadian surgeon, to China. And the opposite truth made me, a Chinese historian, recollect China's past in a daze on a bus in a Canadian city.

When you were living in China, you were out of touch with the world. You could be oblivious to what was going on elsewhere, including the Second World War. Today, no matter where you live, you might be living at the centre of the world. Amazing developments in communications technology have eradicated distance, condensing the globe into a village. Unlike the village in which you were ensconced, this global village includes the entire world. No matter what corner of the village you live in, you can find out about things that are going on all over the world at any moment—even things you don't want to know about. I was completely unprepared, three years ago, to hear the news that Yangyang's father had gone missing. But I made the call to my mother. The news disturbed me greatly. It saddens me to this day.

The day Yinyin and I took the same train for Beijing, Yangyang's father mentioned on the station platform the last time he had seen me. I felt relieved that he did not say more about it. This was another secret in my life I had never told my parents.

Your great friend, whom Yangyang's mother called "another boy," had been dead for a year. I had started second year in high school. At the time, many classic films, both Chinese and Western, blossomed for the second time in local movie theatres like the one in my neighbourhood. One Sunday afternoon, I went alone to the theatre to see Hamlet, with Laurence Olivier, and Yangyang's father was at the entrance, talking with the projectionist. I found this a bit odd, because films had been Yangyang's favourite form of entertainment, and I heard that his family hadn't been to the movies since his death. I wanted to slip behind his father, but it was too late. He saw me, turned towards me, and put his hand on my head. I became his prisoner. And he almost pushed me to a quiet wall.

I had no idea this could happen and did not know how to react. My body and my facial expression became very stiff.

Then Yangyang's father turned my face towards the sun and looked me over with hungry eyes as if conducting a medical examination. There was a fresh cut on his forehead, that he had treated with gentian violet. I was terribly uncomfortable being so close to his face and twisted my head a bit, but Yangyang's father started to stroke my hair with trembling fingers. This situation took me back to the historic afternoon of your great friend's death. I thought that Yangyang's father would soon say, as his wife had said, "if Yangyang were still alive." And I wanted him to hurry up, say what he wanted to say, and let me take my seat in the theatre. I had heard there was no additional programming before the movie, and I did not want to miss any of the film, not even a little bit. I had been waiting for it for three weeks.

To my surprise, Yangyang's father did not say anything at all. He just looked me over and continued to stroke my hair. I do not know how long it lasted. And I did not even hear his breathing. The unexpected silence scared me so much I almost fainted. I did not even know when his hand left my hair.

I stood there stiffly until the ticket taker asked me in a loud voice whether I was going in. Only then did I find that Yangyang's father had gone. I rushed inside and sat down just as the movie started. Like all imported films, it was dubbed. The actor who dubbed Olivier's character of Hamlet had received the best education of all Chinese actors, graduating with a degree in philosophy from the best university in China. And it was said his voice accurately conveyed the conflict in Hamlet's heart, especially when he asked the question that everybody knows. His voice or maybe that blunt question suddenly changed my feeling for Chinese. How I wished Yangyang could sit by my side and share this linguistic miracle with me.

Yangyang's father was sitting in front of me, just three

rows away. His frightening silence just now was like a prologue that kept interfering with my appreciation of the movie. I couldn't help comparing the tragedy in the film with the tragedy in my life. In my real life, the death of a son had left the father living. Which was to say that the tragedy in real life started in the opposite way from the tragedy in the film. A series of questions galloped around in my mind. Would Yangyang's ghost appear to his father? Would he reveal the secret of his death? Would Yangyang's father be punished by God for the suicide of his son? To be or not to be? All of a sudden, the question that Hamlet raised in Mandarin resonated through the movie theatre. Cut to ocean waves hitting the rocks. The fury of the sea under Elsinore drowned out Hamlet's confusion.

To be or not to be? That blunt question churned within me. I couldn't help thinking that this question had caused Yangyang terrible confusion as well. But why had he chosen not to be?

One evening, soon after we were married, Yinyin and I were strolling in a grove in Tiantan Park when I remembered meeting Yangyang's father at the entrance to the movie theatre. I asked Yinyin if she still remembered the scar on his forehead. She said yes, very clearly. She explained to me what had happened. That evening over dinner, Yangyang's mother and father had had another argument about who was responsible for Yangyang's death. Yangyang's mother claimed that the beating his father had given him was a decisive factor behind his suicide. And Yangyang's father insisted that Yangyang's mother had spoiled him, weakening his spirit so much that he could not withstand the slings and arrows of outrageous fortune. Once again, their argument ended in violence when Yangyang's mother picked up a pair of scissors and struck at her husband's forehead. Rushing into the bedroom, the father used gauze to stanch the blood and gentian violet to disinfect the wound. He then went out without saying anything and didn't come back for three hours. Yinyin had no idea he had gone to the movie theatre.

"They were always fighting about how Yangyang's father had beaten his son," Yinyin said. "Do you know why Yangyang got beaten that day?" That was the only time she ever asked about Yangyang's past. I didn't want to talk about that day, the day we went to Graveyard Hill.

After a silence, I shook my head and said, "I don't know."

I don't know why I had to lie to Yinyin. For Yangyang? For his father or for his mother? Or for some other reason? I just don't know.

Dear Dr. Bethune, the first time I chatted with Bob, he told me that it was you who had stimulated his imagination about China and his interest in China when he was a child. And he dreamed that one day, like you, he might go to China to live, to work. He even dreamed of studying Chinese. I remember at the time I almost responded by saying "you are a child of Dr. Bethune." But I didn't say anything. I did not want to have to explain everything we children of Dr. Bethune experienced, which he might never understand.

Having been to China three times, Bob has realized some parts of his dream. But he has never had the opportunity to formally study Chinese. He knows six Chinese phrases, including *nihao* (hello); *xiexie* (thank you), which he mispronounces *shieshie*; *zaijian* (goodbye), which he mispronounces *zhaijian*; and *henhao* (good). All of which are basic words. No wonder he knows them. Even *xiaojie* (Miss), which he knows and mispronounces as *shaoji*, is nothing special. Of course, Bob could not know that in the old regime, this term *xiaojie* was an honorific, while in the new society, it took on a negative meaning as a relic of the exploiting class. And later still, in the era of reform and opening, it went through another semantic shift and acquired a new meaning which some people consider an honorific and others demeaning.

Many Westerners are familiar with those basic Chinese words. They might appear in a simple travel guide or as the first lesson in a Chinese language text. When they came out of Bob's mouth, I wasn't surprised. But Bob knows another word which confused me greatly, because it is much more difficult than the previous five. The first time I heard him use this word, I was sure there must be a special story behind it.

This special story turned out to have two parts, which were separated by half a century.

When he was young, Bob borrowed a book called *Folk Songs of the World* from his uncle. He learned all of the songs in the book, including one Chinese song. He sang the first line for me with feeling and in a powerful voice. "That's a song all Chinese people can sing," I told Bob. "It was originally a song from the period of the resistance against the Japanese. When the Communist Party took control of China, it became our national anthem, though it was temporarily abandoned during the Cultural Revolution." (That will give you an idea, dear Dr. Bethune, about how thoroughly the Cultural Revolution broke with the past: that even our national anthem was discarded when its lyricist was imprisoned as a counter-revolutionary.)

Bob was proud to say he still remembered the name

of the song was *Qilai* (Arise! or Stand Up!). *Qilai* is also the first word in the song and the only word that was not translated into English. And it was in fact the first Chinese word in Bob's vocabulary and the most obscure. Very few people who only know six Chinese words would know this one.

Bob told me he was shaken from the start by the majestic rhythm of that song. "It is so powerful," he said, closing his right hand into a fist and shaking it around in the air. "Such a powerful song. It's no surprise that the Chinese people ended up winning that war."

Bob's understanding of this Chinese song narrowed the distance between us.

His expression suddenly turned stern. "But you Chinese people do not take your national anthem seriously enough."

I didn't know where this comment was coming from, and I said so.

To explain, Bob related an experience on his second trip to China when, on the last evening, the first Chinese word he had ever encountered was given a new and special meaning in a surprising context.

"It was in Guangzhou," Bob said seriously. His tour group was booked into the White Swan Hotel on the bank of the Pearl River, then the most luxuriant hotel in China. In the middle of the night, Bob returned from the bar and was getting ready for bed when the doorbell rang. He looked through the peephole in the door and saw two scantily clad Chinese ladies standing uncomfortably outside his door. He opened the door a crack and asked what the problem was. Those two Chinese women quickly squeezed in, laughed, and asked him if he needed special room service. Bob happened to have such a need. Chinese women were a part of his China dream, the most deeply hidden part, in fact. I remember he once asked me about your relationship to Chinese women, a secret he claimed to be extremely curious about.

Bob recalled that they could speak good English and were obviously well-educated. Moreover, they were naughty and lively, making a deep impression on Bob. The price they quoted Bob found flattering and affordable. "China is a hospitable country," Bob said, regretting that he had come too late and was leaving too soon.

Bob learned a lot from this last night on his second trip to China. He first realized that Chinese people do not like to call each other by name. When he asked those two young Chinese women what their names were, they said that he should call them *xiaojie*. Bob, of course, found this word difficult to pronounce. He mispronounced both *xiao* and *jie*. So instead of *xiaojie* he ended up saying *sha-oji,* which is the correct pronunciation of another phrase meaning *roasted chicken.*

Then Bob asked these two roasted chickens what *xiao-jie* meant. The shorter one told him civilly that it could be translated into *sister* in English. Bob found this hard to understand, because in English that's what you would call a Catholic nun. He did not dare to ask what relationship these two attractive roasted chickens had with the church.

Then he asked a technical question. If the two of them were called roasted chicken, how could he tell them apart? Then they showed they were not just naughty and lively, but also funny. "You can tell us apart by appearance," the tall one said. But Bob said that all Asian women looked the same to him. "Then you can tell us apart by the size of our breasts," the short one said. Bob politely said that both of them had big breasts, so he could not tell them apart by their breasts, either. In the end, the tall one said, "Don't worry, the service we provide is the same."

Bob told me that he had more questions to ask them. Where had they studied English? Were they really sisters? But the two roasted chickens were not interested in his questions. "They just told me to hurry up," Bob complained. "They didn't know that Canadians like to take things slow."

He still insisted on asking another question, asking the two women if they knew you, dear Dr. Bethune. He said it was because of you that he had come to China. In other words, it was only because of you that he had the opportunity to stay in this hotel and receive special room service from such attractive women.

Bob never expected that the two roasted chickens would say, in unison, that of course they knew you. There was no need to ask, they added, because for the Chinese people, your household name was a synonym for Canada.

"I am the compatriot of Dr. Bethune," Bob told them proudly. Then he jokingly asked if he could get a discount.

The tall one was out of patience. She pushed him onto the bed. "Don't embarrass your compatriot," she said. "He truly was utterly devoted to others and without any thought of self. And what *you* tell us is that you want a discount." The short one also tried to hurry Bob up. She reminded him, using another title in the Old Three, that there were more people waiting to be served.

Bob regretted that they did not have any interest in talking. But the pleasure that they gave him more than made up for his disappointment. He said he did not know what magic they used to restore his long-lost sexual vigour. Again he regretted that he had come to China too late and was leaving too soon.

After his moment of climactic passion, lying happily on the bed, Bob suddenly thought of the book of folk songs that he had memorized fifty years before. Then he told these two women he could sing a Chinese song. The short one had just come out of the bathroom. She said he couldn't even correctly pronounce *xiaojie*, how was he going to sing a Chinese song? She simply didn't believe it. But the tall one, still lying in Bob's arms, was curious. She asked Bob what the name of the song was. When he said the name, the two roasted chickens were confused. They had never heard of it. *Qilai* isn't the official name of China's national anthem.

When Bob sang the first sentence, of course, the two roasted chickens immediately knew what song he meant. They laughed out loud, and so hard that they could not contain themselves. Their laughter made it hard for Bob to keep singing. "What's wrong?" he asked, unhappy and confused.

They could not stop laughing. They were in tears, it was so funny.

Bob stared. When they finally quieted down, he asked, "What was so funny?"

The short one was facing away from the bed, putting on her bra. "It's a bit late to sing that song," she said.

Bob asked her why.

"Because," the other one said, "Now it's *qibulai*," adding an extra syllable to Bob's title of the song to turn it into "unable to get up." Then she once again burst out laughing.

Not getting the joke, Bob tried to correct them. "The title is not *qibulai*," he said. "It's "*qilai*.""

"It was *qilai,*" the short one said. "But it isn't anymore."

"To this day, I don't know why they thought it was so funny," Bob said, staring at me. "Were they laughing at my pronunciation?"

"No," I told Bob. "Your pronunciation of *qilai* was correct. What they were laughing at is *qibulai*, which was their own joke."

"Then what does *qibulai* mean?" Bob asked.

"It means 'unable to get up,'" I explained.

"Then what the hell does 'unable to get up' mean in that song?" Bob asked impatiently.

The basic meaning of *qilai* was stand up or arise, I told him, which is what it means in the song. In the room in the hotel, however, the two of them had thought of a special meaning that it doesn't have in the dictionary but which it can have in that kind of context. Unable to get it up. Unable to rise to the occasion.

Bob was embarrassed. The first time he had seen the term was over fifty years before. And he had finally learned that it could be used to convey another meaning. This new knowledge made him all the more nostalgic about the end of his second trip to China. "What naughty roasted chickens," he said, sighing. "They even make a joke out of their national anthem."

Dear Dr. Bethune, I read nothing about your relationships with Chinese women in your papers. I wonder whether, as a man who had retained his vigour and was less than fifty years old, you had any fantasies about Chinese women in the last year and a half of your life. You didn't understand many Chinese words. This was certainly an impediment. But I really hope that you fell in love with a Chinese woman. That would have been the only way to distract you from homesickness and loneliness, from your hopeless waiting for letters from far away. Though who knows? Maybe it would have made you all the more homesick and lonely.

Would it surprise you to learn that your Chinese name was soon a part of the Chinese language? Dear Dr. Bethune, I'm sure you'd find it hard to imagine how popular Chinese is today. Everyone says that Chinese, meaning Mandarin, is the language of the twenty-first century. It is so popular that I can support myself by teaching

Chinese, and I am not alone. More and more students have been studying with me in the past couple of years.

I'm not actually that excited about the future of Chinese. To me, a language is a palace founded on the past. To grasp a language, a person has to listen carefully to the spectres that are wandering around in that palace, to their tears, their complaints, their laughs, their sighs, even their silences. Every word has so many spectres behind it. That's why I always mention you in the first lesson I teach to every new student. Dear Dr. Bethune, I always tell my students that today in this world there are millions, no, tens or hundreds of millions of people who can say that they are your children. I also tell them that memorizing "In Memory of Dr. Bethune" is an ideal segue into intermediate Chinese. I always say so, but no student has ever take me seriously.

A few weeks ago, a student came to speak with me after class. He told me that he was born in Hong Kong and that Cantonese is his mother tongue. He said that he believes the prediction that Mandarin Chinese is the language of the twenty-first century, which is why several years ago he started to study Mandarin in earnest. But his progress was less than ideal. And for a time he even lost interest in studying. He said that he felt lucky to be in my class, because my approach had reignited his passion for Mandarin. After the first class, he told his father on the phone about my feeling for language and my approach to language teaching. His father thought I was an amazing teacher and encouraged him to keep studying according to my method.

I was about to ask this student why his father approved so strongly of my teaching methods, but he told me before I had the chance. His father had memorized "In Memory of Dr. Bethune" when he was studying on the mainland. During the Cultural Revolution, he was one of the many young Chinese who fled to Hong Kong. Later on, he opened a Chinese restaurant, which became a well-known chain in the 1980s. "He said that he is also a child of Dr. Bethune," the student said proudly. He added that "utter devotion to others without any thought of self" had become his father's management philosophy. "It had brought him very good business," the student said. "He had made a lot of money."

I listened appreciatively to the student's story, as if he was teaching me a difficult Chinese lesson. Dear Dr. Bethune, I never imagined that your spirit would ever prove to be profitable.

Your legend has brought so many ironies to our lives and our history.

A QUESTION

Dear Dr. Bethune, it's a lot easier to talk to Bob than it is to talk to Claude. Bob's questions can be described as rhetorical, not needing earnest answers. But Claude is much more serious. His questions are interrogations. He'll only accept a certain kind of answer, one that matches his own value judgments. His my-way-or-the-highway attitude makes me wish I could take his questions as rhetorical. I don't want to reply.

Claude is always asking me why I left my country and why I would choose to live in his. By his country, of course, he means Quebec, not Canada.

Had Yinyin not gone out for a breath of fresh air, of course I would not have left my country. I was just an ordinary university history professor who would, on occasion, discuss politics with students and take part in demonstrations with colleagues. And the ending I dreamed of was very different from what happened. Had Yinyin not gone out for that walk, we might have had a good sleep and found out next morning what had happened the previous night. To this day, I don't entirely know what did happen in the night.

Yinyin's death may have been light as a feather in terms of historical impact, but to me it was as heavy as Mount Tai. It had a subversive influence on my state of mind and completely changed the path of my life.

Because of the massacre, the local universities had declared an early summer holiday. And after dealing with Yinyin's funeral, I too left Beijing. At the time, I had not considered that I would not return to the city that had given me so many happy memories. Waiting on the platform for the train in Beijing Central, the friends who came to see me off all said they looked forward to my return at the end of August.

That was my last trip with Yinyin. That time, I no longer needed to exchange seats with anyone else. Yinyin no longer needed a seat. I kept the urn containing her ashes on my lap. I dared not think about our first trip together. And I refused to look at the scenery outside the window, as Yinyin did, with rapt attention, on the first trip we took together. I just stared up at the luggage rack above the seats. I blamed myself for the tragedy that had suddenly descended into her life or rather our lives.

The train stopped in Hankou for almost five hours, because angry students were holding a sit-in on the tracks not far from the station. There were also some students milling around the railway cars. The slogans they were holding up did not rouse me. I did not believe that "blood could really be compensated for with blood." And I did not need blood. I needed only the night and the pleasure I shared with Yinyin, my wife and my lover.

There were quite a few angry students and onlookers in the square outside the train station in my hometown, and some students were crowded in the entrance asking the emerging passengers if they were coming from Beijing. No one was interested in their questions. But I unconsciously nodded and said yes.

My response attracted their attention. Excited, they followed along behind me across the square. They wanted to know what had really happened in Beijing and what it was actually like when I left. I wanted to get rid of them as soon as possible. "It's very quiet there," I told them. "And very orderly." That was the truth, but it was obviously not the news that they were hoping to hear.

Most of the students turned away in disappointment, but three kept on pestering me. One moon-faced girl asked me exactly how many people had died in the night. This question made me very sad. My eyes were moist. "What does it matter how many people died?" I rebuked them, indignantly. Tears ran down my cheeks. "It's enough that one person died," I mumbled. "One is too many."

My tears and words freaked the students out. As they walked away, I looked down and kissed the travel bag I was holding tightly to my chest. "One is enough, one is too many," I whispered to Yinyin's urn. "Right?"

Before her cremation, I had placed a call to Yangyang's father informing him of the latest tragedy in their family. And I said I would soon bring her ashes home. Yangyang's father asked if I could turn them over to their family. Though I'm not sure whether it would have been against

Yinyin's own wishes, it was in fact what I was hoping for, because I could not take them to my own house. I did not tell Yangyang's father that I had already bought the ticket. I did not want them to take Yinyin home from the station. I knew she never felt like she had gone home.

So I delivered the urn to their home. Looking exhausted, Yangyang's father opened the door. He said that he and Yangyang's mother had been waiting for this moment ever since they got my call. I was sad that they had to face the death of another child. Within fourteen years, they had experienced the deaths of two children.

On the train, I had imagined the worst, that Yangyang's mother would ask me who had killed her daughter when I took the urn out of my travel bag. My reply would be, "I don't know." Or maybe, "Nobody knows." Or even, "Nobody will ever know." I would then say, "Treat it as an accident." Of course, I would not tell her the people who shot her dead—"by accident" according to the government—and the people who had rescued her from the rubble twenty-three years earlier belonged to the same organization. They were all soldiers of the People's Liberation Army. Yes, Yinyin's rescue and Yinyin's death were linked by liberation, the biggest irony in her life. And if Yangyang's mother blamed me for ruining her daughter's life, by falling love with her, marrying her, and causing her to live in Beijing instead of by their side, I would not say anything. I reminded myself that, no matter what happened, I had to keep calm. Even more importantly, no matter what happened, I would never tell them that the ashes in the urn were in fact the remains of two lives. This was the secret I would only share with Yinyin. Just like the pleasure we had shared.

Yangyang's mother's initial response surprised me. Cradling the urn, she looked quiet and calm. In contrast, Yangyang's father seemed disturbed. Thanking me for allowing them to handle her burial, his voice was weak and trembling. "She would feel lonely," he added. "We will bury her right beside her elder brother."

This got a rise out of Yangyang's mother, who started sobbing. Soon, her sobbing turned into howling. "I knew you wanted to follow your elder brother wherever he went," she wailed. "You are the most thoughtful child in the world."

Yangyang's mother's woe shattered the calm I had wanted to maintain since I saw Yinyin's body. I had a sense of being torn apart, a sense of alienation. I felt like nothing was real. I felt hatred in my bones. I hated myself for not preventing Yinyin from going out the door. Or for not going out with her. Had I been by her side at that moment, I could have blocked the bullets for the sake of her and the sake of our child. Or I would've fallen down with her. All of a sudden, the right side of my brain started throbbing. For the first time in my life I had a strong urge to kill myself.

After about a week of insomnia, my parents quietly took me to a mental hospital. They were afraid of being seen, especially afraid of being seen by Yangyang's parents. They felt embarrassed.

Given my clear symptoms, the doctor was able to make a diagnosis, and he recommended I stay in the hospital for a period of time. And then I could go home and keep resting. He reminded us that in my situation I should avoid any environment that would remind me of the trauma. Which meant that, for the time being, I should not return to Beijing.

I stayed in the hospital three months. At the end, my situation noticeably improved, and I started to think about my own future. My university agreed that I could take a year's sick leave. But I knew that I could never stand to live in the city where I had lived with Yinyin. The air in that city, the nights in that city, and the streets in that city were like viruses that would sicken me, body and mind. I needed to breathe fresh air and experience completely new nights and streets.

At the beginning of April, 1990, I succeeded in fleeing China and made my way to Hong Kong, which was still a British colony at the time. Soon I reached Vancouver, the last Canadian city you ever saw, dear Dr. Bethune. After a period of time there, I settled in Montreal. The route I followed was the same as yours, just in the opposite direction.

Please forgive me for omitting the details of how I left China. This is the only thing I cannot share with you.

Let me return to the question Claude kept asking. Maybe your great friend asked you the exact same question when you reached his cave. And what was your answer? That you did it for justice or for the revolution? If so, this was only part of the truth. The core of the truth was the secret between you and your last lover. The core of the truth was the mystery of *must*.

In the past few months I've been wondering what it would have been like if you had returned to Canada at the end of 1939 as planned, instead of dying in China, Of course, your great friend would not have written the essay that turned you into a political icon. Dr. Bethune would never have had any Chinese children. Daily life in China in the 1970s would have been very different. Yangyang would not have left this world at that early age. Yangyang's mother would have not become "that madwoman." And Yangyang's father would not have gone missing. (I prefer to think that his disappearance was more related to Yangyang's death and not to the death of the projectionist.) Yinyin would not have become their adoptive daughter. I would never have come to Montreal. Nobody would have had any need to read a biography about you, authentic or otherwise. And of course I would not have had all these stories to tell to you.

I sometimes ask myself the same kind of question. I am certain that my life in China would not have come to a sudden, absurd ending had Yinyin not died what they insisted on calling an "accidental death." I'm still not sure why Yinyin was so determined to go out for a breath of fresh air so late at night. Indeed, she and the child both needed fresh air. But that night, that historic night, unforgettable and unforgivable, the air in Beijing—saturated with despair, hate, and terror—was anything but fresh. She should have known this. She should have known this ever since the day she saw the fortune teller.

Dear Dr. Bethune, you might find it difficult to understand how that evening influenced the lives of hundreds of millions of your children. That might have been the darkest night of our lives. It has shadowed us ever since. Now I believe that suicide allowed Yangyang freedom from the inevitability of fear that Dr. Bethune's other children have had to bear. His choice was a way of maintaining his dignity.

That evening, three bullets hit Yinyin. The one in the belly hit the child she had been carrying in her womb for three months.

I've never talked to Claude about Yangyang and Yinyin. Nor have I ever responded to his question about why I left China and why I'm here. Dear Dr. Bethune, now I know that in a certain sense my coming to Montreal was your homecoming. It was you bringing your child back to your home soil.

A TERRIBLE ACCIDENT

Dear Dr. Bethune, of all the many events of 1989, you would have found the fall of the Berlin Wall especially shocking. The Berlin Wall was a symbol of the Cold War, and its fall a symbol of the end of the Cold War and the failure of socialism. But the new China, which your great friend founded, escaped this disaster in its own way. Almost twenty years have passed since the year of the triumph of liberal capitalism, and China is still ruled by the Communist Party. Who really cares about this? More and more Westerners come to China these days, "making light of travelling thousands of miles," but unlike you, they do so for profit or pleasure. Do you still remember what Bob said about China? He said China is the largest capitalist country under the rule of a communist party. He may be right.

For Montreal,1989 was also unforgettable year, the year of the December 6 massacre. All the victims were women, all young. They died on the same day, on the same evening, and in the same moment. They were not killed by accident. The man who killed them was a madman, but he knew what he was doing. He hated women, so he shot them. Unlike him, the ones who killed Yinyin "by accident" did not know what they were doing, even though none of them were crazy. There are a lot of ironic contrasts in history.

Dear Dr. Bethune, if you had still been alive, what would your reaction to this tragedy have been? You loved women. You may have hurt them psychologically just like you were hurt by them psychologically, but you would never have hurt them physically. Women often upset you, but they were also lovable in a lot of ways, and you did love them. You hoped the woman you loved would love you back, but this often was not the case. You never seemed to be able to get along with them. What was the problem between you and the woman you married and divorced twice? What went wrong between you and the woman who could see why you *must* go to China?

Dear Dr. Bethune, to have your child discuss women with you must make you feel that time that is like an arrow. So let us continue this discussion. Living in China must have been very different from living in Spain. You were separated from the women around you by the barrier of language. *The Politics of Passion* is the title of a fine collection of your writing, but in the Wutai Mountains, your passion for life could not be united with your passion for politics. A perfect case of alienation! Sometimes, like Bob, I wonder about your relationships with women. Did you think of the Swedish blonde you bedded in Spain when you were suffering from insomnia in China? A declassified Communist International file shows that she might have been a fascist spy. When you made love with her, could you feel her hostility? And if you knew she was an enemy, how could you justify making love with her? What about treating a wounded Japanese soldier? Does this kind of charitable love contradict revolutionary humanitarianism? Or is it the apotheosis of revolutionary humanitarianism?

At the time, we had no idea about the women in your life—we didn't even know there had been women in your life, let alone how many. In our China, the private lives of great revolutionaries were national secrets, highly confidential. To release or gossip about them was counter-revolutionary during the Cultural Revolution. We never thought that, in addition to being a doctor and a revolutionary, you were a man of great sexual vitality and charm. The first time I heard anything about your private life was on the train from Hankou to Beijing when Yin-yin and I met that professor of politics from McGill. And not until I buried myself in your archives did I discover the depth and breadth of your private life. How does it make a child of Dr. Bethune feel to peer into his father's intimate affairs?

The impression I got from your papers is that you changed the direction of your life not of your own accord but because of the woman you loved. The short letter you wrote to your "Pony" when you were on the steamer bound for Hong Kong deepened this impression. You said that she could see why you *must* go to China. This *must* implies a fateful relationship either with China or with her, and I now feel the latter is more likely. Which is to say, the reason you *must* go to China is a secret between you and your lover. Or rather it is *yuanfen*. Or rather it is the end of *yuanfen*. It was this mystery of *must* that gave birth to all Dr. Bethune's numberless children.

I discovered Place du 6-décembre-1989 unexpectedly. It was a gloomy Saturday. I was eating dinner with my girlfriend at the same Vietnamese restaurant I later visited with my parents. After we ordered, I told her that the colour of the new dress she had bought was pretty. "Who are you remembering now?" she asked. "As soon as I heard your compliment I knew it wasn't for me."

Her insight surprised me. Could I be speaking to Yinyin? Like a refugee seeking asylum in the past? Maybe she was right. At any rate, she was extremely unhappy. She looked around for a while and then talked again about a Chinese classmate in high school who was academically gifted but dowdy. For her, that Chinese classmate was emblematic of all Chinese women. I found this insufferable and said nothing more.

When we left the restaurant, I proposed going to the nearby park.

Again, this turned out to be an inappropriate proposal. "If you want to, go," she said coldly. "I'm tired."

I suggested going home together.

That wasn't the right thing to say, either. "If you want to go home, go alone." She didn't even look at me, just walked off in the opposite direction.

I do know why I let myself get tortured like this—

tortured by her, tortured by loneliness and despair. It was all because of Yinyin. But Yinyin never up and left me like this, except that last time when she left me forever. I walked alone towards the Cimetière Notre-Dame-des-Neiges, the largest cemetery in Montreal, wanting to walk among the spirits and hoping that Yinyin, having followed me to Montreal, might be among their number.

About a hundred metres from the cemetery, I happened upon Place du 6-décembre-1989. I was attracted by what appeared to be carvings shaped like tree stumps that were arranged in two rows facing a central walkway, but each with its own path at a right angle from the main one. If I could look down from above, I imagined, the promenade would look like a huge fallen leaf resting against the earth. I counted fourteen stumps. Then I noticed that on every shape was a letter, the first letter of the name of a dead woman; and the rest of the letters arranged along the path. Those fourteen women died the year Yinyin died. More shockingly, their dates of birth were very close together. Two of them were born the same year as Yinyin, and one in the same year as Yangyang and I. This is to say that if those dead women had been living in China, they would have been Dr. Bethune's children.

My discovery made me extremely sad. I sat down on the bench at the edge of the promenade, and my tears flowed down onto the backs of my hands. I could see Yinyin and me in our room in Beijing again, a room about twelve metres square. That was our home. And I returned to the evening on which I held her wake. That whole evening, I could clearly feel her presence, but I couldn't get any closer to her death. She sat opposite me. Between us, a flickering candle. We sat speechless. I did not dare to reach out and touch her. I was afraid that my fingers would sully her existence. Sitting on the edge of the promenade now, I had the same feeling of her presence. I could clearly feel that she was living in this city, waiting for me, waiting for us to reunite. In the ensuing years, this thought has become more and more deeply embedded in my life, in my body.

Dear Dr. Bethune, am I crazy to want to reunite with a wife who died so many years ago? This crazy notion might be the deepest reason I've chosen to tell you about Dr. Bethune's children. Memory is the way I welcomed Yinyin to Montreal as well as a way to set myself free. From that day, I decided not to have another relationship with a woman. I was thankful to my girlfriend for her indifference. Yes, it was all because of Yinyin. I still loved her. I'd never stopped loving her. I believed my love for her would allow us to reunite in a foreign land.

Going home (actually I never considered the apartment my home), I decided to end the relationship with my girlfriend. I also decided to go back to my research and writing, which had been interrupted by Yinyin's death. This was the way I would resume my life with Yinyin. This was how I would welcome her back.

But as you already know, dear Dr. Bethune, it was my girlfriend who ended our relationship. Yes, it's true. I did not break up with her that evening. Blame the injunction against thoughts of self that I had memorized in your memorial as a boy. I thought it would somehow be self-serving to end the relationship, so I kept on putting it off, putting it off until she said it. It was humiliating, but I was grateful. I agreed. I moved into my current apartment tower near Place du 6-décembre-1989.

Close to the largest cemetery in Montreal and with all the windows facing the scenery of death, my apartment is a perfect place for a historian. But my father started to complain about the *fengshui* as soon as he arrived. "No wonder you haven't found a woman who is willing to live with you," my mother chimed in. I did not respond. I did not want to force them to accept that my life is not only heading toward death but also comes from death, that death is my life. This is where I belong, I thought when I first entered the apartment. Through the windows that face the cemetery, I can see another world, the world of Yinyin and Yangyang, the world of my eternal companions.

I did not volunteer to take my parents to Place du 6-décembre-1989. I deliberately avoided it. I wanted neither that sensitive year nor the sensitive topic of death to start my mother sighing with regret. But one morning, when she was strolling back to the apartment, my mother did ask about the little park. "Is it a part of the cemetery?" She and my father had guessed that each stump was a tombstone and the numbers on the ground beside each stump were years. The year of birth and the year of death. And they thought it strange that all of those people should have died in the same year.

I told them it was a special cemetery, and those

people not only died in the same year but on the same day, the same evening, even in the same moment.

My reply shocked my mother. "Who were they?" she asked. "Some were younger than you."

I believed that she had noticed that they all had died in the same year as Yinyin, and that two of them were born in the same year as Yinyin. Of course, she would never reveal the association she had made. "And they were all women," I said meaningfully.

This new detail seemed to provoke my mother. But she did not react in any particular way, besides asking what happened. "I mean, their deaths were on the same date," she said.

I knew that she was intentionally avoiding the fact that they had died in 1989.

I stared at her sadly. "It was a terrible accident," I said. "Just like…" I almost mentioned Yinyin's death. But I did not want to upset my mother any further. Or myself. I did not want to hear her insult Yinyin again.

"What accident?" my mother kept asking. "Was it a car accident, a plane accident?"

I did not want to keep on talking to my mother. Because suddenly Yinyin appeared before my eyes. I could not see her face, and I assumed she would approach, but she did not. I wanted her to tell me about the last few minutes of her life. She closed the door, left the compound in which we lived, turned right and left. When she reached Changan Street, she hesitated before turning towards Tiananmen Square. She kept walking, walking into the darkness, then stopped, put her right hand on her stomach and took a deep breath of that tainted air. I don't know why she insisted on going out so late. That will always remain a mystery. There was no need for her to become part of that night, to pay that kind of price for the sake of history.

"What accident?" my mother repeated impatiently. "What was so terrible about it?"

"I don't know," I said. I was still staring at Yinyin's hazy figure. I suddenly thought of Hamlet meeting his father's spirit. "I don't know how you spent the last few minutes of your life," I murmured. "Can you tell me?"

Yinyin did not reply. At the sound of my mother's voice, she vanished into a layer of mist, which quickly dissipated.

"What do you mean you don't know?" my mother said. "I know that you just don't want to let me know."

In despair, I watched Yinyin disappear. "Maybe it was an earthquake," I said deliberately.

"What does maybe mean?" my mother asked, angry. Obviously she knew why I would mention an earthquake.

To this city, to the entire country even, that tragedy was like a violent earthquake.

Dear Dr. Bethune, when you were young, passionate young people went abroad to participate in war. You were only twenty-five years old when you first went, and World War I left scars on your pride and glory. But about fifty years after you left the world, passionate Chinese young people dreamed of going to a more developed country to study. Can these two passions be compared? Is one better than the other?

Just as you left your country, many of your children were preparing to leave China. We admired our siblings who got scholarships to study in North America, Europe, even Singapore and Japan. Unlike you, they were not going to help the countries they went to. They wanted to get help from those countries instead. By the 1980s, the children of Dr. Bethune had changed. Their slogan was "Everyone is for me, and I am for everyone." Utter devotion to others without any thought of self no longer applied.

Yinyin and I were not as enthusiastic about going abroad as our siblings, though we did occasionally raise the possibility. This is how I discovered Yinyin's interest in Montreal.

Yinyin said she had a mysterious *yuanfen*, a predestined relationship, with Montreal. The fact that I live in this city today is surely a continuation of this relationship. To me, this *yuanfen* has even become a blood relationship. Yinyin's blood, our child's blood. It was blood that brought me here.

Dear Dr. Bethune, do you still remember the baby's glove I mentioned in my letter about Claude, the separatist? When I went skating on Beaver Lake on Mount Royal, I heard a familiar voice calling me. Turning to look, I saw Yinyin standing on the shore of the lake. But just as I was about to skate toward her, she vanished. This was the first time I considered the possibility that Yinyin had followed me to Montreal. When I skated to where she had been standing, I found a baby's glove on the ice. The blood on the glove hit me hard. I knelt down on the ice, trembling and sobbing. This was a testament to the *yuanfen* between Yinyin and me.

This *yuanfen* inexplicably led to a miracle about four weeks before I went to Emergency to get relief from my migraine. And I promised right at the outset that I would tell you why I swung by the supermarket on the way home from the hospital. Now let me tell you, dear Dr. Bethune: I went there for a miracle.

The miracle appeared in the form of the cashier, or rather her profile. I did not know how long she had worked in the supermarket. I was standing in the shortest line, holding a couple of boxes of oats. I dropped them to the floor when I saw her, but then picked them up again and selected the line farthest away from her. But my attention was totally concentrated on her, and I kept on changing position so as not to lose sight of her. I wanted to get a clear look at her before she had a chance to notice me. "Impossible!" I said to myself. "It's totally impossible!" It was a denial that was full of gratitude.

She must have noticed my attention, because her movements became a bit awkward. She even started to blush, and in such a familiar way.

I did not dare go over to her. I was still wondering whether it was possible. What was going on? Was I losing my mind?

On the following Saturday, I dreamt a strange dream, that we were lying in my bed, the cashier and I. I was on my side observing her carefully. Now I was a total believer in the miracle. She was Yinyin. I mean, she was Yinyin herself, not an avatar. Her skin was Yinyin's skin and her figure Yinyin's figure. Even the little scar on her chin was there. Yinyin, I said to her softly. She smiled Yinyin's characteristic smile.

The next day, there were no people in her line. I still did not dare to pay for my groceries there, but I made a great leap forward by going to the next line over. When I was paying, I stared at her, not at the cashier in front of me. She was looking at her fingers, bored. That was a posture that I had not seen in almost twenty years but which was still so familiar. Yinyin! I called silently.

And she heard my silent call! She looked up and smiled at me shyly.

My discomfiture made her blush. Almost twenty years had passed, and her blush was still so fresh and so charming. Yes, she knew that I was looking at her. Yes, she knew who I was. It was bittersweet. While I didn't know how to react, I noticed her lips starting to move. She was saying something to me. Her lips were her lips. They were opening and closing just like Yinyin's lips used to do, even though they were speaking a language Yinyin did not understand. "*Bonsoir!*" she said.

After almost twenty years, I heard the voice of my dead wife again. My eyes were moist. My lips started to move, too. "*Bonsoir!*" For the first time, I greeted Yinyin in a language she learned posthumously.

That evening, I reread Yinyin's first story, and I tried to knit together her disastrous life with imagination and memory. At the same time, I was amazed at the miracle I had experienced. Why would it occur, this repetition across national lines? How could a French-Canadian woman look so much like Yinyin, my dead Chinese wife? And how could she be so aware of my amazement? I am unable to explain this. I do not know where this miracle will take me, and where it will take us. I worry that Yinyin's reappearance, just like her life, will be as transient as the bloom of the cactus called the queen of the night. I vowed to approach her the next day. I had so many questions to ask. Like what happened to her after she left our home that night, that fateful night, that endless night.

Standing in front of her the next evening, I saw that she was just as nervous as I was. She was blushing furiously, and I felt unbearably hot. But our gazes were as one. Almost simultaneously, we greeted each other with

"*Bonsoir!*" The intertwining of our voices recalled the intimacy of our lovemaking the night I read Yinyin's story that first time. I was so grateful to the city I was living in and to Dr. Bethune, who brought me here.

In my nervousness, I forgot everything I wanted to ask her. Over the next two weeks, I passed by her every day. And I vowed every time, before I entered the supermarket, to start talking with her. But every time was like the first. I was too wound up to ask. There were too many things I wanted to understand, too many questions to ask. I wanted to ask her name, her birthday, her hobbies, her telephone number, her email address. Of course, I wanted to ask if she was an orphan, why she kept on blushing. And how old she was, whether she had opened her eyes before Yinyin's closed. But as I said my nerves made me forget all my questions, every time.

I never asked her. I missed every opportunity. Even in my strange dream, I did not ask her any questions. And that day, on the way back from the hospital, I didn't see her. That was the first time in two weeks she had missed our "date." I just had the impulse to write to you, dear Dr. Bethune, to tell you everything your children had experienced in that long period of four decades that passed like the blink of an eye. I believed that my reunion with Yinyin would only add to my passion and inspiration. But she wasn't there. It was her shift, why wasn't she there?

She did not appear for the next three days. I was distraught. If I had not already started to write to you, I could never have borne her disappearance.

The next day I suddenly realized that she would never

appear again. The last time I saw her, two days before I got that terrible migraine, was in fact our last "date." She was scanning the products on the supermarket shelves when I went in. She looked up at me twice, as though she had something to say to me. Her movements were extremely slow that day, abnormally so. There was a shyness in her face, but anxiety showed in her eyes. I was not especially concerned until I realized that this was the same as the anxiety I'd seen in Yinyin's eyes when she said she wanted to get a breath of fresh air. I hadn't been concerned at that, either, or else I would have stopped her. It was afterwards that I was struck by that wave of anxiety, that gesture of farewell. Almost twenty years too late. Now I missed the sign a second time.

When I'd done my shopping and handed her the cash, I saw her lips quivering, thinking about whatever she had to say to me. I smiled at her, hoping that she would speak. But she hesitated and then pressed her lips together and turned to the next customer. Confused and disappointed, I walked to the exit, my heart filled with regret.

Then something else happened that I still find incomprehensible. Just as I was about to walk out of the supermarket, I heard a terrible scream. My first reaction was that Yinyin had been attacked. My God, what had happened?

I turned back to look, but the supermarket was the same as ever. I did not see Yinyin in a pool of blood, just the cashier turning to look at me. Had she heard the same scream? Each filled with surprise, we were once more as one.

The next detail was even stranger. As I prepared to

leave, she raised her arm and waved. This unexpected gesture was the final word of our peculiar dialogue of the past couple of weeks, an ephemeral reunion between Yinyin and me. I did not know what to do. I was carrying two full grocery bags. Hesitantly, awkwardly, I raised my right hand and shook the bag. She nodded, as if she had let me know what she wanted to say. And as if I had understood.

So that was farewell. The cashier knew she was leaving, and she knew her leaving would cause me sorrow. But Yinyin did not know. She had said she would be back soon, and she did not wave.

Dear Dr. Bethune, on the day when I realized she would never appear again, I had been writing to you about Yinyin. Now I know that this wasn't a coincidence. It was a matter of *must*. I was so teary-eyed by the time I finished writing that I couldn't see the words on the screen. Otherwise I might have told you about the miracle then. Yinyin was making me wait—and making you wait, too. She wanted me to tell you about her demise before letting you know about the miracle.

But why did this miracle come to an end? I can't understand it. I regret the time I wasted and all the opportunities I missed. In addition to the questions I failed to ask, I now have even more questions. Have you found another job? Have you left for another city? Have you gone home, returned home to China, a place you've never been?

She hasn't appeared again. I don't believe she ever will.

Dear Dr. Bethune, Yangyang became my best friend

because of you. And because of you he became the first one to leave me, the first one to die. His death brought Yinyin into my life via his family. I had a happy marriage, also because of you, though it was very brief. And in the end, the brief happiness has become a wound, a wound that would not heal. Because of you, too, I came to Montreal, the final home you had before you went to China and the only home I have had since leaving China. Is this what Yangyang's father meant by *yuanfen*? I don't know. I really don't know. And now, this miracle and this loss. What role did you play here? Why would Yinyin vanish just when I was starting to tell you our story?

Now I have even more questions. I vow that if she ever appears again I will not waste a minute, I will immediately take her hand and lead her into my room. I will ask her to live with me, once again. I will tell her that it is the predestined affinity of *yuanfen* that has decided all of this.

The only trace of this miracle is the lottery ticket that I bought from her before she disappeared. I have put that lottery ticket with Yinyin's manuscript in Yangyang's notebook. Immersing myself in work over the past few months, I often feel a painful solitude. This is in fact a syndrome caused by nostalgia and writing. To overcome solitude, I sometimes get out that lottery ticket and the manuscript and hold them fondly. Sometimes I can almost hear the first word Yinyin uttered, after a silence of almost twenty years. And I reply to it with the same word, "*Bonsoir!*" On those solitary winter evenings in Montreal, lost in reveries, I hope against hope that a simple "Good evening" will bring Yinyin back.

A LOTTERY TICKET

Dear Dr. Bethune, Last night, I was wakened by a telephone call at three a.m. I picked up the receiver and heard my mother's voice. "You shouldn't call me so late," I complained. "I mean, it's too early."

"Is it early or is it late?" she said.

I did not respond. I had barely slept two hours.

"I have something important to tell you," my mother said.

"Everything you have to tell me is important," I said. "Whatever it is, you call me at this hour of night."

"Why have you, my son, become so selfish?" my mother said. Then she asked me what time it was. She had never gotten her head around the time difference.

"Your day is my night. We are twelve hours apart," I said.

My mother's brief silence expressed that she had noticed how simple the conversion was and how inappropriate the time she had chosen for her call. "I just wanted to tell you something important," she said apologetically.

I was almost certain that this "something important" had to with Yangyang's mother, who I knew was dying of liver cancer.

After a short silence, my mother said: "That mad-woman was taken to Emergency yesterday." From her tone of voice, she was excited by the news, not saddened.

I waited.

"Last night she was discovered by a janitor slumped on the bedroom floor," she said. "She took an entire bottle of sleeping pills. She tried to kill herself."

I once again recalled how Yangyang's mother had be-haved on the afternoon when your great friend's death was announced, and I met Yinyin for the first time. That crazed look, those ravings, that disconcerting touch.

"I'll tell you tomorrow," my mother said. "You go back to sleep now."

Unable to get back to sleep, I got up and sat in the swivel chair by the desk. The lottery ticket was in front of me.

I hadn't needed anything that evening—this was a couple of days before the farewell. The draw was com-ing up in a few minutes and I just wanted to see her, so I decided to buy a lottery ticket. I hadn't bought one since splitting up with my ex. And I had never won anything in the lottery. It felt strange to buy a lottery ticket from the hand of my late wife.

She didn't find it strange. She seemed to know that I was there to see her. But when our gazes met, she was just as worked up and anxious as I was. I wanted to take her to a quiet corner, sit down with her and talk about our almost twenty years of separation by life and death. And I wanted to know about that night in Beijing in 1989.

But her smile stopped me short. In that smile, I saw a tranquillity that belonged to another world. I did not want to disturb her tranquillity, to awaken her from death. I extended the coins that I was holding. She opened her hands, which I could tell at a glance also belonged to Yin-yin: in shape and touch and gesture, they were so familiar. Solemnly, I put the coins in her tender palms, the palms that had once caressed me body and soul. When I let go of the coins, my fingertips lightly touched her palms. This was the first time in almost twenty years that she and I had had any bodily contact. I did not know at the time it would be her final touch. I trembled like the first time I had accidentally touched her hand on the train to Beijing. "One Lotto 649," I said awkwardly.

She was sharing my rapture, I was certain of it. She raised her hand a bit to draw out the contact as long as possible. Her gesture not only took more time, but also gave more pleasure. In doing so she was telling me that she knew how I felt and what I wanted, and moreover, who I was and who she was. She turned our mysterious contact into a dialogue, extending an instant into an eternity in which all of the loneliness that had built up over all these years of separation was resolved.

I was not paying attention when she turned, printed out the ticket, and put it in my hand. I did not know what to do. I just wanted to hurry up and leave and find some quiet corner to relive the miracle.

At the entrance to the supermarket I took a deep breath of fresh air to calm my nerves. Then I looked back through the glass window. She lifted her arms to stretch, and she, too, took a deep breath. "No, don't breathe like that," I whispered despairingly. "There is no fresh air there." I wanted to dissuade Yinyin from going out into the Beijing evening. Somehow my voice penetrated the glass, because she turned and looked at me. I knew that she couldn't see me, only the glare of the window. She could not see my despairing body fringed with night.

When passing by Place du 6-décembre-1989, I sat down on the bench, exhausted. The air there was even fresher. I noticed a young couple about twenty metres away. The woman was sitting on a bench, her head tucked between her knees, not moving. The man standing beside her was gesticulating and talking fast. I leaned back and stared at the silent starry sky, gulping the cool air. When my parents were visiting, the night sky was the only thing my father liked better here than in China, where there's now too much construction to see the stars.

"Why?" I asked the deep blue sky. "Why would I be blessed with such a miracle?"

I took another look at the couple. The young man threw up his right hand and walked quickly away. The woman called him twice, in a quiet voice, but he did not look back. He walked to the intersection and down the lane by the launderette. The woman watched the empty intersection, and then buried her face again between her knees.

I felt the lottery ticket and looked back up into the heavens. I could not explain why Yinyin would reappear, after twenty years, on the other side of the globe, a deep gratitude pulsed through my heart. Gratitude towards you, gratitude towards life. Dear Dr. Bethune, the solitude that had lacerated me for almost two decades became an impulse to revisit the past. That, I realized, was the original impulse behind writing the stories of the children of Dr. Bethune. "Yinyin," I said to the starry heavens. "I want to go back to the past. Go back to you." The sky blurred, tracked by my tears like veins in a frozen leaf.

The lottery ticket won the second-to-last prize: $10. It was the first time I had ever bought a winning lottery ticket, and this seemed part of the miracle, not an accident. In fact, on the way home from Place du 6-décembre-1989, I had hoped I would not win the prize, because I wanted to keep the ticket as proof that Yinyin and I had reunited. The second-to-last prize was ideal. It bore witness to the miracle, but I didn't have to consider whether or not to cash it in. I put the lottery ticket in Yangyang's notebook, with Yinyin's manuscript. I knew this was the last lottery ticket I would ever buy.

It has been fifty days since the mysterious cashier waved goodbye. Dear Dr. Bethune, all this time I've been writing you letters, telling you about our lives, your children's lives. But have I ever told you who it was who discovered that our lives were rooted in your fate, in the fact that you *must* go to China? This is a secret you should know. This is the secret you *must* know.

At ten o'clock in the evening, Montreal time, nineteen hours after I heard that Yangyang's mother had been sent to the hospital, I called my mother. "Will you go to the hospital to see her?" I asked.

"You should be sleeping," my mother reminded me, in a retaliatory tone. She had finally figured out the time difference.

I repeated my question and, as expected, my mother said no without even thinking about it.

"Could you go once, for me?" I begged.

"No, absolutely not," she said. "It's a matter of principle."

"Please," I said.

"This is absurd," my mother said. "I haven't spoken to her since she tried to break down my door with a brick. It's been almost twenty years."

"I beg you."

"It would be pointless. She's in a coma," my mother said. She sounded like her mind was made up. "If you're curious, I can keep you updated."

"I'm not curious," I said firmly. "I am concerned."

"You should be more concerned about yourself," my mother said.

"I'll manage, Mom," I said. It was years since I had called her Mom, and I don't know why I did so now. Then I reminded her half-jokingly: "Have you forgotten what you always taught us? You always told us we should emulate Dr. Bethune, in his utter devotion to others without any thought of self."

After a long silence, my mother started crying. "You still remember who I am," she said.

"Can you go to see her at the hospital for us?" I begged her again—and immediately regretted that I'd said "us."

The word evidently provoked my mother. "Who is 'us'?" she asked.

"Dr. Bethune's children," I said after a moment's hesitation.

My mother did not respond.

"You must remember," I added calmly. "She's the one who came up with that phrase."

Little did I expect that this would send my mother over the edge. "That's the craziest thing of all! That ruined you. She ruined you, all of you—you damned children of Dr. Bethune," she yelled into the receiver. "She wasn't driven mad by her son's death. She was mad long before that. She's always been a madwoman." Then she slammed the receiver down.

Dear Dr. Bethune, it was just after ten a.m. when I awakened from a fitful sleep. I stared at the ceiling, wondering if there was anything I could do for Yangyang's mother. I was still exhausted. And I had some migraine pain on the right side of my head and was worried that symptoms of depression might follow. I should get up and go outside, I told myself. For almost two months, I'd been spending most of my time remembering and writing. I was so tired of living this way.

I decided to go to the coffee shop across from Place du 6-décembre-1989. I wanted to see if I could make a small change and write to you there. And not on the "typewriter"—my computer—but with a pencil, as your children did back in the early 1970s. This may be the last letter I write you, because Yangyang's mother is dying. She's the one who first understood our relationship with you. She's the one who identified us as the children of Dr. Bethune.

After washing and dressing, I put Yangyang's notebook, two biographies of you, one in English and one in French, and a stack of blank paper in my backpack. As I was heading out, I discovered a note by the door—a note

Claude had stuck through the mail slot. He said he had called me a few times without getting any answer. And he urged me to turn on the television to watch breaking news about China. It was strange that I had not heard the phone ring. I didn't think I had slept so soundly.

I turned on the television. A few channels were reporting on a serious snowstorm in the south of China. An explanation underneath a picture said, "A snowstorm has paralyzed China." The news would have been all the more surprising had it been geographically a little more precise, because it seldom snows in southern China, which is where I come from.

According to the news, however, some areas of southern China had been struck by the worst snowstorm in half a century. And it turned out that the epicentre was near my hometown, which had been cut off from the outside world for more than a week, without water or power. The video shown on the television had been shot about a hundred kilometres away. It was shocking. What would it be like at Ground Zero?

I turned the TV off. It didn't surprise me that my mother had not mentioned the snow in her telephone call. She wouldn't have paid attention to the snowstorm, no matter how disastrous it was. Nothing compared with the death of Yangyang's mother. After years of living in Montreal, I knew the meaning of *snowstorm*. The situation in my hometown must be even worse than it would be in a Montreal blizzard, because people in China had so little experience dealing with that kind of weather. I felt sad on behalf of the residents of my hometown, especially the martyr's bride. I don't know why I thought of her. Was she still alive? How was she managing?

I left my apartment with a lot on my mind. In the entrance, I saw Bob looking around, and he shook my hand as though he'd been waiting for me. "I've never heard about China suffering this kind of disaster," he said. He listed the things he had just read in a newspaper feature. Cars had been stuck on the highway for over a week. People had frozen or starved to death. Hundreds of travellers were trapped in the train station in Guang-zhou, while tens of thousands were stuck in airports in different parts of the country. Most of them wanted to go home to celebrate Spring Festival. Who knows when and if they would get the chance? "The trouble has come before the Olympics even starts," Bob said. "Do you re-member what I said?"

I knew that he was sad about the disaster, but he was also proud of being right about the problems the Olym-pics would cause.

"Mother nature has started to take revenge," Bob said. Then he listed all the disasters that China had suffered in the past year. His moving concern for China was not sur-prising, given his exposure as a boy to the majestic march *Qilai*. The rise of China had been his dream ever since. And his awareness of environmental calamities ensured he wasn't surprised by the snowstorm. To him, this was just one of a series of disasters. "The year of 2008 is not going to be an easy year for China," he concluded. I said goodbye before he had the chance to repeat his classic question about the Olympics.

On the way to the café, my mind was a mess. Innumerable images and imaginings flooded in and mingled together. I thought again of the martyr's bride. I thought of Yangyang's mother. And of course I imagined scenes from the disaster. I imagined I was stuck on the highway, at the railway station, at the airport. All of a sudden, I felt homesick. I wished I could be one of those travellers waiting to get home. I wanted to be one of the victims of the storm.

I ordered a mocha and sat down, facing Place du 6-décembre-1989. I felt discouraged at being plagued by the expatriate complaints of homesickness and nostalgia. Dear Dr. Bethune, I know from the last letters you wrote in China how deeply you were tortured by these two devils. I didn't want to treat you as a role model in this respect.

I got out Yangyang's notebook and flipped through it at random to find out more about his mother. Dear Dr. Bethune, you should know more about her. And I soon found another good story.

One day, Yangyang asked her why the Arabian woman had had to tell a thousand-and-one stories and not a thousand? To him, one thousand was a perfect number. But his mother insisted that a thousand and one was more perfect, a lot more. She had two reasons. First, superficially, a thousand and one has a symmetrical beauty. But the second and underlying reason is more mysterious.

She told Yangyang that he would soon learn the binary system, which, she predicted, would play a key role in the near future. She explained that in base-two, a thousand and one is the same as nine in base-ten, the decimal system. And nine in Chinese is *jiu*, which sounds the same as the word meaning *forever*. As such, a thousand and one is in fact a symbol of eternity.

Was this bizarre explanation a symptom of what my mother had always called her madness?

Yangyang did not learn binary notation as his mother predicted he would—he died before he had the chance—so he never knew how prescient his mother was. Base-two is the logical basis of the modern computer, and it does indeed play a key role in our digital age. But he must have known that the thousand-and-one nights had nothing to do with either Chinese or the binary system. The interpretation his mother gave was sheer nonsense. In his notebook, however, he didn't take this interpretation as a symptom. On the contrary, he praised his mother for her particular insight. It gave him a newfound respect for her.

Discovering our phenomenal relationship with you may have been an expression of her special insight, even if my mother saw it a sign of madness. I was unhappy about her statement, but I had to acknowledge that it wasn't unreasonable. Maybe Yangyang's mother was insane before her son left the world. Maybe she always had been. Or maybe she was a prophet.

I was sad about the way her story had ended. Dear Dr. Bethune, you should know more about this woman.

By discovering our identity, she identified the biggest family on Earth, the biggest in history. Yangyang's esteem for his mother was well-deserved. Besides having exceptional intelligence, she had a keen sense of history. Like a magic wand, this sense of history has left us eternal children. From womb to tomb. From birth to death. Oh, "another boy has died!" Do you still remember that from the historic afternoon when we learned of Chairman Mao's death?

My thoughts were getting crazier and crazier, and were only interrupted by another auditory hallucination— the alarming telephone ring. It was time to go home, I realized, to find out the latest news about Yangyang's mother. I gulped down what was left of my coffee, grabbed my bag, and ran back through the snow to my apartment.

I waited by the phone for an hour, during which time it rang twice. The first time was a recording telling me I had won a big prize. I hung up before the recording ended. The second time it was a stranger, a woman who asked me in an affected voice whether I was interested in Bell's new exclusive offer for internet, telephone, and television.

Assuming that I had missed my mother's call and worrying it would soon be too late or too early in China, I decided to call first.

My mother was not the least bit surprised to hear from me. She didn't complain about the time. Without any delay, she started talking about the most important thing. "Still in Emergency. In a coma."

I heard a subtle change in her tone of voice. "Did you go to the hospital to see her?" I asked.

"Your father went this evening," she said.

So she had arranged for him to go. I was gladdened. This was probably the first time she had ever made a concession on a "matter of principle."

But her conclusion made my eyes moist. "I don't think she will wake up again," she said.

The phone rang again when I put down the receiver. This time it was Claude. He was watching the American democratic primaries on television. He invited me to bet $20 on the sex and skin colour of the next president of the fascist country to the south, which was his way of referring to the United States. "Will it be the white woman or the black man?" he asked.

"As if it could not be a white man?" I asked him.

Claude said he hated the Republicans. It was the Republicans who were to blame for turning America into a fascist country.

Saying that $20 was too much, I did not accept. I thought of the stolen wine glass in the Nixon joke and told him that the next time we went to a restaurant, I would tell him a story that would warn him against betting on an American president.

I overestimated Claude's patience. He immediately lowered his bet. "How about $10?" he asked.

I was feeling listless. I told Claude it didn't matter to me who the American president was.

Putting down the phone, I rested on the couch for a while, and then made a simple dinner. After dinner, I trudged around the building a couple of times, my habit for many years. The snow around the building made me think of the storm in China. I turned on the television, hoping to happen upon the latest report, but was disappointed. All of the channels were breaking news about the Democratic primaries.

Dear Dr. Bethune, it was 10 p.m. when I sat down at the "typewriter" and noticed something was missing. I always put Yangyang's notebook in front of me when I write you a letter. But where was it now?

I fumbled through all the places I could have left it before remembering the café opposite Place du 6-décembre-1989. Yes, I had taken it out of my backpack, flipped through it, and then put it on the table to read the headlines. Then what happened? I heard the telephone ring like an alarm, I gulped down the rest of the coffee, grabbed my backpack, and ran home. Ten hours had elapsed before I noticed I had left Yangyang's notebook behind.

I went out at once and ran back to the café. The two women on duty were a bit irritated when I interrupted their conversation. "Are you sure you left it here?" one of them asked indifferently. The other one pointed me towards the lost-and-found box by the washroom. Then they resumed the conversation. They were talking about a young man who had just died of liver cancer.

There were a lot of misplaced things left by customers in the box, but Yangyang's notebook was not among them. I checked carefully a second time before giving up. When I returned to the cashier, I overheard the two women continuing their conversation.

"What were the last few days like?"

"He was in too much pain."

"He used to be such a strong person."

"But he fell apart in the end."

"It could happen to anyone."

I walked out of the café and crossed the road. The bench that I often sat on at Place du 6-décembre-1989 was covered in snow. I stood beside it for a while and breathed in the cold air. Then I held up a fistful of snow and rubbed it on my face. The shock of cold gave me a sudden release and a deep comfort, so timely, so beautiful, for which I was grateful. Looking up at the sky, pellucid and serene, I knew what had just happened.

Yangyang's mother had finally breathed her last.

I was the first to know this, I am sure. As soon as her own body knew it. My deep gratitude reported this news in real time. Then a weird thought occurred to me, which absolved me of guilt for the loss of Yangyang's notebook. Yes, his mother had taken it. In reuniting with her son and reading his notebook, she would enjoy his praise for her. What a great consolation would that be!

When I returned to our tower, I discovered Bob sitting in the lobby. "The news makes me so sad," he said. Of course he meant the snowstorm in the south of China, not the news about Yangyang's mother.

"I don't want to talk about this," I said, not knowing exactly what I meant by *this*.

My curt response left Bob surprised and unhappy. For the first time, he didn't get into the elevator with me, nor did he ask his classic question about the Olympics.

Just out of the elevator I heard the telephone ring in my apartment. I got out my key, opened the door, and rushed to the phone.

But just as I was about to pick it up, I suddenly changed my mind. I did not pick it up. I did not need to pick it up. I knew who was calling and what it was about. And I did not want to talk about *this*. No, I did not want to hear anything about Yangyang's mother. No more.

The phone rang three times that night, as I tossed and turned in my bed. I did not answer it. I don't know when I got to sleep, but when I did, I had a very strange dream, a dream in which another "terrible beauty" was born.

Dear Dr. Bethune, the poems you wrote did not convince me that you were a poet. But you must have known where this terrible beauty came from.

It was a great square, in the centre of which stood a massive statue of you. After a bloody night, the sun was rising again, on a morning so deadly silent it felt like a vacuum. I saw bodies lying on the edge of the square. Two children in that crowd returned to life. They were Yangyang and Yinyin, no doubt about it. They stood up and started to look among the corpses. They were looking for me, in vain. Then they saw the statue in the centre of the square. Thrilled, they ran hand in hand toward you.

Surrounded by a paralyzing darkness, I shouted their names, wanting to chase after them, but I couldn't catch up with them. We were separated by the diameter of the earth and by a time difference of twelve hours, the difference between day and night.

I saw them stop in front of the statue. I stopped, too. I saw that their eyes were full of reverence as they looked at you. And as I looked, my eyes were full of reverence, too.

Joyfully, their sweet childish voices broke the silence of the morning:

> *Comrade Bethune's spirit, his utter devotion to others without any thought of self, was shown in his great sense of responsibility in his work and his great warm-heartedness towards all comrades and the people . . .*
>
> *. . . A man's ability may be great or small, but if he has this spirit, he is already noble-minded and pure, a man of moral integrity and above vulgar interests, a man who is of value to the people.*

I, too, mouthed the words to the sentences we had all recited so many times. But the cold that surrounded me made my lips tremble. My voice trembled, too, dear Dr. Bethune. My entire body was trembling in the cold and the darkness of Montreal, your last home, my last home.

On Chinese New Year's Eve, I got a call from my publisher in Beijing. In addition to polite well wishes, of course, he asked about my progress on the Dr. Bethune biography. I told him that I had not made any progress at all since the middle of November. Shocked, he asked me why. I hesitated but decided to come clean, telling him what I had written over the past two months. Dr. Bethune's actual predicament in China, I explained, had called up my impulse to write in this way. In the final stage in his life, I learned from my research, Dr. Bethune did not know what was happening around the world. He waited in despair for letters from comrades and friends that would never come. His vain expectation and endless solitude saddened me. "Another biography of Dr. Bethune would not give his suffering spirit any consolation," I said. "Such a spirit needs a new treatment, something special, something radical. For instance, the news that he is a father to countless millions, and what has befallen his children."

The long pause showed that my publisher must have found my distress strange. Then he casually asked me a few questions about what I had written "to and for" Dr. Bethune. In the end, he returned to the original topic and asked when I would resume the biography, reminding me that the publisher was planning to make it one of the major events of the following year, the seventieth anniversary of Dr. Bethune's death.

"The past couple of months of writing has changed, or rather restored, my relationship to Dr. Bethune," I said firmly. "I don't think I'll be able to write his biography."

My admission undoubtedly made my publisher very unhappy. At the same time, it left me in a daze. After the conversation, I sat unmoving at my desk for over an hour. I did not want to do anything. I did not think I would hear from my publisher again, but I did. He called back some time later to ask me to send him what I'd been writing "to and for" Dr. Bethune. He had just talked it over with his colleagues. They were all interested in what I had come up with.

I chose three pieces at random—"A Man Who Is of Value to the People," "A Great Saviour," and "A Little Girl." I did not wait for the response.

Two days later, I got another call from my publisher. He urged me to send him all the rest, saying they were considering publishing the stories as a book.

"But they were not written to be published," I said.

My publisher lost patience with me at this point and launched into a monologue that lasted twenty minutes. He asked me to trust his judgment. Who understood the Chinese book market, him or me? His analysis was that there were several segments that would be interested in a book about Dr. Bethune's children. In the end, he said something that hurt my self-esteem. "Your new book will be worth more than all your previous books put together."

I was not persuaded. I especially did not believe that readers in the digital age would be interested in what had befallen

Dr. Bethune's children. But I agreed to send him the rest in the hope that he would see his mistake.

Satisfied with my compromise, my publisher predicted that our new project would help millions of readers rediscover their long-forgotten identity. "We are all Dr. Bethune's children!" he said.

"We?" I repeated sadly. A strong sense of loss hit me. In the world without Yangyang and Yinyin, "we" was an empty word that meant nothing but loneliness.

I had already moved the cursor over Send. Travelling thousands of miles is no longer a wonder in the digital age. Just one tap on the mouse had sent my memories around the globe, to my father-land, and your final resting place. Dear Dr. Bethune, I know that your spirit is still wandering the good earth, where most of your children are still living. I know you are eager to hear about the children you never knew. Whether these stories would "make your life a misery," I do not know. But I can promise they "will never bore you." (Please forgive my borrowing the words you said to the woman you married and divorced twice, which may bring sad memories to mind.) These stories will finally unveil the mystery your children have wrestled with and that I'm sure also troubled you.

You see, dear Dr. Bethune, why you must go to China?

ACKNOWLEDGEMENTS

A novel spanning the life of a generation over a period of four decades, *Dr. Bethune's Children* has been ten years in the making and itself has a story spanning three countries and three different languages.

My thanks go first to Gail Scott, who encouraged me to join her 2007 fall semester master class in creative writing. The A+ grade she gave to the portfolio written in English entitled *Dr. Bethune's Children* stimulated my ambition to extend it into a novel.

This ambition would not have been realized without the contributions of two close friends to whom I wish to express my deep gratitude. After reading the account of Yangyang's death in the novel, Shirley Cahn confided that she herself had experienced a similar tragedy as a mother; she devoted so much of her time in her last months to this literary adventure and urged me never to give up. Carole Channer, who is a witness to my hard literary life in Montreal, helped me from the first word to the last period.

I am also grateful to Margaret Atwood, the first colleague

to know of *Dr. Bethune's Children* and to Ellen Seligman, the first publisher to show an interest in reading it. These encouraging responses in the fall of 2009 provided me with the first rays of hope I had felt as a writer living in a foreign land.

My thanks go to Bei Dao, the most influential Chinese poet since the Cultural Revolution, who on Christmas Eve, 2009, invited me to write about my childhood experiences for the anthology he was then editing, *The Seventies*. This proved to be a turning point. After completing a long essay for his anthology in Chinese—and essay that was well received—I decided to abandon the English version I had been working on and rewrite *Dr. Bethune's Children* in my mother tongue. This second journey saw the completion of the Chinese version by the end of 2010.

The rest of journey oscillated between hope and disappointment. By February 2011, the manuscript had been declined by major publishers in mainland China, always for the same reason. At this point, the nadir of the life of *Dr. Bethune's Children*, the marvelous Taiwan publisher Guo Feng decided to publish it, first in instalments in the literary magazine he edits, and then in book form. And he made the decision to publish less than two hours after he received the manuscript. A special thank you to Guo Feng.

I would like to pay tribute, too, to the numerous editors, publishers and scholars in mainland China for their courageous and resolute efforts, so far unsuccessful, to bring this novel to readers there. I feel sorry that I cannot release their names at this point.

Sincere thanks are due to that excellent translator and writer Ken Liu, who appreciated *Dr. Bethune's Children* from the day he read it, in 2013, and who helped initiate the novel's return journey into English.

My thanks also go to the late Sylvie Gentil—the distinguished French translator who exerted considerable energy in translating and in attempts to draw French attention to this novel, which she admired—and to Lucie Rault, a musicologist and lover of Chinese culture, who in 2014 translated a section of the first part of the novel into French.

And my deep gratitude goes to the brilliant team that has made *Dr. Bethune's Children*'s return journey into English possible. Linda Leith, my publisher, started orchestrating this new project a few months after launching my first book in English, *Shenzheners* (LLP, 2016). Her passion, her devotion and her insight have ensured the quality of my first novel in English. Darryl Sterk, the translator I see as a magician, has shown tremendous patience and incredible efficiency in a process that has been immeasurably complicated by my constant rewriting. Tim Niedermann, my editor, has handled the text with delicacy, expertise and hard work.

My gratitude also goes to Cai Gao, one of the finest of contemporary Chinese artists, whose illustrations grace the cover.

I would like to thank another colleague, Madeleine Thien, who was responsible for the first propitious sign for the book when she invited me in January of this year to make a submission to the special issue of *Granta* she is co-editing.

My special thanks go to Ha Jin, a bridge builder between the English-speaking world and contemporary Chinese writing, for his unswerving support.

And so begins a new phase in the unusual journey of *Dr. Bethune's Children*. My greetings to the readers who will give this novel an extraordinary new life.

Xue Yiwei
Montreal, May 9, 2017